OMEGA TRAP

LAYNE PARRISH BOOK 3

JIM HESKETT

OFFER

Want to get the Layne Parrish novella **Museum Attack** for FREE? It's not available for sale **anywhere**. Check out www.jimheskett.com/free for this free, exclusive thriller.

PART I

ADD THE BAIT

1

CAMERON PARRISH HURTLED THROUGH SPACE, CLINGING TO the metal chain links of the swing. Her three-year-old body blurred. As Layne waited for her to finish the climb and return in his direction, his ears filled with her frantic giggling. Pure joy streamed from her vocal cords.

He couldn't recall the last time he'd witnessed such flawless, unadulterated exultation. Maybe that was the point of having children; experiencing sensations through the eyes of someone not yet jaded or burned by the world.

Layne stood behind her—the primary pusher—and Cameron's mother, Inessa, was in the front. She would hold up her hands so Cameron could bump her feet against them. Each time it happened, Inessa beamed. Her smile, a mile wide, lit her face. Layne rarely pined for his ex-wife, but it wasn't hard for him to remember why he'd been attracted to her in the first place.

Also, too easy to remember why he'd divorced her.

"Okay!" Cameron shouted. "I'm done."

When she returned his way, Layne grabbed either side of the swing and slowed her until the thing came to rest in the middle. He lifted her out of the contraption and set her on the playground, a soft area consisting of a sea of recycled tire bits. He held her there a moment to make sure she wasn't dizzy.

"What next, little one?" he asked as he pushed up his shirt sleeves, revealing the tattoos blanketing both of his arms from shoulder to wrist.

Her head swiveled around to evaluate the many wonders of this little park in Broomfield, Colorado. Close to where Cameron lived with her mother, some of the time. On this one compact block were the small city's grade school and high school.

As Cameron deliberated, Layne could even hear the classroom bell ringing at the high school at the edge of the park.

"Slide," Cam said. "I wanna go slide. A whole buncha times."

"Slide it is," Layne said. As he stood back up, he met Inessa's eyes, and both of their smiles faded. These co-parenting play dates had been his idea, but that didn't make it any more pleasant to see his ex. Sometimes, he was even still mad at her.

Layne had lots of practice in the art of being civil, and he considered himself to be quite skilled at it.

"We should talk about something," she said in her abrasive Russian accent. "It's important."

"Can it wait?" Layne said. "I have a thing to—"

But before Layne could finish the sentence, a booming noise raced across the park. A crack, loud enough to interrupt his thoughts. The sound peaked and then dissipated with a rolling echo, like thunder.

Except it hadn't been thunder.

When it happened the second time, Layne knew for sure. That had been a Kalashnikov AK-12 in a semi-automatic mode.

A few more shots ripped across the courtyard. By instinct, Layne pulled Cameron close to him. He knelt, folding his arms around her. As Inessa gasped and covered her head with her hands, Layne's eyes darted around, searching for the source of the blasts.

Within a couple seconds, he'd found their origin.

The shots were coming from inside the high school, just beyond the park. Layne studied the grounds adjacent to the school to be sure there were no shooters outside before he released his grip on his daughter.

He then spun Cameron around and took a breath before speaking. He didn't want her to notice the spike in his heart rate. "I need you to go with Mommy."

Cameron nodded dumbly as he pushed his daughter back, toward her mother. Inessa stood there, frozen in a state of near panic. Layne took Cameron's hand and inserted it into Inessa's hand, pressing it there.

He stood up and snapped his fingers in front of Inessa's face. This broke his ex out of her trance. She stared at him as more gunshots echoed across the park, an echo of shouts and screams coming from the school. Whatever was happening in there, it had escalated. The gunfire came at a more rapid clip now.

"What's going on?" Inessa said, licking her lips, chest heaving.

Layne removed his car keys and placed them in Inessa's hand. "Take Cameron. Put her in the car and drive back to your house. Do not stop, no matter what you see. Understand?"

Inessa gulped air, her eyes darting around the park.

"I need you to say it. Do you understand?"

She nodded, head jerking up and down. "I will take her back to my house. I can do this."

He pointed them both toward the car, dormant on the opposite side of the park from the school. With a little push, he set them in motion and then drew the Colt Peacemaker from his concealed hip holster. He held it behind his back so Cam wouldn't see.

As Inessa hustled their daughter toward safety, the little girl looked back at him. He gave her a wave and forced a smile.

Once they were out of sight, Layne turned and sprinted toward the school as echoes of new gunshots sped across the park. He kept his breaths even as he heaved long strides across the grass. In the nose, out the mouth, blinking so his eyes wouldn't dry out. At times like this, elements of his training engaged in quick succession like pistons firing in an engine.

All the tools he thought he'd locked away, never to be needed again.

Near the school's front walkway, he hunkered down next to a trash can and kept his eyes on the street. He waited and watched Inessa buckling Cameron into the car seat and then scrambling around the other side of the car to start it up.

Safe. They were safe and free.

As soon as Inessa had left her parking spot and started to drive away, Layne first removed a small tube from his pocket and popped a nicotine lozenge into his mouth. Instant relief flooded his bloodstream.

Then, he burst from his hiding place and rushed inside the school. He flung back the door, unsure what he would find, but telling himself to be ready for anything.

He first saw a security guard face down on the floor, arms splayed wide. A puddle of blood next to his head. Layne stood in a wide hallway, lockers lining each side. Windowed classrooms at intervals. Paper banners promoting an upcoming baseball game, torn and littering the hallway like chunky confetti.

The resemblance to the incident sixteen years ago throbbed inside his head. The shouts, the screams, the blood. But he couldn't allow himself to become distracted now.

He closed his eyes and focused on slowing his thumping heart so he could listen. With no knowledge of the school's layout, he had to be careful before committing to a path down any of these maze-like passageways.

Layne then heard shooting, somewhere to the northwest of his current position. Not in this hall. He pointed the Peacemaker low and crept along the tiled floor. The locker area opened up to a series of classroom doors.

At the first door, he peered through the window and saw an empty classroom. Same with the next. Of course, there could be kids or teachers hiding in the closets beyond his field of view, but he decided to let them be. If they were hidden well enough for now, maybe the shooter would leave them alone.

Shooters. Could be more than one. Layne knew so little right now.

At the third door, he saw a foot sticking out from behind the teacher's desk. He opened the door, slowly, with his pistol pointed at an angle toward the ground. "If you're in here, please come out. I'm not going to hurt you."

A head poked out from the other side of the desk, and a wash of relief passed over the male teenager's face when he saw Layne. Handsome, white, well-dressed, with hair carved like a politician.

"Who are you?"

"I'm a friend," Layne said, hovering in the doorway.

"Is it over?"

Layne shook his head. Something in the kid's face said he had seen action today. "How many of them are there?"

"One," the kid said, stuttering through the word. "Just one, I think. He was asking for me. He said he was looking for *me*. Why is he looking for me?"

"I don't know, man. It doesn't matter right now. We have to get you out of here." Layne waved him out, and the boy emerged with two other girls.

"But he's out there," a girl said.

"Yes," Layne said. "Inside. If we get you out the front door, then you'll be fine. Let's move quick."

The teen boy babbled, making no sense. They looked so young, so terrified. Just kids who'd found themselves trapped in a nightmare.

"Come with me," Layne said. "It's a straight line to the outside. I know this is terrifying, but you need to be a little brave. You can do this. Be brave, just for a minute, then it's over."

At first, they wouldn't move, so Layne entered the room and holstered his gun. He held out a hand and beckoned them to come to him. "Please."

The three kids shuffled forward, clutching each other. The kid who'd said the shooter had been looking for him led the way, biting back tears.

Layne pointed them out the door and then escorted them into the hall. He had to physically push the three of them down the hallway. Their legs seemed to stop working every few steps.

At the door, he pointed at the street on the other side of the park. Sirens echoed in the distance. "Go there. Wait in the street. The cops will be here any second. You're safe now, as long as you stay far away from the building."

Layne shoved them out the door and then slammed it shut behind them. He drew his Peacemaker and met the eyes of the teen boy one more time. After a quick nod, Layne rushed down the hall, toward the continuing sound of gunfire.

He threw back a door to find another perpendicular hallway, and his eyes landed on a young teacher with bullet holes across her stomach. Her mouth was open, blood spilling out. Leaning back against a trophy case. Dead. Eyes wide and fixed on a water fountain behind Layne.

He had no time to mourn for her. This hallway led to the gymnasium, and he could see it through a window crisscrossed with safety glass. Inside the large and open space, dozens of kids sat in the bleachers on either side of the basketball court. In the center of the court were a podium and a microphone. The students had been in the middle of a pep rally when this had begun.

Standing behind the podium, a brown-haired white kid held that AK-12, waving it around, menacing the kids in the stands. His back to Layne. An adult was at his feet, sprawled on the ground. A streak of blood cascading out from his body like a river.

Layne had seen no students killed so far, oddly enough.

"Where is he?" the kid shouted at the students sitting in the bleachers. There was something familiar about his voice.

The young man leveled his rifle toward a cluster of kids in the first row, and Layne burst through the door.

The kid turned. His eyes met Layne's. For an endless fraction of a second, Layne's understanding of the situation formed, piece by piece. His mouth dropped open.

He recognized this school shooter.

"Noah?"

Noah Smith's eyes turned into giant white saucers as he lowered the assault rifle and cocked his head. "Mr. Parrish?"

2

LAYNE STOOD FIVE FEET AWAY FROM THE SHOOTER.

While Noah's eyes were still wide and his rifle lowered, Layne leaped forward and popped a quick right cross at Noah's chin. The punch jerked his head to the side and made him drop his AK, which went slack. The carrying sling over his shoulder kept it from falling away from his body.

But, since Noah had several other weapons strapped to various locations on a utility vest, Layne had to get in close. He would need to restrain Noah's hands to keep him from accessing any of them.

While the teenager was still recovering from the punch, Layne grabbed one of Noah's elbows and applied pressure, turning his body perpendicular to Layne's. Then, Layne looped his hands under Noah's armpits, backed up, and he linked his hands together behind the kid's head. This forced Noah's arms into the air, keeping the pistols and knives on his vest out of reach. Layne then leaned back until they toppled, sending them both to the ground. Layne below, Noah restrained while on top of him.

On his back, Layne wrapped his legs around Noah, keeping him in place. From down here, Layne couldn't move, but neither could Noah, which was good enough. Layne would sacrifice his own mobility to neutralize the threat.

All of this had taken place over the span of two seconds since Layne had first met Noah's eyes. All in a blur of sound and motion and Layne hadn't even consciously made any of those moves. They'd happened automatically as a result of years of training.

By now, Noah's shock seemed to be wearing off, and the young shooter tried to struggle free. He wriggled left and right and tried to pull his arms down to escape from Layne's grip.

Layne applied pressure, keeping the kid's limbs locked in place. The sound of sirens outside filtered in through the open gym windows. Any moment now, they would have company.

"Noah," Layne said, his mouth a few inches from the kid's ear. "Noah, what are you doing here? You don't even go to this school. Does your dad know where you are?"

Instead of answering, Noah swore and rambled and struggled to break free. Layne held firm, tensing his muscles to keep the kid from wriggling out of his grasp. Layne had a hundred pounds on him, but the adrenaline motivating the young man had changed him into a powerful force.

"Is there another shooter? Noah? Answer me. Are you alone here?"

Noah continued to thrash and grunt, and he did not

answer Layne's question. The gunshots had stopped now that Noah had been restrained, so Layne had to assume he was the only threat.

In the stands, dozens of teenage onlookers sat, paralyzed by fear, waiting for help.

But Layne didn't have to wait long for help to arrive. Within a few seconds, the doors to the gymnasium opened. A crew of SWAT team members came pouring through like water rushing over a burst dam.

And, oddly enough, a detail of private security followed the SWAT.

Who here had private security? How had they arrived so quickly?

The SWAT team members, their rifles held firmly in place, marched straight toward Layne and Noah. Barking orders as they swept forward in a fan formation.

"Sirs," Layne yelled against the din of shouts and gear rattling, "I have him subdued. He is still armed, but he cannot access his weapons."

"Who the hell are you?" said one of the SWAT. Still pointing their guns at both Noah and Layne.

"I'm not law enforcement," Layne said. "I made a citizen's arrest on this shooter. As far as I know, he's the only one."

Layne flicked his chin at the Colt Peacemaker on the floor, which had fallen out of his pocket when he jumped forward to punch Noah. "That's my revolver on the basketball court there, but otherwise, I'm unarmed."

The cops hesitated for a moment, weighing Layne's words.

Then, they swarmed and relieved Noah of all his weapons. By now, the young man had ceased his attempts to wrestle free. His fate had seemingly settled on him as his face drooped and his chest heaved and vibrated.

Layne relaxed his grip as the young man went slack and tears streamed down his cheeks. Next, the cops went to work untangling him from Layne.

3

THEY PUT HANDCUFFS ON LAYNE, BUT ONLY FOR A FEW minutes. He had to explain how he came to be armed with a loaded revolver inside a school while an active shooter situation had unfolded.

At first, Layne had trouble finding the words. The unbelievable nature of the situation had taken its toll on him. The shooter was Noah Smith, the son of Goran Smith, a man Layne would sometimes meet in the ring at a downtown Denver boxing gym. It took him a few tries to put aside his initial confusion so he could converse with the cops.

The SWAT and personal security team didn't want to hear much of what Layne was trying to tell them, anyway. Their faces turned increasingly dour as they demanded he recount his part in it over and over again.

But, a cop named Barry recognized Layne, because they used to ride together in a short-lived Colorado motorcycle club a few years back. This cop uncuffed Layne and returned his weapon to him.

The security detail was not so forgiving. Even when directed to leave Layne alone, they all eyed him from across the gym floor. Arms crossed, foreheads crinkled as they stared at him and muttered back and forth to each other.

"Who are those guys?" Layne asked Barry, nodding toward the men in the black suits.

"Senator Carroway's detail," Barry said.

"Why is a Senator's security detail here at the scene of a school shooting?" As soon as the words had left his mouth, Layne snapped into awareness. The kid in the classroom had said the shooter had been looking for him. The brave and terrified preppy kid who Layne had led out of the building.

And, when Layne had barged into the gym, Noah had been demanding to see a specific person. Trying to get the answer out of the terrified students in the bleachers.

That kid in the classroom had been the son of the senator. Noah had come here to kill or kidnap that specific kid. The deaths of these teachers and the security guard had been incidental.

Personal beef, or something bigger? What could possess him to go to such lengths to shoot up a school to take out one teenager?

As Layne watched them dragging Noah across the gym in cuffs, the young man made eye contact with Layne. "They're going to kill him now, you know that? That's on you."

"Who, Noah?" Layne said. "Who are they going to kill?"

The young man only shook his head, his sullen face pointed at the ground. At that moment, he no longer looked like a teenager to Layne. He'd transformed into a grim and aged person, resigned to his fate.

"You know the shooter?" Barry asked.

"A little. His dad and I box at the same gym in Denver sometimes."

"Understood. We will need a statement and the whole rigamarole down at the station. If anyone gives you shit, come see me. You're a hero, Layne, so don't let them push you around."

Layne spread a flat smile. "I don't know about the 'hero' business, but I appreciate your help."

"Don't sweat it. It's an ugly situation, no matter how you slice it." Barry craned his neck around as a new crew of official-looking people filtered in the gym doors. "Let's get out of here so the tech guys can get to work."

Layne watched officers escorting the children down from the bleachers, all of them stunned. Some crying, some in states of near catatonia. Had they all been gathered here for a pep rally or school-wide announcements?

Layne stood. "No problem. I'm ready to go."

"You got the senator's son out," Barry said. "His dad is going to be very excited to meet the man who saved his kid's life. Photo ops and free dinners are in your future."

Layne considered this. "Is there press out front yet?"

"By now? Probably."

Layne pointed at Noah. "Can I assume they're taking him out a back entrance?"

"Definitely."

"Then I'll go out with him. I have no interest in being on the news or meeting the senator for a key to the city."

"Suit yourself," Barry said, then pointed Layne toward

a line of cops escorting young Noah toward the back of the gym.

Layne's phone dinged in his pocket, and he pulled it out to see a text message from Inessa. She and Cameron had returned home safely. In a rare show of post-marriage concern, she asked for a reply text to confirm he was still alive.

Layne marveled at how much had happened during the fifteen minutes it had taken her to drive home. Lives had been lost. Others wrecked, maybe never to recover.

He sent a quick message to let her know he was fine, then he joined the line of cops escorting Noah out the back. They opened the rear door of the gym to bright sunshine, a warm spring morning in the Northwest Denver metro area.

And, as soon as they were all outside, Layne knew something was wrong. A sense of foreboding saturated the air. He could feel the cops around him tensing up as they noticed it, too.

A loud crack echoed across the expanse of the courtyard. Layne recognized the sound instantly. A sniper rifle.

Before anyone could do anything to stop it, a bullet punched a hole out the back of Noah Smith's head, sending a shower of red and gray across the brick facade of the building.

He was dead before his body even hit the ground.

And, as the cops all dropped to a crouch and hunted around for the shooter, Layne knew their efforts to stop any further attack wouldn't matter. Whoever had fired that shot from the rooftop of some nearby building had already commenced a hasty exit.

4

Even before the echo from the sniper's gunshot had faded, Layne took off. While the cops swarmed on Noah's dead body, they formed a circle in front of the door, guns out, crouching. They probably expected more attacks, but Layne knew better. With one shot, the sniper had taken out his target. No reason for him to stick around.

Layne set his sights on a three-story bank building across the street. He didn't know for sure that's where the sniper had been, but it made the most sense. It's the spot Layne would've selected. Close enough to guarantee a high-percentage shot, but far enough away to give the shooter options for his or her escape. All the other structures in the area were either houses or smaller buildings, making a getaway tricky.

Layne sprinted, although he didn't hold out much actual hope of catching the shooter. In the space between him and the bank building, collective panic had spread out and taken hold. Cars that had been previously plodding along the suburban streets now sped away to the adjoining streets. Pedestrians either screamed and ran or screamed and dropped for cover.

Layne was the only one rushing toward the chaos. Not the first time he'd done such a thing, but the first time in a long time.

He made it to the bank building in about fifteen seconds, and he immediately rounded the side, toward the back. There was no fire escape with ladder access anywhere he could see. Obviously, the shooter wouldn't try to escape from inside the building. Exterior access made the most sense.

The only way Layne found to descend from the roof to street-level was a storm drain. He approached it and noted a deep scrape running all the way to the top of the building. He tapped a finger against the scrape and found it hot to the touch, which didn't surprise him. The shooter had cinched something around this storm drain and then rappelled all the way down. Ballsy, but efficient. Aside from jumping, this had to be the quickest way down.

Climbing up after him or her was a waste of time. The shooter wouldn't be up there any longer. No doubt about it.

Layne flashed back to ten years ago, in Mexico City. He had been there with his team, chasing some Venezuelan gangsters who had fled across the border in Brownsville, Texas. A brutal crew. The gangsters were holed up in the Torre Insignia, a giant pyramid bank building. While Layne and his colleagues had searched the place floor by floor, the Venezuelans had scaled down the exterior of the pyramid with ropes and suction cups. Then, they'd escaped into the city, never to be seen again.

Layne had failed the mission that day, something he didn't know how to properly view when he was younger. Barely thirty years old then, and thinking he would be a spy forever. Thinking those losses would even out when compared to the potentially unlimited number of successes he would have throughout his career. Only a few years working on the team, Layne didn't yet know how each failed mission would weigh on him like a new stone added to a backpack he couldn't take off.

Now six years retired from that team, he still felt those stones back there at times, weighing on his shoulders.

Layne spun around and found an empty parking lot behind him, backing up to a neighborhood. Trees, power lines, wooden fences. Sidewalks and mailboxes. Nothing stood out as being out of place.

This assassin was good. Professional. The shot had been less than sixty seconds ago, and he or she had already fled. And now Noah was dead, so whoever had sent him into that school to kill or kidnap the senator's son was cleaning up the liabilities.

If he hadn't had a personal connection to this grim situation, Layne might have been tempted to tip his cap to the sheer skill of it. Send in a kid to kill, then take him out before he can do any damage to the mission's handlers. Brutal but effective.

Layne waited another few seconds, letting his heart rate slow and tuning his ears to find anything to give him a hint of a direction to hunt. Nothing appeared.

Nothing left to do.

All Layne had done was rush headfirst into something that was none of his business to begin with. But, like it or not, it was his business now.

He flexed his hands and rolled his head around his neck as he walked back toward the cops at the rear of the school. Noah was there, dead on the ground. His killer—most likely the same person who had armed him and sent him into the school to neutralize the senator's son—was in the wind.

5

Layne spent the next two hours at the police station. Fingerprinting, making statements, shuffling from room to room. Repeated scrutiny over the Colt revolver he'd had on him. Especially, why. Layne launched on a three-minute monologue about how he was always packing when out in public with his daughter. He had a concealed carry permit, which he readily showed them.

Aside from the gun, they were quite curious about the timeliness of his proximity to the shooting. It took some work for them to believe the *dumb luck* explanation. But, it was the truth.

Layne Parrish was no stranger to interrogation. They weren't too hard on him since most considered him a hero. They didn't even dig too deeply about how a forty-one-year-old retired security consultant with no sanctioned military or law enforcement training could enter an active shooter zone and restrain an armed hostile without taking a bullet. Maybe his tattoos and body-builder frame were enough of an explanation.

With a cup of coffee in one hand and a donut in the other, Layne waited on a bench outside of a detective's office to get the final permission to leave for the day. The skies opened up for a sudden and fierce rain, pelting against the windows. Such heavy rain was unusual for Colorado. It reminded him of Singapore, when the clouds would rage against the earth for hours at a time.

His mind swam and his body dragged. The mental exhaustion had pulled him down physically as well, one side effect of getting older. On the wrong side of forty, thinking too hard for too long could make him tired.

Barry, the cop Layne had recognized at the scene, stopped in front of the bench and extended a plastic pouch to Layne. His gun, wallet, and other personal effects were inside it.

"Sorry about the trouble," Barry said.

"It's okay. I don't blame anyone for being thorough, actually, and I'm happy to help."

Barry sat on the bench and looked Layne in the eye. "You okay? You think you can prepare for this, but no one's ever prepared for a live fire scenario."

Layne didn't want to admit to Barry that this wasn't the first shooting he'd ever seen. Not even the first school shooting he'd ever been unfortunate enough to experience. "I'll be okay. Just need to get home and crash on the couch for a bit."

"The senator was miffed that his son's savior isn't interested in meeting him."

"I'm not much for photo ops," Layne said.

"His people called here, trying to get your info. More than once."

Layne looked his friend in the eye. "Can you keep it in-house? I know it's a big ask, but the public attention is really not something I'm looking for right now. Tell them I'm an illegal immigrant, and I'm too scared I'll get deported."

When Barry cast a frown down at Layne's lily-white skin, Layne shrugged. "Or something like that."

"Sure. I can keep your involvement quiet."

Layne dropped a meaty hand on Barry's shoulder. "Appreciate it, man."

"The shooter's dad, he's a friend of yours?"

Layne tilted his head back and forth. "We're not close. Gym buddies, I guess you could say. Do you know if anyone's called him yet? I haven't seen him here."

"Sorry. Don't know."

Barry shook his hand and then walked away. Layne held up the plastic bag and shifted the contents around. Besides checking in with Inessa at some point, he thought he might call Goran Smith about his son. Layne thought he probably had Goran's number in his phone.

The detective's door opened, and he leaned out into the hall. "Mr. Parrish? Just need a couple more minutes of your time."

TWENTY MINUTES LATER, Layne was on his way, headed back toward his car outside of Inessa's house in Broomfield. The detectives had asked him not to leave town since they'd probably want to speak with him again in the course of investigating the shooting and Noah's death by a sniper.

Layne stared out the window as the patrol car navigated through the park. The school adjacent to it was a swarm of press and parents, standing amid the police tape flapping in the breeze.

Layne thanked the officer for the ride and hustled over to his car. He thought about going in to see Inessa and Cameron but decided against it. This was right around Cam's nap time, and Inessa tended to nap with her daughter. Better not risk it by knocking on the door. Then, when he noted the fan in the window of Cameron's room, that sealed the deal. Inessa only turned on the fan for nap time.

Instead, he looked at his phone and tried to call the shooter's dad Goran, for the third time. Straight to voicemail again.

Something about this bothered Layne, so he put the car into gear and headed toward Goran's house. He'd been there exactly one time, for a barbecue last summer. Layne thought Goran had only invited him that day because Layne had overheard about the party while Goran had been discussing it with some friends at the gym. They hadn't ever been close enough to socialize outside of the gym.

At that barbecue, Layne had spent more time talking to Noah than anyone else, actually. They'd been paired up for a horseshoe tournament in the backyard, and Layne coached the kid into becoming a solid horseshoe thrower in a short amount of time.

Hard to believe the same pimple-faced and bright-eyed kid had murdered multiple people and then himself taken a bullet, only a few hours ago.

Layne piloted his car across Broomfield to Westminster, the next suburb in the sprawling spider web of interconnected towns that made up the area of Greater Denver.

And, as soon as Layne turned off 94th and onto Perry Street, he knew something was wrong. First, a single police car streamed by. Then, a second cop car. Finally, an ambulance, rushing directly toward Goran's house.

Since his son had been involved in a school shooting, the cop cars made sense. But an ambulance?

When Layne was within sight of the house, his mouth dropped open. Goran Smith's two-bedroom brick house with the powder blue siding had been cordoned off with police tape. The reflection of flashing lights bounced off the house's windows. Two plainclothes detectives stood in the front yard, and a third headed toward a neighbor's house.

Layne parked as close as possible and left his car. He wandered down the street, trying to get a look, but trying not to seem like a lurker. At the edge of the property, a detective noticed him, and held up his hands, keeping Layne back.

But, a few seconds later, Layne saw what he'd expected to see. Paramedics wheeling a stretcher out the front door. Underneath the sheet, a male figure, Caucasian, at least 6'3" and muscular.

It had to be Goran Smith, Layne's gym acquaintance who boxed like a wounded animal but always had a fresh and clean dad-joke for the locker room afterward. A man who spoke with a hint of an Eastern European accent, but often talked about how much he loved America.

Now, father to a school shooter.

He was dead underneath that sheet.

They're going to kill him too, Noah had said, only moments before the sniper's bullet had erased the young man.

"Officer," Layne said to a uniformed cop standing near the ambulance. The cop turned around and raised his eyebrows, waiting for Layne to say what he wanted.

"What happened here?"

The cop swished his lips around for a second as if debating whether or not to answer. "Heart attack."

"Really? Why all these cop cars and police tape for a heart attack?"

The cop's expression changed, and he launched into full suspicion mode. "That's none of your business, sir."

The cop lingered for a second as if he might pull out a pad and pen to take Layne's name, but Layne held up his hands in surrender and walked away before the cop could do anything else.

Layne supposed it wasn't unnatural for all these cops to be out here, given what Goran's son had done a few hours ago. The cops had to know something was up. No way could this be a real heart attack.

First, the people behind this had set up his son to pull a job, then they'd killed that son, and now they'd taken out Goran, too.

6

Layne waited a few hours before he took any action. He needed the time to process things and decide on next steps. Pieces of the puzzle were scattered all over the board.

He went to Inessa's house to see his daughter Cameron. Inessa bombarded him with questions as soon as he entered her house. With Cameron there, who was oblivious to the gravity of the whole episode, Layne said little about it. All that mattered was that the three of them were safe. He offered a few curt answers to close off any conversation, and Inessa eventually dropped her investigation.

Since he still had a few days left of his week in their alternating shared custody cycle, he considered taking Cam back to his apartment in Boulder. Instead, he suggested to Inessa they all have dinner together at her house. The events of the day had shaken Inessa enough to make her agree.

After dinner, Cameron asked questions about the loud

noises and why daddy was running across the grass at the park. Layne answered what he could without delving into any specifics. A three-year-old didn't need to know about the horrors that had happened inside the school. Someday, she would have to be aware of school shootings, but not today.

Layne's mind drifted to Goran and Noah Smith, the lives of two people he'd known, cut short within a few hours of each other. Erased. Noah had ventured into the school, armed to the teeth, to find the son of a senator and put a bullet in him. Why? The most likely answer was revenge against the senator, or to put pressure on him for some reason. Leverage.

Layne considered calling his old teammate Harold Boukadakis to ask him to look up the senator and find out what dirty secrets he might have to warrant such a harsh measure. But, he held off going in that direction for now. Maybe best to give it another day or two to think it through.

This puzzle had multiple dimensions. Noah hadn't accomplished his task inside the school, so there had been a contingency shooter outside, to take out Noah, to make sure he couldn't confess and give up the names.

That meant he *knew* the names of the people who had put him up to this.

And, more troubling was the death of his father, Goran Smith. The timing suggested the same people had silenced him, too. That meant Goran had known what his son was doing in the school. And he had approved, or he had at least known enough about it to become a problem for the organizers.

Goran had known something dangerous enough to warrant his death. Layne needed to find out what.

Near Cameron's bedtime, he helped Inessa put their little one to sleep there, then he drove to Goran Smith's house in nearby Westminster. He made a slow approach and parked far enough away to leave his car out of sight. Head down, Rockies baseball cap pulled low, he shuffled along the sidewalk until he was within sight of the house.

Layne observed a single cop car watching Goran's front door, with one officer inside that car. Layne found a bench that put him out of sight of the cop's rear and side mirrors, then he waited. Somewhere around eleven at night that officer fell asleep.

So Layne went to work.

Hunkered down, he crossed the street and approached the house. He figured he had twenty or thirty minutes until the sleeping officer woke up, either naturally, or due to a squawk from his radio.

But Layne told himself to be in and out faster than that. After setting a timer on his watch, he approached the backyard and hopped over the fence. Positioned in the rain-soaked grass was a wooden ramp for skateboard tricks. Stickers all over the side of the thing. Noah's skateboard sat at the base of the ramp. Eventually, someone would come to take these things away. Maybe Goran's ex-wife, or a sibling or cousin. They would languish in storage for a while, then maybe end up sold for cheap at a garage sale.

Layne skirted to the back door where he found a single piece of yellow police tape across the entrance. The door wasn't even locked. Layne checked the tightness of his gloves, slid it open, and pointed his ear to the inside, listening. No sound came back.

Layne eased inside the house. "Okay," he whispered, inhaling to center himself and letting muscle memory take over. The subterfuge of the home invasion was a skill Layne had learned long ago, and one he often told himself he no longer needed. Since his retirement, that had turned out to be untrue more times than he wanted to admit.

From experience, Layne knew to go straight for the bedroom closet and the home office. Maybe the garage if Goran kept important items out there. Layne wasn't sure what he was looking for, but he would know it when he found it. Something to indicate why the people behind this would have killed Goran immediately after sending his son to die.

Names or dates or locations written somewhere. That was what Layne needed to discover.

He first checked a built-in desk in the kitchen. There he found all the usual items like scratched out to do lists, bits of paper with phone numbers scribbled, and shopping lists. When he turned around from the desk, he noted a framed portrait hanging on the wall next to the sink. A picture of Goran and Noah standing arm in arm, up near Rocky Mountain National Park. Layne recognized Longs Peak behind them. That snowy and jagged structure of rock towering above the area northwest of Denver.

Layne averted his eyes. While he and Goran weren't close, he still didn't want to think about losing him. Maybe Goran had it easy; he didn't have to adjust to life without his only son.

Layne moved on to the bedroom where he searched around for a safe or for file cabinets. He found neither. But, Layne did find one interesting detail in the room. There was a record player that was not plugged in, sitting on top of a stack of rubber bins. The odd part wasn't Goran owning a record player, it was that the record player was the only thing in that area of the room not covered in dust. Even the bins below looked untouched for months or years.

There were stacks of records on the shelf next to it, but they were all dusty. Unused.

A giant red flag appeared in Layne's mind.

He approached the record player and thought about how to handle it before he made contact. The base of the player was large enough to conceal a bomb, or some other boobytrap. With his ear turned to it, Layne listened for vibration or any sort of active mechanical sound coming from inside the thing.

He tore off a piece of paper from a nearby legal pad and tried to slide it underneath the bottom of the record player. When it passed all the way in with no obstruction, Layne felt satisfied there was no pressure switch underneath it.

After a few more seconds of complication, he decided there was no threat.

He made sure his latex gloves were tight and had no holes in them as he lifted the record player and then set it on the ground. Underneath the player, inside the first rubber bin, were more scattered documents and pages but something nestled underneath all that stuff caught Layne's interest. A brochure from the school where the shooting had taken place. It was a pamphlet describing a proposed expansion to the school. This pamphlet also effectively acted as a blueprint for the current school layout.

Noah didn't go to that school, so there was no reason Goran should have this pamphlet.

Goran had known about the operation today.

Next, Layne found his smoking gun. Underneath that brochure was a yellow legal pad. On that legal pad, Goran —or someone—had sketched an image of a phoenix rising from the ashes. Below that phoenix were the words Winged House, a phone number, and an address. Also, as Layne studied the phoenix image, he noted part of it looked like the flag of Belarus.

The address for Winged House was in Golden, about thirty minutes south of where Layne lived in Boulder. Alongside the address were a series of dates. Many of the dates had been scratched out, except for one date in particular, underlined: today.

And, next to the date, the initials *AB*. Circled many times.

Layne took out his phone and snapped a picture of the yellow legal pad. He didn't know if it would amount to anything, but Layne's intuition told him he needed to dig into the Winged House and *AB*.

7
———

Layne arrived in Golden bright and early the next morning. Golden, Colorado was a little town on the edge of the mountains west of Denver, home to the Coors brewery and meandering suburbs of identical houses. Rolling green hills strangely absent of trees, endless bike lanes, and shadows from the mountains towering to the west.

Winged House was an educational program center and a halfway house for recent graduates of prison. They'd based it in a former hotel a little west of town, butting up to a hill. Four stories, with residential housing, group therapy, both live-in and outpatient. The website contained info about the organization's tax-exempt status and vague text about charity work.

Layne parked in a large lot in front of the repurposed hotel, and took stock of the aging building. The thing was massive. His research online indicated that Winged House occupied only the first two floors of the hotel, for residents and classroom areas. The upper floors were home to spiders and raccoons. Those areas had been marked for future renovation.

As he left his car in the lot and started toward the building, Layne first heard music booming from a nearby truck. Something in the metal genre, grinding and dark, with a guttural scream of vocals to accompany the hard guitars and churning drums. Loud, but not loud enough for anyone to call the cops.

There were two men in the back of the truck, sitting in the bed, playing cards. Rough types, both looking like they'd spent time behind bars. They glared at Layne with slanted eyes as he strolled by. Their gazes tracked him, and they held their cards in their hands, pausing the game to check him out.

Layne waited for either of these white men with buzzed haircuts and visible face tattoos to say something to him. But, they seemed content to give him a nonverbal stare-down until he'd left their immediate area. He could feel their eyes drilling into his back as he passed them and then came to a stop before the door to the front entrance.

Layne paused before entering the building.

If he did this, he was embarking on a course he couldn't reverse. Committing to see this all the way through.

With gritted teeth, Layne opened the door.

When he entered the building, he came upon a large reception area dead ahead. To his left were locked glass doors, leading off to hallways in a restricted area. To his right was the entrance to the cafeteria and meeting rooms past that. Tall ceilings, wooden paneling, exposed ductwork. Unlike the exposed ductwork in hipster restaurants in Denver, this didn't look like a fashionable design choice. More like another prospect for future renovation.

"Can I help you?" asked a frumpy Slavic woman in her fifties, standing behind the reception desk. She had a razor-sharp haircut dyed purplish-red and a boxy frame below that. Her eyebrows arched down over her eyes, pulling them into a perpetual glare.

He nodded. "I called about a tour."

The woman scanned a clipboard page, and then her eyes brightened when she landed on the name. "Mr. Haskell?"

Layne Parrish nodded. "That's me."

The woman grabbed a walkie-talkie from the desk, whispered something into it, and then exited via a little door in the side. She escorted Layne over to the locked glass doors and then pressed a small key card against a panel. The door beeped and hesitated a moment before opening. Layne glimpsed the security panel near the door, and the high tech nature of it struck a dissonant chord, given how dilapidated everything else appeared. Layne had spent a few years after his retirement from espionage ops working in the security business, and he knew this was an expensive system. Top-dollar kind of expensive.

"I'm Raisa Sokolov," said the frumpy woman. "Your message said you were seeking outpatient. Do you have documentation from your PO? You didn't say anything about it on the phone."

"PO doesn't require anything specific. This is voluntary for me. I'm just having trouble adjusting to life outside, if you know what I mean."

Raisa gave him a grave nod. "I do, Mr. Haskell. Let me show you what we have to offer." Layne's guide escorted him down a long hall which branched off into several conference rooms. She explained how these conference rooms were meeting spots where both inpatient and outpatient Winged House guests would meet every morning for group discussion sessions. Raisa then escorted him up a stairwell, into the male-only dormitories.

In addition to male-only, Layne noted he saw not a single person of color anywhere around. Lots of white men with shaved heads and bargain-basement tattoos.

As they worked their way back down through the halls and toward the front, Layne cataloged everything he could see. So far, nothing seemed too far out of the ordinary. He'd expected a halfway house filled with ex-cons to feel like a grim and foreboding place, and Winged House did not disappoint.

But, he had not yet figured a reason Goran was in possession of this place's info, or why the address and the dates held any significance.

But, when they entered the cafeteria, all of that changed.

Raisa had continued her sales speech all the way back down past the lobby and then walked him to the right side, where they found a large mess hall and more meeting spaces.

The sizable cafeteria was empty except for two groups of people. One was the food workers preparing breakfast, putting stainless steel bins filled with food into troughs for a breakfast salad bar. The other was a small group of men and women, well-dressed, seated around one of the long dining tables. And, as soon as Layne entered the room, he heard the accent. At the head of the table was a tall and sturdy man with jet black hair and crystal blue eyes. He had a sharp nose and angular features.

But his accent made Layne take notice. Belarus. Almost like Russian, but just different enough to stand out.

There was no mistaking it. Goran Smith had always spoken with a hint of the same accent. Even though Layne had never directly asked Goran about his heritage, he'd always suspected "Smith" to be an adopted American name.

The people at the table stopped talking when Layne and Raisa entered the room. They looked up at him with suspicious eyes. Layne's guide blushed. "I'm so sorry," Raisa said. "I didn't know you were having a meeting, Mr. Borovitch."

The lanky man stood, buttoning his suit as he did so. He strutted away from the table, long limbs slicing through the air as he walked. He grinned, exposing a gold tooth shining near the back of his mouth.

The man stuck out a hand. Bony fingers marked with a hint of nicotine stains, although Layne smelled no smoke on his clothes. A surreptitious smoker, no doubt.

"Artyom Borovitch," he said. Layne stuck out a hand to shake, and when he gripped the man's hand, he immediately knew this was *AB*, the bastard who had sent his friend's son to die in a school shooting.

8

A FEW HOURS LATER, LAYNE RETURNED FOR HIS FIRST session of the day. Outpatient. He spent time with the front desk woman Raisa, filling out paperwork. She was apparently also the primary Intake Counselor. Once he was a paying customer—and paying in cash no less, instead of insurance—Raisa lightened her gruff attitude by a few degrees.

Layne hadn't been to prison, so he faked all his details. He still had contacts in the government who could help him make it look as if he had actually spent time in the Limon Correctional Facility. Just a few phone calls to make sure all her database searches would check out.

He wasn't concerned about faking all that info, though. He was more interested in figuring out how he could earn a chance to get close to Artyom, the Winged House director. Clearly, a man with something to hide. In an organization such as this, Layne had two options: the indirect espionage of spying, or the direct espionage of gaining Artyom's confidence. Either route had its complications.

Layne attended his first actual educational meeting in the late afternoon. A roundtable discussion of a dozen ex-cons, sharing life skills needed in the real world. Without exception, every single one of them regarded Layne with a suspicious eye. Fresh meat. But, not only that. They all looked at him as if they knew something he didn't. In a place like this, Layne suspected there were drug runners, clandestine gambling circles, and who-knew-what else. Of course, they wouldn't let him into any of their cliques until he'd proved his trustworthiness.

Layne held back, watched, and observed. He knew better than to make waves or to give anyone less than their respect due. Avoid prolonged eye contact and keep to himself.

Another odd practice Layne noticed: frequently, counselors/teachers would enter the classroom and pull individual students out of the session to talk alone. No one seemed to regard this as suspicious, but they never explained these absences.

Definitely, something deeper was going on here.

After a half-hour, they took a break and were allowed to wander the halls and venture outside for a smoke. Years off cigarettes, Layne was still a slave to nicotine, but he ingested all of his in lozenge form now. The smell of cigarettes made him ill. Funny, since he used to suck down a pack a day at his worst.

Layne explored the inner hallways alone since no one had allowed him into any social circles yet. Apparently, outpatient attendees had fewer restrictions than the residential halfway house guests. Neither group welcomed him, though.

Layne noted one thing right away about this current hallway: the exposed ductwork above his head looked sturdier than the ducts in the main lobby, even large enough for a person to fit inside. As he navigated the halls, studying the paths, he was trying to use it to make a mental map of the layout. Never knew when it might come in handy.

Raisa hovered near him as he explored. Mostly, she glared at any of the ex-cons who seemed to take an obvious disliking to Layne. She was offering him some sort of "new guy" protection. He wondered how long that might last, and what they would do when she backed off. Layne wasn't afraid of confrontation, but he preferred to keep a low profile for as long as possible.

Eventually, Raisa's walkie-talkie chirped, and she returned to the front desk area. Without his protector, the other outpatient people didn't swarm him, but they made no moves to accept him into the group, either. Layne played it cool like he didn't care.

And then, he saw Artyom at the end of the hall. He was walking along, cell phone up to his ear. Gesticulating with his free hand. Looking upset and arguing with the person on the phone.

For a moment, Layne did nothing as a sudden and unexpected swirl of rage filled him. He had to bat it back down. Young Noah Smith had almost certainly died because of this man. If Layne let that thought skulk around in his brain too long, he might try to kill Artyom with his bare hands. But he couldn't do that. Not yet.

Layne needed to get closer to know more. Any information would be useful at this point.

He removed from his pocket the little guide that showed him where classes would be and then he ambled down the hall, feigning confusion about which rooms were which. As he drifted toward Artyom, Layne could pick up bits of the conversation from a reasonable distance. Definitely, not speaking English. It sounded like Belarusian—or maybe Russian—but Layne wasn't certain. Since his ex-wife spoke fluent Russian, and the languages were similar enough, Layne could understand many of the words. It had been a long time since he'd traveled to Minsk or Moscow or had paid much attention to either language.

As Layne neared Artyom, the halfway house director took notice. Layne averted his eyes, positioning his face away so Artyom wouldn't get a good look at him.

Artyom told the caller to hold so they could resume their conversation in private. Now, Layne's interest had definitely been piqued. And, he was becoming increasingly certain it was Belarusian Artyom was speaking, which tied into the flag of Belarus Layne had seen on the brochure he'd uncovered at Goran's house.

Artyom ducked into a nearby room marked *Conference Room Eagle* and closed the door behind him. Layne considered leaning up against the door, but there were others in the hall. Too risky. Especially since they were still giving him the "new guy" eye.

But, he remembered the ductwork. Using the exposed piping as a blueprint guide, he skirted down the hallway past two more doors, until the ducts turned right and vanished into the wall above a maintenance room. Layne opened the door and entered the little room. He found himself inside a dark closet, with no other way out.

Bingo. The duct passed through the room, with an open grate providing air. Layne shined his phone's flashlight around and located a chair among the cleaning supplies and mop buckets, then he scooted the chair under the grate. He pushed his ear against it and closed his eyes.

After a few seconds of concentration, he could hear Artyom speaking in Belarusian. Layne lost another few seconds of precious conversation by playing catch-up in his head and reminding himself how to translate the language on the fly. But, when he was able to get up to speed, the words streamed by like watching captions on a TV show.

"The senator," Artyom said in a Belarusian dialect that Layne mostly understood. "No, the child failed." A long pause. "Yes, the committee. The Senate Intelligence Committee. The important one. He's the only one who can make it happen." Another pause. "Well, I don't know. As much as we want to avoid triggering that situation, maybe it is time—"

Before Layne could find out what the situation was that Artyom didn't want to trigger, the door opened behind him. Light flooded in, making him blink a few times against the brightness as he spun.

There stood Raisa, a scowl on her wrinkly face.

"What the hell are you doing in here on that chair? Sneaking drinks from a hip flask? Some little vapor marijuana device? Jerking off into a sock?"

"Excuse me?" Layne said.

Raisa unclipped the walkie-talkie from her belt. "I've

seen it all, Mr. Haskell. Everyone thinks they're clever, and they're usually wrong."

"I wasn't doing anything like that," he said, which did not ease her scowl or make her lower the walkie. "Just needed a moment alone. I get panicky, sometimes, talking to other ex-cons. You didn't see the way they were looking at me out there."

Raisa's eyes fell down to Layne's chest and biceps, which were bulging and pushing the limits of his shirt. Layne didn't often sell *intimidated* well since he looked like someone who flipped over monster truck tires in his spare time.

"Panicky?" she said, finger hovering above the walkie button.

He nodded. "I'm feeling better now. Just needed a second to myself. Sorry I didn't ask for permission first. It won't happen again."

After a deep breath, she put away the walkie. "Okay, fine. But, you can't do your quiet time here. This room is off-limits."

As she took a step back and beckoned him to follow her, Layne cast eyes at the grate in the ductwork. He could still hear the mumbling of conversation, but the words were too faint to catch.

9

After his aborted attempt to eavesdrop, Layne returned to afternoon sessions, keeping his distance from Raisa. Her protective "new guy" overwatch ended immediately, though. She scrutinized him for the rest of the day. Layne pretended not to notice.

The next session was all about basic mechanical life skills, discussing topics like paying bills on time and nonviolent conflict resolution. Layne was a bit surprised how well these gritty ex-cons took to such basic advice. Even the ones sporting teardrop tattoos across their cheeks would scribble notes when the lecturer talked about how to make a schedule so the trash cans could arrive at the corner once a week.

Not that Layne had much room to judge when it came to tattoos. He had ink from his shoulders to his wrists, covering up various scars and bullet wounds. Also, the end product of years of undercover and espionage work. Sometimes, an hour or two of gritted teeth in a tattoo artist's chair was the only way to unwind. After some of the things he'd seen, the vibrating sting of a needle was a welcome release.

When classes finished for the day, Layne wandered around on campus, trying to formulate his next move. The pieces of the previous conversation he'd overheard rattled around in his brain. Something about the Senate Intelligence Committee and "the child" not succeeding. The child was obviously Noah Smith. The detail about the intelligence committee seemed to confirm Layne's suspicions that Noah had gone into that school to kill or kidnap the senator's son, who was a student there. Yet, nothing explained how any of that tied back to Artyom. Or, what purpose killing the senator's son would have on the intelligence committee.

At the beginning of these investigations, Layne always felt like he didn't even know which puzzle piece to set down first. The corners of the puzzle were lost among the haphazard collection.

And then, when Layne came to a window overlooking the courtyard in the middle of the complex, an idea materialized. Artyom was again on his cell phone, wandering around the courtyard, walking lazy laps.

Layne didn't need to be within earshot to record. He had a way to eavesdrop on conversations with software as long as he had a high-quality video capture.

He pulled out his phone and centered Artyom in the frame. Too far away. He zoomed in, but that made the picture too grainy. Layne needed clear, high-resolution video of Artyom's mouth to make the software work.

Time to move.

Layne hustled down the hall and back to the first floor. Raisa was near the front desk, so Layne pivoted and headed for the door out to the courtyard. She followed him, and Layne watched out of his peripheral, but he kept his eyes forward.

Past her, he opened the door to find a grass-lined area populated by ex-cons and counselors walking and talking, enjoying the sunny afternoon. There was one active spot where groups played yard games like horseshoes and cornhole.

Layne spotted Artyom sitting on a bench not far away, still on the call. His face scrunched, his free hand slicing the air like an orchestra conductor. Too far to hear, though. Also, he was isolated, which suggested he might be engaged in a conversation worthy of eavesdropping.

Layne whipped out his phone, pointed the camera at him, and then proceeded to record video. He covered his tracks by kneeling and angling the camera in the general direction of a ladybug crawling along the stem of a leaf. Artyom was still mostly in frame, but Layne could definitely make the claim he was shooting a harmless nature video.

Layne stayed in place, following the little ladybug around, keeping an eye on Artyom and ensuring he stayed in focus. To sell the move, he had to keep his head pointed in one direction, which exposed him to approach from the rear. He had no choice but to hope no one interrupted him.

For the next sixty seconds, he got his wish, until the shuffling of feet in the grass appeared nearby.

"Hey," said a deep and gravelly voice.

Layne shifted his eyes from the camera to see a giant of a man towering over him, fists balled. Scowling down at Layne.

"Can I help you?" Layne asked.

"What do you think you're doing?"

Layne shrugged. "Nothing much, man."

"No pictures or video recordings at Winged House. HIPAA compliance. We got a right to privacy and what you're doing is against the rules."

Layne wasn't sure if he had enough video recorded to glean anything useful, but no sense in getting in trouble twice on his first day. "No problem. I had no idea." He slipped the phone back into his pocket and stood. He extended a hand toward the guy, who had about three inches and fifty pounds on Layne's sinewy frame.

"We're good, right?"

The guy sneered at Layne's hand and then stomped away.

LAYNE HAULED ass to Broomfield to retrieve Cameron from her daycare before closing time. They charged a hefty per-minute fee for late pickups. Whenever it was his custody week, and he and Cam weren't at his cabin in the mountains, he often arrived in the nick of time. The watch would chime six pm just as he was typing in his personal code to access the building. But, the flirty women who worked there didn't mind at all and tried to chat him up any time he appeared.

On the way from Broomfield to Boulder, he and Cameron talked about trains and horses and bicycles and traffic lights. Cameron also recounted a suspenseful tale of how another preschooler kept making faces at her during nap time, getting them both in trouble for giggling.

At his modest two-bedroom apartment, Layne plugged his phone into his laptop moments after setting down Cameron's dinner in front of her. Around her second birthday, she refused to sit in a high chair at the dinner table. Layne had bought her a step-stool-with-guardrails contraption for her to learn how to wash her hands at the sink, and after that, she only wanted to eat her meals at the table, standing up. Layne had dubbed it Cameron's Command Tower, and he carted it back and forth between the cabin in South Fork and the condo in Boulder.

A TV in the background droned on. News coverage of the shooting. Layne had muted the TV so Cameron wouldn't hear it, of course. As the debate flared on news media between second amendment people vs. gun control people vs. mental health people, Layne wondered how far the police would reach in their investigation. A school shooter killed immediately after his shooting. Some of the detectives wouldn't push too hard, thinking the kid had gotten what he'd deserved.

Of course, the conspiracy sites would go nuts if they didn't solve the crime. An assassin killed by a sniper, and no one could find the sniper? The debate over this incident would persist for months or years.

Cameron thumbed on her iPad and dug a little plastic spoon into her tray of blueberries.

"What do you say?" Layne asked.

"Thank you, Daddy."

"You're welcome, little one. Eat your vegetables, too."

"So I be big and strong?"

"That's right."

When the laptop recognized the phone, Layne waited a few moments for the software to load and read the video files. This little gem of a program had been gifted to Layne by Harry Boukadakis, the hacker extraordinaire who had written it himself. Using facial recognition and linguistics, this program could take a clear video of a human speaker and translate his or her lip movements into text.

Layne had never thought he'd need it. Until today, he hadn't.

While the thing chugged and churned and tried to process the data, Layne's thoughts drifted to the last time he'd seen Goran at the gym. Maybe six weeks ago. He'd been in a foul mood, and when they'd met in the ring that day, he'd taken out his aggression on Layne. They were evenly matched as boxers, so Layne didn't mind Goran turning up the effort.

When the round ended, they both leaned over the ropes, dripping sweat. Goran then apologized and said he'd been having a hard time at work. He and Layne tapped boxing gloves, and all was forgiven.

That man was dead now. Could he have actually been involved in this plot to gain leverage on a US senator? Could he have helped send his son to die, or did he not know about it?

The software traced a rough replica of Artyom's face as the video frames ticked on. Across the table, Cameron sang along with a cartoon theme song, leaking from her iPad's speakers. She picked up a hunk of broccoli and shoved it in her mouth. She made a sound to get Layne's attention, then stuck her tongue out at him.

When Layne grinned at her, she giggled back.

"Not such big bites, Cam."

"Okay, Daddy. Small bites only, I promise, forever."

He chuckled as the software routine finished and a text document loaded in its place. Layne clicked on it and scanned over the contents. Several parts had translated as garbled and unreadable, marked by (()), but he could understand enough to get the gist. He read it a few times before it all settled over him, and then the implications clicked into place.

No, no. (()) The senator. Yes, Carroway. Senator Carroway. (()) It was his idiot son who got away from the school. (()) Yes, he's the one keeping Pavel at the dark site. Not too far from the beach, we think, but it could be several miles in the jungle... if we knew that, we wouldn't still be looking, obviously. Maybe on the north end of the island. The Americans whisked him away there, but we've been unable to find him. (()) Carroway knows where he is for sure. (()) Treating him as a common enemy combatant. No, I do not know the conditions. The only one who can bring him home to us is the senator. (()) I've been thinking lately it's time to initiate the Omega failsafe. (()) Yes, then we move on from the alternate to the primary target. (()) I don't want to do it, either. But, if things don't look up soon, we may not have any choice. We have a window coming up in a little over one week, and if we're going to move, that is the day we must do it.

INTERLUDE 1

FORT COLLINS, CO | SIXTEEN YEARS AGO

Layne Parrish blinks as the sun emerges from behind puffs of clouds. On his back in the grass, the wind makes water from the lagoon lap against the banks. He's on campus, and the sounds of bike tires grinding pavement hum around him like birdsong. People stroll by along the grass next to the canal, toward the bookstore. Undergrads already trying to cash in on their used textbooks. Finals week isn't even over yet.

He checks his watch and realizes he still has thirty more minutes until a meeting with his advisor. Probably the last meeting with his advisor. Their mutual career is coming to a close.

It's coming to a close because Layne is almost finished with his master's thesis. Twenty-four years old, a psychology grad student at Colorado State University in Fort Collins, Layne is tired of the relentless grind of education. He knows he will have to spend a couple more years of grunt work to get his LPC before he can actually practice real therapeutic work. Supervised sessions, then unsupervised, working for someone else in a mental health facility somewhere, or in a drug rehab, or maybe a hospital. It will still be a few years until he can open his own private practice. Maybe down in Denver, or maybe Austin, or New York. He's keeping his options open at this point.

But today, Layne doesn't care about that. Today he's not thinking five or ten years into the future. No thoughts of settling down and buying a house and starting a family, worrying about school districts and life insurance.

He's also not thinking about the past. Definitely not thinking about *her*. He does still reminisce about her from time to time, but not as much as he used to. When the incident first happened, it was all he could think about. So much that it almost wrecked his chance at college.

When Layne was younger, his father had said this about memory: *over time, you will only remember the good parts*.

Layne's not sure if that's true now, or if it will ever be true, but he does think about his girlfriend's suicide less frequently as time goes on. He can see her eyes and her face, her smile, and not as much of the way she ended. He can hear her laugh and feel her fingers on his skin, sending electric shocks when she touches him.

Layne sits up, now in a strange headspace after transitioning from thinking about clouds and his advisor and his future to her.

It's okay, though. Most days, he doesn't dwell on her.

He's supposed to meet Samir and Logan at the Town Pump bar for happy hour soon, but now he doesn't know if he feels like going. Logan said there's a good chance the cute teacher's assistant from their Social Psych class will be there, but Layne's not sure if that sweetens the deal or not. He doesn't expect to be in Fort Collins much longer, and neither a one-night stand nor a long distance relationship sound appealing. No, he should have asked her out last fall, when he first saw her in class. They shared a look, and he wanted to approach her then but opted not to do anything about it.

He feels okay about that decision now, though. There will be other cute women at other bars in the future.

Layne shoves a few books in his backpack and zips it up as he lights a cigarette. He gazes at the brick and stone building of the Lory Student Center in front of him, the gargantuan gathering place on campus.

The cigarette feels harsh in the heat of this late Spring afternoon. He prefers to smoke in the cold, to pretend it's warming him, even though he knows cigarettes have no magical healing powers.

And then, the sound of a gunshot cracks the silence. The dozens of other students on the lawn across from the Lory all look around, pausing their games of frisbee and their picnic study sessions to figure out what's happening.

Another gunshot. Layne is now sure that's what he heard this time.

He makes eye contact with an undergrad crossing in front of him. The kid's eyes are wide, full of fear. Maybe nineteen years old. He apparently knows that sound too, because he doesn't linger. Clutching his backpack, he does the smart thing and sprints away, toward University Ave.

One of the glass doors at the front of the Student Center flies open, and a young woman with shoulder-length dreadlocks charges out of the building, her hands in the air, waving frantically.

"Gun! Shooter inside!"

She stumbles down the stairs and lands on the pavement, and then bounces back up on her feet as she resumes her panicked jog. "There's a shooter inside the Lory! Assault rifle!"

Layne watches the young woman race across the campus toward the street. Several others are still paralyzed by confusion, turning left and right, unsure if they should flee, or in which direction to go.

Layne lets his backpack fall to the ground.

And although he does not know in the moment why he does this, and he may never truly understand, Layne snuffs out his cigarette and runs toward the building.

10

Artyom Borovitch frowned at the small recorder on his desk as the journalist fiddled with it.

"So sorry," the woman said. She was a short and plump Belarusian, with liver spots on the backs of her hands, and threads of gray through her hair. While Artyom himself had quite a few strands of gray running through his midnight hair, he'd always found it a distasteful quality in a woman. Perhaps if she were old enough to qualify for a nursing home, but any woman who could still drive a car should take better care of herself. Simple pride in one's appearance was a basic human necessity.

But mostly, Artyom didn't like the way she seemed to have so much trouble with her equipment. It was as if she had not tested her recorder before coming to Golden to meet with him. That was the first fact about her professionalism Artyom thought disagreeable.

Second, how she probed him. She wanted to conceal her lack of knowledge and her disheveled appearance by *acting tough*. The little questions designed to make him spill things he shouldn't, to open him up for further probing. He wasn't stupid. He knew full well when someone was trying to ply him with compliments or soften him with praise. Threats almost seemed preferable. At least those were out in the open.

"Is it fixed yet?" Artyom asked.

"One more moment," she said. She slid in a fresh AA battery and then set the recorder back onto the edge of his desk. "There. My apologies. Please, continue."

"We built a business in America because they call it the land of opportunity. But, everything we do here is to help Belarus. All is always for Belarus."

The journalist leaned forward, her fat little chin wiggling as she shifted to the edge of her chair. "How so?"

"Because I say it is. Because the United States does many underhanded things to fund bad politics in my home country, and we will fight it with funds for good politicians of our own choosing. We will not let them install a puppet government."

The harshness of his tone made her eyes creak open, and she returned to a normal sitting position, which had been his hope. No reason for her to become too comfortable. She was here to serve *his* purpose, after all.

"Tell me again the name of your *blog*," he said, drawing out the last word to show his disdain.

"I run a respected website in Kansas City, dealing with issues related to Belarusian ex-pats and their lives in new countries. We're one of the top-ranked Google searches for *Belarus*. I wouldn't call it a *blog*, per se."

He tented his fingertips. "Very well. Let me ask you a question. My wife and I keep a fan in our bedroom. When I am hot, I will say, 'I am going to turn on the fan,' and then I rise from bed to turn on the fan. When my wife is hot, she will ask, '*can* we turn on the fan?' Now tell me: is my wife's inquiry politeness, or is it weakness?"

The journalist blinked as if she did not understand the question. "I wonder if you see the irony of coming to the United States to fight the United States."

"I do not fight the United States."

"You said you did. Those were your words."

Artyom gritted his teeth and took a breath. "Then you were mistaken. We are not fighting. We are using the freedoms afforded in America to make a better Belarus. You should appreciate it since you are one of us."

She made no reply to the reference of their shared heritage. Instead, she narrowed her eyes and stared at him. "How far will you go to help our home country?"

"Winged House and our LLC are an organization of peace."

"What does that mean?"

"It means only what I said."

Her eyebrows raised, indicating she was awaiting further explanation. This annoyed Artyom, so he held firm, not blinking. He said nothing. For a few seconds, a deep silence bloomed between them.

"Tell me about Pavel Rusiecki. You spoke about him at a rally a few months ago, but you've gone quiet on that topic lately. Why?"

"What is there to tell? He is a political prisoner of the United States. He is innocent of the charges leveled against him. Which, I might add, they have given him no chance to fight."

"The US officials said he killed an American dignitary

at an embassy in Uganda. There is evidence to support these charges you claim are fallacious."

"Bullshit. He is innocent of all charges." Artyom leaned forward and jabbed an index finger at his desk. "When I say I do all this for Belarus? I mean people like Pavel. Belarusians at home and abroad, fighting the good fight. Here, we teach people fresh from prison new ways to view the world. We reduce American recidivism and make society more productive. With the revenue from this, we can build, expand, and send money home to Belarus. We can raise a legal defense for Pavel Rusiecki and others like him. In a few days, we will hold a fundraiser here. With the money we collect, we will open the third and fourth floors of the facility and can take in dozens more residential patients and even more outpatient. We're only starting to realize the vision of what we can do."

She tapped a button on the recorder and Artyom raised his eyebrows at her. "Everything okay?" he asked.

"Yes, it's fine. What would you say to your critics back in Belarus?"

Artyom darkened. "What critics?"

"There are some who question your methods, Mr. Borovitch. The ones who claim you're doing more harm than good with your attention-seeking speeches and flashy public persona."

"What critics?"

"News organizations in Belarus have questioned if you really are as peaceful as you say."

"That is ridiculous. We support no terrorists. We commit no crimes. Instead, we make business to raise money for causes important to Belarus, and our ex-convict services here directly benefit Americans, as well. We do more for this country than most of its own citizens do. There is nothing questionable about that. And, I am not flashy and attention-seeking. I'm not on the evening news every day like some activists. I have a small corner of the world, and when I seek attention, it's attention for my home. That is all."

"You know who Senator Carroway is?"

Artyom's pulse rose, and a lump formed in his throat. Her sudden change of topic had caught him off guard. Artyom did not like being caught off guard. "Yes, I know this name."

"The school Senator Carroway's son attends was infected with violence only two days ago. Four died, and more were injured when a student opened fire on his teachers and other school staff."

"So?"

"So, Senator Carroway is someone who could help to release Pavel from custody, is he not? And the young man who committed this crime had a father who was born in Belarus, and he suffered a fatal heart attack the same day. A strange crossroads of information, don't you think?"

"I don't think anything about it," he said, feeling the pressure build behind his eyes. A headache was coming.

"Violence involving Belarusians and people of Belarusian descent happened thirty miles from here, and you don't have an opinion on the matter? I find your silence rather curious."

Artyom pretended to check his watch, then he leaned forward again. "You can find it however you like. Our time is up. I'm afraid I must show you out now."

"I only have a few more questions."

He stood and picked up her recorder, thumbed the button to turn it off, and then handed it to her. "You will have to wait until some other time to continue your witch hunt. I have an important meeting I must attend now."

Taken aback, the journalist shoved the recorder into her purse and then hitched it over her shoulder. "I understand. But if you think the story is going to magically go away, then you are mistaken. I'll get a quote from you about the shooting sooner or later."

"You are Belarusian, yes?"

The journalist nodded. "I was born in Ukraine, but I grew up in Belarus."

"But your accent sounds mostly American. You have been in this country for too long. You have grown fat with American complacency and entitlement."

She shook her head, wearing a wry smirk. "No, I moved here because I was tired of dealing with old-world assholes like you in Minsk. Good day, Mr. Borovitch."

She strutted out of his office, and he waited a couple seconds before he followed. He ventured into the hallway as she was waiting for someone to buzz her out into the main hall. There was a back way out of his office, through the kitchen and cafeteria, but Artyom like to keep that route private.

A security guard nearby pressed his keycard to the panel, and the journalist glared at Artyom one last time before exiting. Her fat, smug face made him want to punch a hole in a nearby wall. But, he resisted. She would definitely include a detail like that in her article.

From a side door, Artyom's top assistant Raisa emerged. "Everything okay, sir?"

Artyom glanced at the security guard, and then he

pulled Raisa back in the other direction, out of his earshot. They stopped a few feet down the hall. He leaned close to Raisa and whispered in her ear. "That woman."

"Yes, sir?"

"She has a recorder from our conversation. Have her followed and make sure it does not leave the property."

Raisa nodded. "Understood. And, the journalist? Does she need to disappear as well?"

"The journalist," he mused as he stroked his chin with a finger. "No, no need to kill her. But do send someone to follow her back to her hotel. She needs to be taught a lesson about respect. And tell them not to leave her until they're sure she's learned it."

11

Layne slid into his car in a parking spot out front and watched Cameron play through the window of her daycare. A yawn raced through him. He'd dropped her off two minutes ago, and she was already mingling with the other kids. She was standing in a plastic kitchen play-set next to another preschooler about her same age. A little boy with olive skin and spiky hair. Both of them tinkered with the kitchen set, side by side, but not exactly together. Parallel play, they called it.

Layne slipped his phone out and checked the news. They'd plastered the school shooting all over every news site, understandable given the strange nature of the shooter's death by sniper immediately after. Nothing about a shooting in a school could be normal, but this one was beyond what people were used to. And the police seemed to have no idea who to investigate. Not that they would want to put out much effort to find Noah Smith's killer. Most of them probably thought he got what he deserved.

The senator would put pressure on them, of course, since his son had been in the school.

With a sigh, Layne dialed the routing number to mask his phone call. After a few beeps, as the call bounced through various VOIP servers in Europe and then back, it finally connected.

"Hello?" said Daphne Kurek's sultry and smoky voice.

"Hey, Control," Layne said.

Daphne made a sound as if she'd taken a bite of something delicious. "Well, good morning, Mr. Parrish. I wasn't sure if I would hear from you again."

A woman emerged from the car parked next to Layne. He didn't remember her name, but she sometimes smiled at him and remarked on how cute Cam was. Car keys in hand, she gave Layne a hearty grin and a wink. He lifted a hand to wave at her as she opened the back seat to unbuckle her child.

"I know, Daphne," he said into the phone. "But it hasn't been that long since we spoke."

"It feels like forever. We used to talk every day, back before you went off to do your own thing. Your short-lived stint in the private sector as a security installer. But, you retired from that, too, didn't you?"

Layne sniffed. Daphne had a way of twisting conversations to her own benefit. She'd want to talk about him quitting the team, severing ties with her, and how hard life was without him under her employ. Layne had no interest in reminiscing or indulging her in a guilt trip. So, he pushed forward to keep it on track.

"This is business. I need to ask you about something. A favor."

Daphne sighed as Layne watched Cameron abandon

the boy at the kitchen set and proceed to run laps around the room. Her blonde hair trailing behind her head, hands with tiny fingers waving in the air. A fearless smile on her face. Her complete and total joy made Layne grin.

"Of course," Daphne said, "whatever you need."

"I need to ask about someone the US government is keeping in a dark site, probably in Africa or Asia."

A pause followed, with a bit of static on the other end of the line. "I'll try, but I don't know if I can help you with that. You know how those other agencies can get about their little secret prison projects."

"I know," Layne said, "but this is important. There's a Belarusian guy named Pavel I need to find. I don't have a last name yet."

"You're trying to track a Belarusian? Does this have anything to do with that school shooting near you from a couple days ago? I heard that kid had a parent from Belarus."

"That's right," Layne said, "It's related. I'm investigating a guy named Artyom Borovitch, and I need to know why he's interested in this Pavel person."

"My dear Layne, how do you get yourself involved in all these petty local squabbles?"

"I knew the kid. His dad and I used to box together."

The snarky quality evaporated from her tone. "Oh. I'm sorry."

Layne shifted in his seat, car leather squeaking. "It's okay. We weren't that close. But I need to know what's going on here."

"And what does this have to do with this person in a secret prison?"

"I don't know. Something, for sure. But I don't have all

the pieces yet. Anything you could get for me on this would help out a lot."

"What was the name again, dear?"

Now, Layne gripped the phone a little tighter. He knew Daphne remembered the name because she wasn't the type to forget sensitive information. She was stalling for time, which meant she knew something she didn't want to admit. "Pavel. Unknown last name."

A few seconds ticked by in silence. Finally, she said, "I can't help you."

"Why not? What can't you tell me?"

"There are a few secret prisons across Asia that I know of. And none of them are supposed to be found, hence the name. You're retired from the team and therefore no longer an employee of the US government. I could get into trouble telling you as much as I have. Now, if you decided to come back to work for us, maybe we could…"

She drifted away, letting the words hang in the VOIP cyberspace between them.

"Not going to happen, Control," he said. "I'm retired."

"Then you're on your own with this one. All I can tell you is this: if we do have him, he's never supposed to be found. If I go around asking about your Pavel—if it's who I think it is—then it's bad for us. Bad for you and me, both. Worse for you as a private citizen."

"Fine, Daphne. I'll do this by myself."

Again, she sighed. "That doesn't mean I can't help you. Just not with this."

"How do you mean?"

"I assume you think this Artyom person has an ulterior motive?"

"I do," he said.

"If you decide you need to take him out, let me know. I can make it go away. I'll clean it up for you and remove any trace of your presence in his life. It's the least I can do."

Layne considered *Omega*, which, given the name, sounded like the grand design implementation for whatever Artyom was planning. Layne had to know more about it. What if he took out Artyom, and that triggered Omega, or else it proceeded without him?

"I can't do that yet. There's not enough info, and I need him alive until I've learned what I need to learn."

"I understand," Daphne said. "Please, in the meantime, keep your nose clean. It would really suck for me if you died or got arrested before I managed to convince you to come back and join the new team."

"Understood, Control. I appreciate your concern."

He ended the call as he watched Cameron twirling in place, her little fingers flying through the air as she moved faster and faster and faster.

12

BETWEEN CLASSES, LAYNE STROLLED AROUND THE courtyard as per usual. The smokers gathered in their clusters and so did the non-smokers. During the quick breaks between life skills lectures and group sharing sessions, there weren't many other places to go.

While Layne hadn't been to prison, he had been in a situation once that reminded him of his current daytime routine. In San José, he'd spent almost a month in a hostel there. The building had been located in a bad part of the city, so he and other guests at the hostel didn't go out much. It was a multi-story square building with an interior courtyard, just like Winged House. Most of the time, everyone occupied the courtyard unless the skies opened up with rain. But, Layne wasn't there for undercover incarceration simulation. He was there to locate and assassinate a particular South African spy due to pass through the walls of that hostel at some point. Layne was working for Daphne Kurek's team, with his teammate Alicia acting as backup, and Harry Boukadakis providing remote technical and operational support. The spy finally appeared during the fourth week of their stay, and Layne and Alicia took him out the same day with no trouble. After a month of sunning himself in the courtyard, Layne had been ready for the action. The spy's plan to proceed to America and kill the governor of New York never came to fruition.

Layne didn't tour the rest of Costa Rica on that trip, as he and his teammates were on a plane back to the US later that same evening, to gear up for the next operation.

Here at Winged House, Layne didn't have any on-site backup or remote operational support. In some ways, he liked going it alone. No more following questionable orders. No more post-op dissection of choices made. Complete autonomy.

But, if the whole thing went south, he'd have no one to pull him out. Every decision carried weight. Every move irreversible.

On his second full day as an outpatient guest here, Layne seemed to inspire less antagonism in the others. At least, they weren't rude to him outright. They'd progressed mostly to ignoring him.

Although Layne wasn't supposed to have his phone, he kept it in his pocket on vibrate, because he was waiting for a text from Harry Boukadakis regarding the parts of Artyom's recorded conversation that Layne hadn't been able to transcribe. Harry had said he would look at the code and see if he couldn't improve the level of recognition to take a second pass at it.

Until then, Layne would just have to wait. Mind his own business and look for opportunities to gain knowledge using old-fashioned, boots-on-the-ground sort of espionage.

As Layne wandered around the courtyard, thinking of ways he could insert himself into conversations to learn more about his fellow ex-convicts, Omega weighed on his mind. Figuring out what it was, what it could be used for. Figuring out a way to get closer to Artyom so Layne might know how to stop it when the time came.

Omnipresent in the courtyard and other common areas was the woman named Raisa. In addition to being an intake counselor and occasionally working the front desk, she also appeared to be security and something of a personal assistant to Artyom. Layne kept a close eye on her. She might be the way in. He did everything possible to stay at arm's length so as not to draw her attention while also noting her movements and mannerisms.

Maybe he could get something juicy on her and then turn her. He'd have to learn how deep her loyalties went, and that might take too much time. Brute force was risky and messy, but often much more expedient. They don't teach you that in spy school.

Layne stopped at the edge of a circle of residents playing cards. Not one of them paid him any mind as he joined their little circle. He hovered there, thinking of asking to be dealt in during the next hand. Couldn't hurt. Maybe he could learn a lot more about the place from the residents as opposed to the employees and administration.

But, as Layne opened his mouth to speak, a flash of color zipped by in front of his face. Without warning, one resident took a swing at another one. From two feet away, a stocky bald guy launched a fist at a skinny man's face, cracking him across the jaw. Then the skinny man leaped to his feet and balled his fists. Layne only needed a fraction of a second to see that the guy balling his fists also had taken something from his pocket and concealed it in the palm of his hand.

Layne burst into action. He leapfrogged a man still crouched at the edge of the circle to land in front of the skinny guy with the object in his hands. Years of training told him to neutralize the biggest threat first, which had to be that mystery object.

Layne first jabbed the man in the chest to push him back a step so he could create room. Then, he grabbed hold of the guy's wrist and twisted it inward to shift him off balance and angle his body to allow Layne access to him from behind. Then, Layne snaked his other hand underneath the guy's opposite armpit, to twist him away from any potential oncoming attacks from the stocky guy.

Layne used his leverage to shuffle the skinny guy toward the edge of the circle, away from the action. The ex-cons gathered there parted, allowing him through.

The skinny one tried to swing his fist at Layne. But, Layne was too fast. He swept his foot forward, tripping the skinny guy and bringing him off his feet. Half a second later, Layne slammed the guy into the grass, pushing his face down. He pinned both arms behind his back, and could now see the object in his hand was only a roll of quarters. Probably reserved for laundry later tonight.

"Get off me, you son of a bitch," the skinny guy said, growling. But Layne didn't budge. He drove his knee into the guy's back, making sure he couldn't gain any leverage.

The other fighter stood back, mouth open and staring down at Layne.

The onlookers in the card circle all took a step back, letting Layne have his space. Their facial expressions indicated awe. Layne thought maybe he shouldn't have intervened so quickly, publicly demonstrating his prowess, but the hidden object in the skinny guy's hand had worried him.

Sometimes Layne didn't have the luxury of choice before he acted. His muscle memory would take over and thrust him into the fray.

Despite the ferocity of the man on the ground squirming below him, Layne didn't let him up. A few seconds later, Raisa and a couple of beefy security guards stepped in. She leaned down and put a hand on Layne's shoulder.

"Okay, Mr. Haskell," she said. "You can let him go now."

Layne stepped back, and the security guards helped the guy up, then escorted him toward the doors leading back inside. He sneered at Layne on his way out, but he said nothing. No one was saying anything, actually.

What mattered more to Layne was the look Raisa gave him as she escorted the resident away. She met Layne's eyes and offered an appreciative nod. Layne felt the respect in that glance. It was the first time Raisa had viewed him with anything other than indifference or suspicion since he'd joined the Winged House patient list.

Perhaps the way in *should* go through the staff. If he could convince Raisa he was an asset, maybe he could get close to Artyom that way. The boss might need muscle, and Layne certainly looked the part.

An interesting possibility.

Almost as quickly as it had happened, the event faded, and everyone resumed their normal courtyard activities. Layne's phone buzzed, so he pivoted away from the group and hid under the shade of a nearby tree to check the notification. A text message from Harry Boukadakis.

```
Harry: I unscrambled a little more of the
video you sent me. This part: Maybe on
the north end of the island. The Ameri-
cans whisked him away there, but we've
been unable to find him. (Broken)
Carroway knows where he is for sure.

Layne: What did you find?

Harry: The broken part took some doing,
but I got the speech rec to run at 96%
confidence for that section. That short
broken part makes a reference to Patong
Bay. Does that mean anything to you?
That's in Thailand, right?
```

Layne stared at his phone for several seconds, reading over Harry's comment about Thailand. Artyom's object of desire Pavel was being held in an American secret prison in Thailand.

Then, like a light bulb flicking on above his head, Layne knew exactly what to do. Patong Bay was on the island of Phuket, and Layne knew someone there who owed him a favor.

Omega Trap

```
Layne: It does mean something to me. I
have a local there. Thanks, K-Books

Harry: No problemo. Good luck out there.
Let me know if you need anything else.
```

Layne checked around before stashing his phone to make sure he wasn't being watched. No one seemed to care, or else they were steering clear of the guy who had so handily disarmed the man about to start a fight with a roll of quarters.

Patong Bay was on the west side of the island, south of mainland Thailand. And, if that's where the US government was keeping the enemy combatant Pavel, Layne knew what steps to take next.

He needed to talk to this Pavel person and find out why Artyom would take such extreme measures to have him released.

But, he couldn't leave the country now. He still needed to learn more about Artyom and Omega here. The words from the transcription played in his head: *The Omega failsafe. Then we move on from the alternate to the primary target.*

What was the primary target?

Layne thought he had just the trick to poke his nose in a little closer.

13

Layne discovered Artyom's office was on the first floor, past the admin area only accessible behind the main desk. At first, this seemed like a major roadblock, since he would need a keycard to breach that barrier.

But then, in the afternoon, he noticed something interesting. While hardly anyone went back to Artyom's office via the entryway behind the admin offices, Layne realized a few people—Artyom included—were disappearing and reappearing via the kitchen door at the back side of the cafeteria.

Secret entrance. Another way in.

The next morning, Layne prepared for the occasion. Since his retirement from Daphne's nameless espionage agency, he'd rid himself of most of his toys. But, he did like to keep a few around, for special occasions such as these. A MemoQ USR-1000 recorder had sat in his pocket all day. It was shaped like a little USB power brick to provide backup juice for a cellphone, and it even had actual reserved battery life, in case someone tried to do that very thing. But, it was also a remote transmitter, capable of recording a few hours of audio at a time and then spitting it over Bluetooth whenever the transmitter neared a dedicated transfer app on his phone.

No bigger than a tube of lipstick, if Layne could drop this thing into a drawer or file cabinet in that office, he'd be set. Come by once a day and walk near the north end of the kitchen and then let his phone automatically leech the most recent audio recordings to keep the device clean and ready for more. Maybe. It depended on how far away the office was from that end of the kitchen. Bluetooth had a limited reach.

Layne found an excuse to stroll into there not long before dinner. There was an attractive redhead named Jenna who he approached to strike up a conversation. He found it easy. Jenna was short and skinny and boasted a splash of freckles across the bridge of her nose and under her eyes. She was wearing an apron stained a deep red, with pink corduroy pants. While she was stationed at a prep table, dicing tomatoes in a splicer thing that looked like the Eiffel Tower with a chopping grate at the base, he asked her about those pants.

"Don't you get hot, wearing thick pants in a steamy kitchen?"

She grinned at him as she set a tomato on the grate and then slammed the top down to split it into a dozen wet chunks. "I'm used to it by now. Plus, I didn't have to shave my legs today." She tapped a knowing finger against her temple.

Layne chuckled.

"You're awfully cute," she said, "all worried about me getting too hot back here."

She was probably about half his age, but she displayed no hesitation or wariness in her flirting game. He respected her forward nature.

"It is what it is," he said, then he flicked his head at the door in the back of the kitchen. "Do you know where that leads to?"

"Back hallway to Artyom Borovitch's office. It's the worst-kept secret in the whole place."

Layne peeked through the glass doors, trying to earn a better angle to see how long the hallway was. A straight shot to Artyom's office back there. A straight shot to finding out more about Omega and Pavel and how all of this tied into a school shooting near Denver.

Maybe it was close enough to establish a Bluetooth signal, but he couldn't tell for sure from here.

"What are you looking at?" Jenna asked.

Layne eyed her, not sure how much he should say about his plan. Obviously, he couldn't tell Jenna that he intended to place a bug into Artyom's office and then swing by the cafeteria kitchen daily to flirt with her while he downloaded recordings via Bluetooth. So, instead, he shrugged and tilted his chin toward the door. "Borovitch is the guy who runs the place, right? The owner or president?"

Jenna rolled her eyes. "Yeah. Real prick. He's Russian or something like that. And he acts like it, too."

"He acts like what?"

"Sexist, racist, you name it." She wiped her hands on her apron and put aside the bin full of chopped tomatoes. "Dinner tonight?"

"Why in the world would you want to go out to dinner

with an ex-convict like me? Don't you know we're dangerous and not to be trusted?"

Jenna smirked. "Maybe I like a little bit of danger. How about your phone number, to start with? Maybe we can talk sometime when I'm not covered in tomato guts."

Layne agreed to exchange phone numbers with this paragon of youthful confidence. He had absolutely no intention of dating a woman seemingly half his age, one who should be in college right now instead of working in the kitchen of a halfway house. But, he did think it would be valuable to be friendly with her. She provided an easy excuse for daily trips here to the kitchen. Back in his career in espionage, Layne often had to misrepresent himself to certain people to accomplish a goal. He'd never enjoyed that part of the job, and he promised himself he wouldn't lead Jenna on.

She said she would call him later, and he made some noncommittal response about how busy he was in the evenings. "You should know I have a daughter."

"Cool," she said, putting an empty bin underneath the tomato slicer. "My dad also has a daughter."

"That's okay with you?"

Jenna shrugged. "Sure, unless she sucks."

"She doesn't suck."

"Excellent. That works for me."

Something flashed out of Layne's peripheral vision. Emerging from Artyom's office were a trio of men in dark suits. Each of them carrying a briefcase, they strutted down the hallway toward the cafeteria. Layne moved a little closer to Jenna so he could spy them while keeping her body between them and him.

When the three men emerged from the door, Layne

watched them via one of the curved mirrors placed at the corner of the entrance. In that mirror, he saw something in the hands of the man in the rear. For a second, he couldn't tell what it was, then he squinted, and it came into focus in the mirror.

His heart sank. The man was carrying a device like a nightstick with a ball on one end, no bigger than the man's palm when collapsed. Harry Boukadakis used to call these gizmos *zappers*, like the electrical devices on porches to eradicate insects.

As the men marched through the cafeteria and the guy in the rear put the zapper inside his jacket pocket, Layne shook his head.

"Damn," he said.

Jenna's brow furrowed. "What's wrong?"

"Nothing," Layne said. "Have you seen those guys before?"

Jenna nodded. "Yep."

"More than once?"

"For sure. At least three or four times a week, they come through here."

He pursed his lips. Layne knew this meant implanting his bug was no longer an option. Artyom was too clever for that. He used zappers to sweep for bugs on a regular basis. If Layne wanted to eavesdrop on the conversations going on inside that office, he would have to get creative.

And that meant reaching out to the source for a better tool.

14

Layne tucked his daughter into bed and placed her stuffed frog and owl next to her. Cameron snatched up her bedtime companions and squeezed them as if she were trying to snuff out their existence.

"Daddy?"

"Yes, little one?"

"Are we going to the cabin soon?"

He frowned down at her. "Not this week. We're going to stay in Boulder, so we can be close to Mommy."

"Because you're working?"

He nodded. "Because I'm working. But we'll go to the cabin in South Fork again soon. I promise."

He didn't feel the need to tell her that he also couldn't leave town because he'd been involved in a school shooting only two days before, and the cops would probably want to speak with him again. Maybe multiple times.

"Can we get donuts at the Rainbow Grocery when we go?"

"Yes."

"Can we stop at the playground across the street and swing on the swing?"

"Yes."

"Can we..." she drifted off, face scrunched, trying to think up another question to delay bedtime.

"Time for bed, Cam."

"Okay. Night-night, Daddy."

"Night-night, little one. Love you."

She blinked a few times, her eyelids already drooping. Layne backed out of the room and slid the door almost shut, but not all the way. As soon as she'd turned three-and-a-half, Cameron had insisted on the door being left open a crack. Fine with Layne, as long as it didn't encourage her to stay up late.

He waited at the door for a few seconds and then paused in the living room, watching the lights of the cars driving by on Highway 36 into Boulder. The air conditioner in his apartment kicked on, momentarily shaking the walls. A bit like an earthquake.

Layne took out his phone and dialed the first of the two numbers he had on his to-do list this evening.

"Hello?" said a hoarse and tired voice.

"Did I wake you, Harry?"

Harry Boukadakis grumbled on the other end of the line. "No, Layne, I'm still up. Just fighting a sinus infection that's got me blowing my body weight in snot into tissues every day."

"Gross, man."

"You're telling me."

"Sorry about that," Layne said. "How's Virginia?"

"Muggy. How is Colorado?"

"Weather's perfect, as always."

"And you're still enjoying retirement?"

Layne cracked a smile out of one side of his mouth. While Harry didn't work as hard as Daphne to recruit him back to the team, Harry dropped little hints from time to time.

"Retirement is great," Layne said. "No complaints."

"I heard about that school shooting out there," Harry said. "It's been all over the news. They said a tall, muscular guy with light hair ran into the building and single-handedly disarmed the shooter. They also said he elected to remain anonymous, and the press hasn't been able to track him down."

"Hmm. They said that, huh?"

"Yep, they did," Harry said.

"Well, I think that person, if asked, would probably say anonymity is rare in the world today."

"Gotcha. You and yours doing okay?"

"We're doing great. You?"

"My son's in a growth spurt, so my wife's been hiding the grocery store bills from me. I'll tell you what, Layne. The wisdom of age is the cruelest joke the gods ever played on us."

"If you could turn back time, eh?"

"Exactly," Harry said. "You get it."

"Yeah, knowing now what we didn't know then doesn't do us a lot of good. Anyway, since you're sick, I'll get right to the point. The fallout from that school shooting is why I called."

"I should have known you'd find a way to involve yourself, Boy Scout."

Layne gritted his teeth at the mention of his old and annoying operational handle. But, he opted not to say anything. If anyone had earned the right to use that nickname, it was Harry Boukadakis. "I need your help."

Harry coughed for a few seconds before responding. "Sure, whatever I can do."

"I need a bug that can't be discovered."

The hacker laughed with a throaty gurgle. "And I need to win the lottery."

"I'm serious, Harry. Something an electronic sweep can't find. Old school, manual kind of surveillance."

The phone went dark for a second, and Layne listened to the sounds of Cameron snoring through the crack in the door.

"Well, I might be able to help," Harry said. "I do have a bug like that. Mostly mechanical, with all the active electronics completely shielded from detection. It records to a memory card, and there's no OTA transfer. You'll have to swap out the battery and memory yourself, in person. Battery life is going to be your main issue since it will only run on a single, standard AAA."

Layne considered this. He'd have to break into Artyom's office every time he wanted to listen to the surveillance, but that was a risk he'd have to take. "I can manage that."

"Okay. I'll drop it in the mail first thing in the morning, and it'll be there day after tomorrow. I'll follow it up with an email containing all the tech specs and how to use it. Good enough?"

"It's much appreciated. Thanks, Harry."

"I assume you don't want me to tell Daphne about this?"

Layne sighed. "It doesn't matter to me. I know you're still working for her, but I'm not, and she has no sway over me. She knows I'm investigating something related to the shooting out here, so tell her whatever you want. Tell her you gave me the bug if you think she'll either ask or find out about it. The last thing I want is to get you in trouble."

"Fair enough." Harry paused, then sneezed. "Sometimes, my wife can't sleep. She gets up in the middle of the night and then goes out to the couch and sleeps there."

"Okay," Layne said, waiting for more to the story.

"When I wake up in the morning, and she's gone, there's this split-second of panic, because something is different. You know, the world is not how it should be. It takes me a moment to figure out what it is when my brain is all fuzzy with sleep."

Layne pursed his lips. "Why are you telling me this?"

"Sometimes, things aren't what they seem. And you might think you know what's real, but you don't have all the info. Basically, I'm just telling you to be careful."

"Roger that, Harry."

"Anyway, it's good to talk to you again, Layne."

Layne said his goodbyes, and then the call ended. He pivoted back toward Cameron's room and stared at her almost-closed door for a few seconds. It stayed still.

One more call to make.

He stared at his phone, his eyes on her contact page. A part of him didn't want to make the call. A part of him whispered that this whole enterprise would end in chaos and it would be all his fault.

He had to do this, though, didn't he? No other option appeared. No better way.

Layne made his second call. The call that could land both him and her in trouble. He hated to make such a large request, but he didn't know a better person for the job.

She picked up after the second ring. "Hello?"

"Hi, Serena."

Serena Rojas was a twenty-eight-year-old operative on Daphne Kurek's team. She had actually replaced Layne when he'd retired a few years ago. And despite her youth, Layne knew her to be effective. Also: ruthless, logical, and efficient.

And, most importantly, discreet.

"Hi, Layne. Everything okay?"

"In a manner of speaking."

"Please explain."

Layne smiled. Serena had never been one for small talk in the short time he'd known her. Her ability to get to the point was one thing he admired about her.

"Don't worry about it. Thing is, I need a favor."

A second or two of dead air followed. "Okay."

"Are you free for the next few days?"

"I am, actually. Is there something you need?"

"It's a big ask."

Serena sighed. "Anything, you know that. Just tell me what's going on. Or, if you can't do that, how about you tell me what you need from me?"

"When I ask you, if you want to say no, or if you're worried about what Daphne might think, I won't hold it against you if you say it can't be done."

"Spit it out, Layne. It's late, and I'm tired."

For a split second, another tinge of guilt prickled the back of his neck. The feeling he was about to take advantage of her generosity. Maybe he should let it go and find another way to get the information. He was already lying to the cute kitchen worker Jenna to achieve his goals, was he preparing to send Serena into a death trap?

But no, this was the only way. And it was important that it not only happen now, but also that it be handled by someone he trusted.

"How would you like to go on a trip to Thailand?"

PART II

SET THE TRAP

15

LAYNE SLIPPED INTO THE DOOR AT THE NORTH END OF THE cafeteria, leading into the kitchen. Post-lunch, the room swarmed with workers in aprons and hairnets scrambling to clean up after a meal of hamburgers and fries. Layne strolled through the kitchen until he saw Jenna near the back, in the dish pit. No one paid any attention to him, which was the best possible outcome.

She rotated a handle to raise a set of metal doors on a rectangular contraption built atop a long, stainless steel table. A fog of steam ejected from the open doors of the contraption as she reached inside and yanked out a scarred plastic tray full of bowls and cups. He could feel the humidity on his exposed arms and face from several feet away.

"Isn't that hot?" he asked.

Jenna grinned, and Layne noted the long sleeves on her shirt, despite the blistering temperature in the vicinity.

"Hey, big guy. Yes, it's very hot. But I'm used to it by now, so it's all ones and zeroes to me."

Her hands moved over the bowls and cups so fast as she organized them, bits of still-hot dishwater whipped through the air like shrapnel.

"Wow," he said.

"The trick is stacking."

"Stacking?"

"Yep," she said, "stacking. Doesn't matter if they're clean or dirty. After a meal, the dirty dishes come in fast and furious. If you don't separate bowls, plates, cups, silverware—whatever—into their own little areas of stacks, then you run out of room on the dirty dish side real quick. Same with the clean dish side. You gotta run your clean dishes out to the staging stations as soon as they're stacked, or you can't push the dirty dishes through, then it's all backed up, and you can't get to your next meal prep. Then it's a big nightmare."

Layne pushed out his lower lip, admiring her expertise. For someone so young, she implied a wealth of wisdom when she spoke. It made him think of his daughter, and what she might be like in her early twenties. Would she be wise and skilled in anything? Would she take pride in her work or her projects?

Layne positioned himself so he could chat with Jenna while still being able to see out the back door of the kitchen. The door leading to his destination, Artyom's office. As he watched, a security guard emerged from the back hallway and paused there, in front of the door. Layne averted his eyes.

"Stacking," she said again. "Know what I mean?"

"I do." Layne did not share her dishwashing expertise, but he knew about stacking. He knew about entering an apartment building to face multiple hostiles, and the necessity to isolate them to reduce their collective power. Not the exact same principle as stacking dirty bowls into one tall pile, but the danger of letting things spiral out of control was the same.

"Sorry I didn't call you yet," Jenna said. "I've been moving from an apartment in Golden to this little house in Eldorado Springs, and it's a big mess, and I don't even really want talk about it."

Layne waved a dismissive hand. "I get it. I've been pretty busy over the last few days myself." With his other hand in his pocket, he fingered the little device he'd picked up from UPS this morning, sent to him by hacker extraordinaire Harry Boukadakis. A tiny recording device meant to look like a thumb-sized flash drive. Inside was a 200 gigabyte SD card, enough to record several days worth of audio at low fidelity.

But the capacity of recording time wasn't the issue. The main problem was Layne would have to manually swap out the battery when it was in danger of running out of juice. Harry's follow-up email had recommended daily changes, or at the most, every other day. This meant repeated break-ins to Artyom's office.

Because, since Layne had discovered that Artyom regularly swept his office for bugs, old-school mechanical trickery appeared to be the only solution. Such a low-tech device undetectable to electronic surveillance sweeps had severe limits.

That was the price Layne had to pay. The price to pay

for Layne to learn about Omega, and about the spy named Pavel held prisoner at a dark site in Thailand. The only way to figure out why Artyom had orchestrated a school shooting to put pressure on a senator.

Omega was a failsafe, Artyom's transcribed conversation had said. *Then we move on from the alternate to the primary target.*

"Maybe this weekend?" Jenna asked with a hopeful rise at the end of her sentence.

"Maybe," he said in a noncommittal tone.

Layne looked toward the door again, and the security guard who'd been standing nearby checked his watch and left his post. Layne lowered his head and angled his body more toward Jenna as the guard marched across the room. He headed through the kitchen, toward the cafeteria, and disappeared from view.

Layne had seen Artyom wandering the far side of the campus a few minutes before. The office was empty.

Layne had to move, now.

"If you'll excuse me a second, Jenna."

"Sure thing. Don't be a stranger." She spun around and set to work stacking the dirty bowls and cups next to the dish pit.

Layne disappeared through the door, focusing on speed. He skulked right up to Artyom's office door and picked the lock in ten seconds flat. It was an easy job. If a silent alarm had been triggered somewhere, well, he couldn't control that. Push forward and get the job done.

On the other side of that door, Layne found himself in a large and lavish office. Belarusian flags and maps decorated most of the available wall space.

Layne told himself to focus first on accuracy, and then access. He had to position the device where it would not only pick up sound but also not falsely trigger based on air conditioners or hallway noise and record bad audio and therefore burn through the battery too fast.

Second, focus on a location where he could easily retrieve it, while also placing it somewhere Artyom was unlikely to find it.

After a few seconds of searching, Layne decided on a spot. Atop a file cabinet in the northeast corner sat a bowl full of junk: paperclips, thumbtacks, and even a couple other flash drives. Good chance Artyom would never bother to look inside this little bowl. It seemed like a worthwhile risk. Also, the file cabinet was as far away as possible from the vent in the room, so if the air kicked on, it wouldn't muddle conversation or falsely trigger the bug to start recording.

Serena suddenly appeared in Layne's mind, and he wondered if she'd landed in Thailand yet. Their conversation had been two full days ago, and there had been minimal contact between them since then. They'd agreed to only touch base for emergencies, given the sensitive nature of her operation over there. But, he worried. She was going alone, and that was never a good idea.

No time to waste on that now. Layne flipped a small switch on the inside of the USB connector and then dropped the bug into the bowl of random objects. He had no way to determine how long the battery would last. That depended on Artyom and how often he was in this office; how many times the device clicked on to record, chewing up the battery life.

But, one thing Layne knew for sure: if the battery died, any audio spoken after would be lost.

He checked his watch. He would allow himself twenty-four hours to return here to replace the battery. Not one minute more.

16

Serena bounced around in the back seat of the van as it traveled from HKT Airport toward Patong Bay in Phuket. She focused on not barfing. After a full day and night trapped on various airplanes, her stomach was not happy with the quality of the local roads.

The van also made stops and starts every few seconds as motorcycles and scooters cut across the street in front of it. It seemed as if, the smaller the vehicle, the less obligation it had to follow traffic directions. Not that Serena knew much about the traffic laws in Thailand. She hadn't been to this specific country before. Never had she learned more than a few phrases in the language, and she didn't know her way around.

But, none of that mattered. She had a contact, a goal, and a self-imposed directive to keep her head down and not attract too much attention. Get in, learn about the spy, and get out. Leave no trace.

It was easy to fade into obscurity in the back of the van because an Australian couple closer to the front were making plenty of noise as they argued with the driver. They kept raising their voices. Accusing the driver of having no idea of where he was going, and fleecing them for additional money to deliver them to their hotels. Trying to make eye contact with the rest of the passengers, to recruit them to the Australians' cause.

Serena slid her sunglasses on and stared out the window at the surroundings. Patong Bay was the strangest place she had ever seen in her life. Touristy beach elegance mixed with abject poverty, hand in hand along the way. A jet ski rental shop sitting next to a shanty with a toothless man selling liter bottles of gasoline from atop a folding card table. Twelve-story hotels next to alleys where packs of wild dogs bloodied each other to win a scrap of meat from the dumpster.

Eventually, the van dropped Serena off at the Kalima Resort at the northern edge of the bay. She gave the driver a couple hundred baht as a tip, and when his eyes widened, she wondered if she'd egregiously misunderstood the exchange rate. Oh well.

The lobby was extravagant. Spotless marble and shiny wood, huge vaulted ceilings. Head swimming with jet lag, she lugged her bags up to the front and set her passport down on the counter. Her eyelids were like fifty-pound kettlebells. If this process took longer than thirty seconds, she thought she might scream.

A man with dark skin and a blinding smile bared a mouthful of teeth at her. "What a great day, miss. How can I help you?"

She ignored the "miss" comment. Too tired to get into it right now. "Susan Baker," Serena said. "I have a room reserved for four nights."

"Ahh yes, Miss Baker. I am so happy to help you."

He snatched up her passport and flipped it to the photo page, then he held it up, looking back and forth between the book and her face. Back and forth, back and forth.

Serena stood tall, breathing in and out, waiting for him to finish. Her knees wanted to buckle from fatigue. The customs official at the airport hadn't scrutinized her passport this intensely.

The man's eyes flicked back and forth a few more times. Then, with a sigh and a smile, he folded the passport book and scooted it back across the counter to her. "Very good, Miss Baker. Your room should be ready now."

Serena accepted a keycard and her passport, then she backed away from the counter. The desk clerk was still talking, but she didn't catch a word of it. So beyond caring right now.

She checked into her room, a modest Queen size with a view of the bluest water she'd ever seen. Outstanding. If only she had time to appreciate it and maybe to rent a quality camera to shoot a few sunsets over the water.

A quick shower expunged her body of the international travel grime, and then she opened a Diet Coke from the mini bar and chugged it. Serena didn't know if there was enough caffeine in this room to kill her jet lag, but she would try.

With one towel around her wet hair and another around her midsection, she stood in front of a full-length mirror. "You can do this," she said to her reflection. "In, out, no drama. Then, on a plane back home before anyone even knows you're gone."

Her reflection didn't seem convinced.

Since talking to Layne two days ago, she had focused all of her efforts on getting here. Her current boss (and Layne's ex-boss) Daphne knew nothing about it. Daphne would probably be furious if she found out Serena had engaged in espionage work off-the-clock as a personal favor to a retired shadow operative.

And, Serena didn't care. Layne had earned the right to a favor. Maybe many favors. If Daphne had a problem with that, she could cram it between her clenched butt cheeks. It's not as if Control didn't already yell at her enough.

Serena used a fresh towel to dry her hair, but she couldn't rid it of all the moisture. No matter. She could pull off the wet hair look if she had to.

She napped for a couple hours and then changed into her single sexy outfit to meet the contact. *He's both a lech and a pushover*, Layne had said. *Flash a little skin, and he'll do whatever you say.*

Serena wasn't a fan of the seduction tactic, but she'd had success with it before. And, she reminded herself that despite how distasteful it might seem, this was all part of the favor. A favor for someone she now considered a friend.

She touched up her makeup in the mirror and then rode the elevator down to the first floor. When she stepped out into the lobby, a few heads turned to follow her. Not her intention. She was only looking to catch the eye of a single man in the hotel bar today. If any of these random European tourists came up to flirt with her, they might earn a kick in the nuts.

After a meal and a couple drinks, she settled in and waited for the contact. Layne had said he would arrange for the guy to come by every afternoon, since, at the time, neither had been sure when Serena could get away to travel to Phuket.

And, after about an hour total, it finally paid off. A man, short and thin with brown skin and bald on top except for a few wisps of a comb-over meandered into the hotel bar. But, what made Serena positive she'd found the right man was the prearranged orchid pinned to his lapel.

He had a nervous look about him. Eyes swishing left and right, his hands flexing and unflexing as he searched around for an empty table to occupy. That sort of effort would make him stand out. Not in a good way.

So, Serena went to him first, which hadn't been the plan. But, better to get this meeting over with as quickly as possible before they became memorable to the population.

She held her purse out in front of her as she glided across the room, stopping in front of him. His mouth dropped open as he looked her up and down.

"Not many good places to sit in here, right?" she said.

"No. Not many," came his thick-accented reply.

She pointed at a table away from the rest of the bar patrons, and he sat. He had a little nervous tic which made his lower left eyelid flutter every few seconds.

"What's your name?" she asked.

"Niran. And this is not good idea to be seen."

She sat back and kept him in the center of her vision, but let her peripheral scan the room. She couldn't find anything out of the ordinary, but she did have that strange feeling of being watched. Hard to tell, though, with the jet lag weighing on her like a cough syrup hangover. She wasn't sure how much to trust her innate sense of danger right now.

"Are you expecting someone in particular?"

He shook his head. "No. No one."

"Do you have many enemies, Niran?"

He gave a chirp of an uncomfortable laugh and reached for a packet of sugar from the table. His bony fingers worked the sugar inside back and forth as he passed it from one hand to the other.

"No," he said. "No enemies."

"Then why are you concerned?"

"I am man who pay my debts. I only do this as favor to L—"

Serena whipped a hand up, interrupting him before Niran could say Layne's name out loud. "You said it was bad to be seen. *Why* is it a bad idea?"

"Your government," Niran said, leaning forward. "They do not want to… let public the place you are seeking."

"But you know where it is, don't you?"

"Not for certain. Maybe I know the area. But, maybe I wrong. Maybe it all for nothing."

Sounded like he was trying to strike a bargain. "You need money? Whatever it is you want, Niran, I can get it for you."

Niran shrugged. "What good it do to get what I want, if I dead before I can enjoy it?"

17

Zabojca sipped his drink and stared at the bowl of limp and uninspired noodles in front of him. The waiter had described the sauce as *brown*, but it seemed more beige to Zabojca. The potential amount of tap water in the sauce concerned him more than the color, though. He supposed if the cooks boiled it, the water should be fine, but he didn't want to take the chance.

Enough people had told him never to drink the water in Thailand that the advice felt like it was engraved on the back of his eyelids. And, as nice as the Kalima Resort restaurant appeared to be, Zabojca could not storm into the kitchen and demand to see how they prepared their food.

He'd been asked to take a lot on faith, and faith was something he could not spare.

So, instead, he ate packaged crackers and sipped his drink, which he'd insisted not contain ice cubes. As he consumed this meager meal, he studied the Latina woman across the bar. His heart skipped a beat when he saw her, for more than one reason. He'd watched her check in a couple hours ago and had prayed she would come down here this evening. The position of his table afforded him a view of the street, but he'd hoped he wouldn't have to follow her through the hectic neighborhood today.

Her slinky dress shined, and her hair had been coiffed quickly but with ruthless efficiency. He admired a woman who could make good look easy. But, he could still see the jet lag in her slumped shoulders. The drooping of her eyelids that suggested she'd spent the last thirty-six hours as a prisoner of various airports and Customs lines. Maybe she'd taken a quick nap in her room, which had only made her dreariness worse?

He had first spotted her at the airport, and he'd known right away she was the one he'd been waiting for. Something about her said *spy*. And, not only that, it said *American* spy. He tailed her from the airport to her hotel, and every time he looked at her, he became more confident: she was here to find Pavel.

The woman reminded him of someone he'd known when he was much younger. That woman had not been Latina, of course. Zabojca had not seen a person from that part of the world until later in life. But, he had known a girl in Minsk who'd originally come from Mongolia and had the same earthy skin tone as this female spy. While Zabojca couldn't remember the girl's name, he remembered how they flirted with each other as teenagers, her a year or two older. And he remembered how crushed he was when she moved back to her homeland.

Why her name was a mystery, he couldn't say. Her

face, though, stayed etched in his mind, all these years later.

In the bar, after the female spy had consumed her meal and a couple drinks, the Thai man entered, and she took notice of him. The way she paid attention to him, seemed like she was waiting for a date. Given his slovenly appearance and her trim and curvy figure, one might assume she was a prostitute introducing herself to a client. But Zabojca knew better. This was the meeting he'd been waiting for.

Fate had smiled upon him.

He said a little prayer of thanks because he was on his fourth whiskey and Coke and didn't know if he could handle too many more to maintain his right to this table near the bar.

The woman spoke to the Thai man, and they sat. Zabojca wished for a parabolic mic, but it didn't matter what they were specifically saying. That they were here, together, told him all he needed to know. He could find out their names and details later. This was enough to start.

Now he knew he'd been right to follow her from the airport, and they would lead him directly to the clandestine prize they were all seeking.

Now, the only question was: which one to follow after their meeting?

18

Layne exited the front door of the Winged House after the final afternoon session. Surprisingly tired. In his younger days of espionage, playing a character for hours or days at a time invigorated him. Now, he found the pursuit draining. He wanted to snuggle with his daughter on the couch and watch cartoons for a couple hours. It seemed like the only activity that might revitalize him.

Only a few hours before, he'd planted the bug in Artyom's office. He already worried about its battery life, particularly since Harry had said it was significantly older tech. Surveillance gear aged even worse than computer gear. He'd given himself twenty-four hours, but what if it didn't even last that long?

Nothing Layne could do about that today, though. All he had left on the agenda was a stop by Children's Academy—Cameron's daycare—and then preparing a dinner of sliced nitrate-free turkey hot dogs, broccoli, and raspberries. Then, couch time until bed.

As he stood there, drinking in the fresh air of the

spring evening, Raisa passed him by on her way through the parking lot. She gave him a non-committal look, something ambiguous enough that Layne had no idea what it was supposed to mean. She'd been antagonistic to him in his first couple days, but that had cooled off since Layne had broken up the fight in the courtyard the other day.

Layne followed her, fishing his keys out of his pocket. No sense in standing around any longer. A few feet later, she craned her neck around, then turned her boxy body toward him and lowered her chin in a nod.

"Afternoon, Mr. Haskell."

"Hi, Raisa. Going home?"

"No, of course not. Always more work to do here. Only out for dinner, then back for paperwork and whatever else Mr. Borovitch requires."

"Ahh, well, we appreciate how hard you and the counselors work to keep this place running."

Raisa eyed him, maybe trying to evaluate if he was serious or not. "Indeed. How long have you been here, now?"

"Today was my fourth day."

"And how are you liking Winged House?"

"Great," he said, then he swallowed as he struggled to come up with a concrete example. "Like, today, the after-lunch roundtable was on conflict resolution. Really useful."

"And what did you learn?"

"In prison, there isn't such a thing as conflict resolution. You back down, you're weak. At least, with some guys. With your celly or your buddies, it's different. But with someone you're not close to, finding a compromise is basically impossible. And, if that person has a different skin color, forget about it."

He'd thrown in that last bit as a calculated wager. Judging by the lack of anything but white people inside the walls of Winged House, he hoped she might relate.

She raised her eyebrows, waiting for him to continue.

"I guess I'm learning that it takes a whole different set of skills on the outside. I think I knew that once upon a time, but I have to relearn it."

"I see. Adjustment can take effort, and it doesn't happen as quickly as we would like. What is the name of your P.O.?"

He blanked. He'd established a fake one for the intake paperwork, but for some reason, the name had been deleted from his memory. But, he had to say something. No time to stammer. "Johnson. Up in Boulder County. I just switched because I moved."

"You have a new address?"

Now, the lies were starting to stack up. So many tracks to cover. He clenched his teeth, mad at himself for making such a rookie mistake.

"Yes, new address."

"I see. Please come by the office in the morning to update your information."

She gave him another curt nod and then walked away. Layne bit his lower lip and blew out a sigh. Making a change to his cover story on such short notice could prove tricky. He only had so many favors he could call in before his contacts would tire of making exceptions for him.

Oh well, nothing he could do about it at the moment.

He bounced his car keys in his hands a couple times and then continued on through the parking lot.

From out of the corner of his eye, a flash of buzzed red hair stood out. A large man's head, spied from an angle where the side and back window of a car lined up. The redheaded man was standing next to a dark-haired man, and they were leaning in close to each other. Almost as if embracing, but not quite. Their stances were odd; unnatural.

As Layne navigated through the parking lot far enough to reach a better viewing angle, he confirmed his suspicions. Not embracing, they were in the middle of a drug deal. The redhead guy was holding open a tiny baggie of light powder, and the other guy was about to dip his pinky into it to sample the goods.

From the other corner of his peripheral, Layne now noted Artyom, strolling through the lot, headed toward the building. He and Raisa were about to cross paths.

An idea formed, like a flash of lightning inside his head. Layne had no time to think it through. He had to act, as quickly as possible, while all these things were converging.

"Hey," Layne barked at the two men, huddled between the cars. "What are you doing back there?"

Now, both Raisa and Artyom took notice. Layne had to act before the rats scurried. Both of the guys angled their bodies away, probably to stash the powder.

"What's in your hand?" Layne said. "Is that drugs?"

He sprinted to narrow the distance as he watched the redheaded guy lower his hand to shove the baggie down into his pocket. Layne leaped the last couple steps and snatched the guy's arm, a mere two inches away from his pocket.

Layne looked down. The baggie was still open. To maximize the impact, Layne jerked his hand up, causing the baggie's contents to whoosh into the air like the puff of a mushroom cloud. A mist of white powder coated the guy's arm and face. Perfect.

The dark-haired one turned to flee toward the other side of the parking lot, and Layne opted to let him go. He only had to catch one to make his point.

Layne applied pressure to the redhead's wrist to bring his body around. The guy tried to shy away, which put him off balance. Layne now yanked him out from the cars and into the open space of the parking lot. Spinning his body around, Layne positioned himself behind the guy.

Now, with an arm-bar, Layne pushed, lowering the cocaine-coated man to the ground. He held him there until footsteps halted nearby.

"What is the meaning of this?" Artyom said.

"I caught him, Mr. Borovitch," Layne said, pretending to be startled and out of breath. "I caught him with this powder. Looks like drugs."

The guy lifted his eyes to Artyom, a layer of powdery cocaine coating his face. Guilt was written right there, plain enough for all to see. Even Raisa had now joined their little circle, slowly shaking her head back and forth.

"You deal drugs in my halfway house?" Artyom said.

The man shook his head as a line of sweat dribbled down his forehead, creating a wet divider along the powder. "No, it's a misunderstanding."

Artyom flared his nostrils. "Let him go."

Layne obliged, and the guy scooted back a few feet,

thumping into the tire of a nearby car. As soon as he could, he swiped a hand over his face and neck, trying to smear away the powder. Too little, too late, though.

Layne stood, dusting off his hands in an exaggerated show of heroics. He put his fists on his hips and kept his mouth shut as the weight of the situation settled on everyone present.

Artyom extended a hand. "Thank you, Mr. Haskell. You have done an excellent job helping Winged House today. We need more like you."

Layne grinned down at Artyom's hand and then shook it.

19

IF THE REFEREE PULLED OUT HIS YELLOW CARD ONE MORE time, Artyom vowed he would hunt the slimy bastard down and yank out his toenails. It was bad enough that Americans refused to call this sport by its proper name. They had to over-officiate it too, every chance they got. It was as if they didn't want the children to strive and succeed.

Typical of this country. Americans all wanted something handed to them for nothing, simply due to their privileged status of being born within the confines of this land mass. Artyom didn't raise his son that way. He pushed him to never settle for the status quo.

"Mikhail! Shoot!" Artyom called out to his son as he accepted a pass from a midfielder. Only a few meters away from the goal. But, the young Borovitch lacked the confidence, so he passed toward the edge of the penalty box. His idiot teammate attempted a poorly-conceived shot, and the opposing goalie had no trouble deflecting it.

The collective crowd in the stands tensed and then

relaxed as the attempt on goal fizzled and failed. Artyom took a breath and blew it out rather than bellow over the heads of other parents in attendance. He'd already received a few too many snide looks for his exuberance. Not that Artyom feared what they might think or say, but he knew he would be wise to keep a low profile. Especially given all that had happened, and all still to come.

Just then, the lights around the field flicked on. Artyom glanced at his watch. The spring days had stretched on later and later, and he'd almost forgotten to check the time.

The call was late.

In his pocket, his phone buzzed, on cue. Artyom whipped it out to find an international number on the screen. He had a good idea who he'd find on the other end of the line. After pressing the button to accept the call, he scooted to the edge of the stands and dropped to the ground.

"I am here," he said in Belarusian as he strolled away from the other parents. He settled on a spot about five meters away, a table stacked with red Solo cups for Gatorade and orange slices to eat at halftime.

"Enjoying your evening?" said Zabojca.

Artyom hoisted himself onto the table. "What time is it there?"

"It is morning in Thailand right now. Very early. But not too early for a glut of Australians and Americans already drunk in the room next to mine, waking me up."

Artyom clenched his fist as one of his son's teammates took a new shot on goal, and then he blew out a sigh when the shot attempt missed. "Perhaps they are still drinking from the night before and have not yet gone to sleep."

"Perhaps."

"What news, Zabojca?"

"Yesterday, a brown-skinned American woman arrived in the country. I followed her from the airport, and she came to this hotel. Later, she met with a short and squat local. They were not lovers or business partners."

"Sounds promising."

"I anticipate they will have another meeting at some stage today, so I will keep an eye on both of them."

"More than an eye, I hope," Artyom said.

"Do not worry. I always clean up any mess, whether or not it is mine."

This little jab made Artyom grin. "You are still mad at me, Zabojca?"

"Not at all, Artyom. Not at all."

"Excellent. I will have news on Omega soon, perhaps even before you are finished there. Our time is running thin so I will have to make a decision, one way or the other."

A few seconds of silence passed, so Artyom made a questioning sound.

"Sorry," Zabojca said. "Like I said, it is still early here. I need to flush the sleep from my body and prepare for the day. I have her name. Serena. I don't know her last name yet."

"Quick, clean, and no trace. Understood?"

"Understood," Zabojca said.

20

Serena sat in the passenger seat as Niran drove. The jungle roads were mostly dirt, with tree roots slashing the path like speed bumps. She bounced around in the seat. Her stomach vibrated, swirling the rice and fish she'd eaten for breakfast. Even after a full night's sleep, her body still felt the low-grade tinge of a jet lag hangover.

Around the next turn, Serena jumped in her seat when a massive gray elephant rumbled across the road. Patchy skin like a dried-up desert.

Niran giggled at her skittish reaction as he hit the brakes to let the giant beast pass. "I tell you a true thing. Thailand has number one elephant football team in entire world. Number one. Does America even have elephant football team?"

"Not as far as I know."

"That's right. Not even have one. Thailand always number one for many years now. Very proud."

Serena had no response to this, so she pursed her lips and nodded as the road meandered through a collection of shanty towns north of the bay. Trees framed either side of the passage, almost turning it into a tunnel.

"You look afraid," he said.

She shook her head. "I'm not afraid. Just focused. There are a lot of moving parts here, and I'm not sure what's going to happen inside that prison. Crashing into an elephant on the road doesn't help our cause much."

"Is not elephants should worry you. Much more dangerous things on this part of the island. People not happy for outsiders to pass through."

He didn't elaborate, and Serena didn't want to think about additional complications, so she held her tongue.

Deeper and deeper into the jungle they went. At times, the tree cover was so thick, it almost felt like passing from day to night. Then, the punishing overhead sun would resume when they ventured into a clearing.

For a moment, she thought they were being followed, but she couldn't isolate anything particular. Just the swishing of vines in the breeze and bird sounds. Niran's old car coughing and sputtering as it ran up and down hills and snaked around curves.

"What favor do you owe Layne?" Serena asked.

"Hmm?"

"You said you were only helping me as a favor to Layne. I want to know what the favor was."

Niran made a face as if he were considering whether to elaborate. "Many years ago, when we were younger. I was in Bangkok, and he was working for your government. I *think* he work for your government, but he never tell me, exactly. Smart enough to know I should not ask. But, I'm in trouble and in the streets because my wife was mad at me. She moved back to Phuket and leave me on mainland. Very bad situation because I'm also sick at the time. Layne, he find me and very kind to me. Give me food and new clothes, let me sleep on floor of his hotel room for two days until I get past the stomach illness. He even take me to airport and buy me plane ticket back to Phuket. And he still check on me, once a year or so since then."

Serena considered this. She didn't know Layne was the sort of person to help a homeless person in a foreign country. Then again, she and Layne rarely discussed personal matters, so she didn't know his non-work side much at all. Serena wasn't even sure of his daughter's name. Carly? Cassandra?

Maybe Layne had only done the favor as a quid pro quo. But, whether Layne was securing a return favor for future use, it had certainly paid off now.

If Niran could deliver, that was.

For ten more minutes, the faceless jungle whipped by the car as Niran piloted his junker deeper into the tunnels of trees.

Suddenly, he stopped at the edge of a clearing. He pulled over to the side of the road. A few clicks and thumps came from the engine as it idled. With a shudder, he turned the key in the ignition, letting the car fall silent.

"Why are we stopped?" Serena asked.

Niran pointed into the jungle expanse on her side of the vehicle. "See how it curve that way? Low space between two rises?"

Serena noted that the jungle opened into a valley with hills on either side. "I see."

"If you walk down that way, you come to place where the hills same distance either side. Turn north, only a few meters, and there you find a cluster of trees. In those trees is a door. Seems like magic. This door, it's very hard to see because of lots of fake vines and bushes around it. But, when you clear all that away, it leads underground, to the place you are looking for. The prison."

Serena opened her door and stepped outside. She rounded the vehicle, opened Niran's door, and said, "Show me."

He balked, jerking his head back and forth. "No, no, no. The men with guns. White men. I don't want to go anywhere near there. They sometimes wander outside, too."

Serena pulled him out of the car and pushed him up against the side of the vehicle. Not hard enough to hurt him, but she needed to get her point across as quickly as possible. Her bloodshot eyes caught his gaze and held it. "I'm not asking you to go *inside* this door. I just need to make sure I understand where it is. You've seen it in person?"

He nodded.

"Then I need you to show me where to find it. I don't have a lot of time to go hunting around down there. Understand?"

Before Niran could respond, a trio of vehicles arrived on the road behind them, driving side by side, clogging the entire road and blocking them in. Three jeeps. Thai men with machine guns appeared, their eyes fixed on Niran and Serena.

It all happened in a flash. One moment, alone, the next, blocked off by an armed welcoming party.

Niran said something Serena didn't understand, but the meaning was clear. Niran had indicated these men were members of some local gang who didn't take kindly to Niran, or maybe to Serena. Either one. Didn't much matter.

Serena had stocked weapons in the trunk of Niran's car, but the men with the guns were too close, and the trunk was locked, as far as she knew. So, she made the sane choice and offered the universal symbol of surrender by raising her hands in the air. They might begin negotiations if Niran could calm himself enough to act as translator. Most likely, they wanted a toll for passing through their territory.

While Serena stayed calm and offered surrender, Niran however, quaked in his shoes. His eyes darted in every direction.

Serena watched him, and he grew worse by the second. His quaking turned into convulsions of fear.

She knew it would happen, maybe even before he did.

Niran swallowed, a gulping sound drowning out the jungle for a split second. His eyes narrowed. He pivoted and then sprinted into the jungle, leaving Serena to face these local gangsters all alone.

INTERLUDE 2

FORT COLLINS, CO | SIXTEEN YEARS AGO

Layne bounds up the stairs and enters the Lory Student Center through the glass doors, with the bookstore on his right and a hallway leading to the main floor's open atrium area to his left. Panting, head throbbing. A streak of blood runs across the marble floor in front of him, but no bodies in sight.

He rushes forward, but he isn't sure where the shooter is. He assumes one, with a pistol, is probably upstairs. The previous blasts didn't sound like shotgun fire or automatic weapons fire.

Layne doesn't know much about guns. His father taught him how to shoot soup cans in the woods when he was young, definitely, but that's the general extent of his knowledge.

Today, though, he will have to come of age. Twenty-four years old. There's a dim blink of thought in the back of his head claiming he might die in the next few minutes, but the thought stays in the back and Layne doesn't let it swell.

His tennis shoes squeak on the marble floor as he sprints toward the stairs leading to the second floor. When close, he crouches to squint up the stairs before venturing blindly. He can't hear well enough to discern the source of the commotion, but he can definitely hear voices and the shuffling of feet. Frantic rushing. No one in direct sight, but there *are* people up there.

Layne knows he has to hurry. Each second the shooter is active, lives are at risk. He leaps up the staircase, three at a time, heart pounding and mouth dry. His tongue wriggles like a congealed lump of dirt, rattling against his teeth.

At the top of the stairs, Layne encounters his first dead body in the Lory Student Center. It's a woman from the cafeteria. A cashier. Layne doesn't recall her name, but he remembers previously seeing her wear a name tag proclaiming that she is from Boise, Idaho. He remembers this because he remarked on it once, and she corrected his pronunciation of the city's name.

Whatever her name was, now she's dead in the middle of the floor, with a puddle of blood spreading out around her midsection. Eyes open, staring up at the ceiling, unfocused and unblinking. The *not blinking* part is what Layne will remember for years, and sometimes he will see other dead bodies and recall this cashier, her eyes pointed at the ceiling.

Layne hurries forward, stepping around the blood so as not to leave footprints. He might need to be stealthy before this is over. Not sure why he thinks this, or how he knows to avoid leaving a trail of blood, but half of his actions are on autopilot. As if adrenaline and fear have become little gremlins piloting a control center inside his head.

The weight of his actions hasn't even sunken in yet. He's only dimly aware that he's done the exact opposite of what everyone else within earshot of the weapons fire has done. He's run headfirst into the melee instead of running away.

But now, he's here, and he has to do something about it.

There are office rooms on either side of the hallway, and several of the doors stand open. Layne, hands spread and lowered to keep his center of gravity flexible, creeps foot over foot until he can see inside each office door as he passes. Without a weapon, he looks around for a glass case, maybe with a fire ax he can take.

How will he deal with a shooter when he's unarmed? That thought didn't occur to him before.

Doesn't matter. Layne presses forward, hunting. He doesn't know if he's looking for students or the shooter, or both. He's mostly thinking about placing one foot in front of the other and pondering how he will walk out of here alive today.

Something in the air changes. A sound echoes from nearby, and he can't tell where it's coming from. Halfway down the hall, his quest ends abruptly. From around the corner runs a young man, combat boots pummeling the ground as he hustles. White guy, long blond hair, and pockmarked skin. Utility vest littered with guns. No, not guns. A utility vest with several knives. No, a single knife.

Layne's not sure of anything right now.

In the young man's right hand is a pistol, his finger on the trigger.

The blond shooter's head tilts up, and he goes wide-eyed at the sight of this grad student standing before him. Layne isn't sure which one of them seems more surprised.

The shooter raises the pistol.

About ten feet between them.

Layne does the only thing he can think of. He sprints directly at the shooter. Legs pumping, his body angled toward the ground, at a breakneck pace to close the distance.

The shooter squeezes off one shot and in the marble hallway, the blast of the gun echoes like thunder between Layne's ears. But the shot flies over his head, missing him completely. Somewhere behind Layne, glass breaks.

The shooter closes one eye to aim down the sight, but it's too late for him to press the trigger again. Their bodies collide.

Layne grabs the shooter, wrapping both palms around the hand clutching the gun. Since he's bigger than this scrawny kid, Layne uses his body weight to force them both over toward one of the nearby office doors. Layne slams the shooter's gun hand into the door frame next to the door. Bones crackle from the force.

The guy shrieks and drops the gun. But, he's not done yet. He reaches his free hand toward the knife on his utility vest.

Without thinking, Layne applies pressure to the shooter's forearm, bending it back toward his elbow. He rotates it away from his body and presses until he hears the bone snap.

With a wail that sounds like it came from a tortured cat, the shooter wilts away from Layne's grasp, crumpling to his knees. Tears stream down his face as he struggles to catch his breath.

A splash of surreality washes over Layne Parrish. He's broken this guy's arm, without even thinking about it. It wasn't even that hard. A little pressure, a little leverage, and *pop*, it snapped like tearing apart a chicken leg.

If he stops to think about it, he'll be sick. No doubt.

The shooter, sitting next to the door, tries to move his free hand out to push himself up. Layne curls his fingers into a fist and punches the kid in the nose with all his might. His head snaps back and thuds against the doorframe, then he slides down to the floor. His eyes shut. Out cold.

For some reason, Layne thinks about his friends Samir and Logan, waiting for him at the bar for happy hour. He wonders if they already know about this active shooter situation. What will they think of him if they learn he could so easily break this kid's arm and then knock him out? Will they consider him a hero? What will the cute Teacher's Assistant from the Social Psychology class think?

It doesn't matter. Layne acted accordingly to stop a threat. He didn't think about it. He seized opportunities, and that's why he's still alive, and not a casualty, like the cashier from Boise.

Layne snatches the gun from the floor. Adrenaline throttles his brain. His nose itches because his jaw is vibrating.

Is it over? Has Layne stopped the threat?

As terrifying and bizarre as the situation is, there's a small part of Layne that almost feels... good. A rush has taken over his body, sort of like a pleasant whiskey buzz on a cool afternoon.

It's power. The guilty rush of power.

While he's pondering the oddity of this feeling, more gunshots ring out from beyond a closed door at the end of the hall. A second shooter.

21

Zabojca watched the men in the Jeeps arrive and train their weapons on the woman and her guide Niran. Safe in his perch in the tree, Zabojca didn't worry about being spotted. But the situation had taken quite a surprising turn, for sure.

As expected, Serena—the brown-skinned spy from America—lifted her hands in the air and showed no visible signs of panic. She was well-trained and much too smart to let her enemy see distress on her face. Zabojca assumed she would take control of the situation and barter some financial arrangement with them. With a satisfying payday, these local thugs would be on their way.

Of course, nothing of the sort happened. The whiny little Thai man Niran succumbed to an immediate anxiety attack, which was a predictable response. Shaking in his boots, Niran would not be able to handle whatever would come next.

Zabojca didn't know for certain the identity of the

gangsters confronting these two. But, they did have tattoos like the Oros gang, a relic of mainland Thailand. Supposedly, they'd all been taken down by the law over the last couple of decades, but that's exactly the sort of propaganda the law would publish. Make the people feel safe to go out and stoke the economy. Buy cars, buy houses, all the while forgetting about the tangible dangers that should have all of humanity quaking in their boots at all times, just like little Niran.

For a moment, Zabojca thought he would have to intervene, which he did not want to do. While he had been to Thailand many times, he considered himself an impartial visitor to this country. He had no desire to insert himself into its politics. If both Niran and Serena died, he would not find the entrance to the secret prison. They had stopped their car here, but that didn't mean the bunker was nearby.

Also, if he did intervene, he could end up dead. The gangsters were small in stature, but the size of the rifles more than made up for their physical limitations. Zabojca was smart enough to know not to take on so many hostiles.

The operation to find the dark site and Pavel within it was important, but not enough to die for. Zabojca still had many important things left to do in his life. And, all of them depended on him surviving the day.

When Niran planted his feet and fled into the jungle, Zabojca drew a silent breath and reseated himself in the nook of his tree branch. At his age, his back and butt muscles weren't cut out for this flavor of espionage anymore. Out of practice? Definitely. Prone to making mistakes? Not at all.

So, when an impulse to watch Serena and observe her end of the situation unfolding tugged at him, he ignored it. No, he needed to stay on Niran. Find the location of the hidden door in the jungle. Get inside and recover Pavel. That was the mission. This Serena woman was merely another competitor for Pavel's affections, although Zabojca didn't know why. She was American, from what he'd learned about her in the short time since following her from the airport. And, the Americans managing this prison wanted to keep Pavel hidden away until the end of time. Curious.

Unless she was some brand of anti-American terrorist.

"Forget her," Zabojca whispered to himself. Stay in place and wait for Niran to pass by this tree.

As he waited and stared at Serena, the lookalike girl he'd known as a teenager again appeared in his thoughts. Except this time, he recalled her name. *Marta.* Marta from Mongolia. Strange that he had forgotten it all these years, and possibly more strange that he could so easily associate her name to her face now. But, then again, his life of late had been filled with recollections. Recollections and regrets and a desire to travel through time and make better choices.

Such a pointless waste of time. Still, on occasion, the mind went to places where you wish it wouldn't.

He and the girl had met one night as teens, at the Minsk-Pasażyrski train station, actually. Her dark skin intrigued him. Bundled up in long pants, a wool coat, scarf and hat, he could only see a sliver of her face then. But those eyes, he would remember those eyes for the rest of his life.

How would his future have changed if she hadn't

moved away from Belarus? Might they have married? Maybe he wouldn't have moved away, either. Maybe everything would have been different.

Shuffling came through the jungle below.

With eyes on Niran scrambling through the trees, Zabojca dropped from his hiding spot and flexed his knees to make a soft landing in the spongy grass below.

He unsheathed his machete. Long strides placed him on Niran's path within a few seconds. The leafy vines and bony fingers of tree branches whipped by as he narrowed the distance between them.

Zabojca could hear Niran's panicked breathing when he was five meters behind him. Running in a panic like that, the little Thai man would probably surprise a cobra and earn himself a nasty bite. Or worse, run into another group of those tattooed gangbangers looking for a payday.

Zabojca sprinted to save dumb little Niran from himself. As Zabojca gained, Niran's panic kept him blind to the pursuit until the very last second.

Niran spun, a look of horror on his sweaty face. Zabojca grabbed him by the shirt and shoved him against a nearby tree. The sounds of the jungle continued on around them, and Niran's haggard breathing now came in hiccups and snatches.

"You left your friend back there," Zabojca said in Thai.

Niran's head shook back and forth, his eyes like little black marbles rolling around. "She's not my friend. I don't know her."

Zabojca lifted the machete and let the tip rest on the skin just below one of Niran's eye sockets. He squirmed and tried to pull his head away. Zabojca resisted the urge to draw a little blood to set the proper expectations. The fear of pain was usually more effective than the pain itself.

"Easy," Zabojca said. "If your eye comes out, it will be your doing. Now, breathe, my little friend."

Niran tried to calm himself, gulping big lungfuls. Eyes still wide and full of terror.

Zabojca nodded. "Good, good. That's better. Now, you should know: I don't care about the woman. Do you understand?"

"Yes. Yes, I understand."

Now he had Niran's attention, so Zabojca decided to press a little.

He pushed the knife blade in a couple millimeters, producing a drop of blood. Niran whimpered and tried to pull back, pressing his head into the tree.

"I only care about the dark site. Tell me where it is, and you get to keep both of your eyes today."

22

Layne clucked his tongue against his teeth as he surveyed the courtyard. On this overcast day, the sky threatening to open up and storm, there wasn't much activity out here. He'd sat with the few other Winged House outpatient participants at a trio of benches in the southeast corner. Lounging around, killing time in between classes. Making small talk at times, at others, long stretches of silence played out.

Layne had been coming here for five days now, in-between time with his daughter and fielding multiple phone calls from detectives investigating the school shooting.

One interesting tidbit: the senator had not so far turned it into a publicity stunt for himself. That his son attended the school was public knowledge, but Noah's declared goal of kidnapping him had not been released to the media. Maybe the cops were keeping that detail secret to use as leverage against the architect of the shooting.

Either way, it didn't matter right now. Earning points at Winged House was Layne's top priority.

Although he hadn't been fully accepted as one of their own, the other ex-cons weren't outright antagonistic toward him as they had been in his first few days. The decisive way he'd broken up that courtyard fight had earned him a little juice from some.

Others, though, had put even more distance between themselves and Layne. The incident in the parking lot yesterday had naturally made him a few enemies. Wherever the river of the Winged House drug trade flowed through, the ones involved in it would not have appreciated the extra attention he'd brought by involving Raisa and Artyom.

He'd made inroads with management by stopping the fight and the drug deal in the parking lot, but he didn't yet feel any closer to inserting himself with important people. The choice between gaining leverage with management versus gaining leverage with the general population had been a tricky one. Layne wasn't sure if he was progressing in the right direction.

During classes, he kept his mouth shut, except for when disagreements broke out. Then, he would speak up, usually in defense of someone, especially if that person could provide a social benefit. Among these several dozen residents and outpatient guests, there was a caste hierarchy just like high school. Cool kids, medium cool kids, not-so-cool kids. Layne accepted that he would have to work his way up. Not every step was forward progress.

Across the courtyard, with her hands behind her back and a matronly pouch proceeding her, Raisa strolled along the courtyard's outer rim in a nonchalant manner.

Looking as if she weren't out cataloging and inventorying details about everyone.

Layne had given her fake details about a new address and a new parole officer yesterday, and then he'd had to scramble to set up the contact info on the back end, in case Raisa called to check up on him. If she'd done so, she hadn't given him any indication she could see through his ruse. At least, not yet.

"That bitch got her eyes on you," one of Layne's classmates said.

"You think so?"

"Hell yeah," the guy said. "Just make sure, if you get up in that, she at least gives you a good review in your chart after y'all put your clothes back on."

This spurred a round of snickers from everyone at the benches. Layne checked the temperature by casting his eyes around and found that they seemed to be jovial and not mean-spirited about it. From person to person, Layne could never tell how each might interact with him.

Then, something across the courtyard caught his eye, so he lumbered to his feet. "Be right back."

The object of Layne's attention, Jenna the redheaded cook, was crossing the courtyard with a large covered dish in her hands, looking flustered in her apron, long-sleeved shirt, and baggy pants.

She'd tried to call him a couple times the night before, and Layne had not returned her calls. He'd been with his daughter, of course, and Jenna would've known that. But, Layne didn't want to make Jenna mad or turn her off. He needed that cafeteria kitchen connection. Besides, he would need to retrieve the active surveillance bug from Artyom's office within the next four or five hours.

Also, she was growing on him, to a certain extent. Not that he intended to date her, but their little kitchen chats were fun. She could be feisty when flirting.

"Hey," he said before she could cross the courtyard completely to slip away via a door on the east side. She paused and turned to face him. Beads of sweat dotted her forehead and neck, her face looking strained from carrying the covered pot.

Layne swooped in and took it from her hands. "Let me get that."

Jenna let out an appreciative sigh as she shook out her hands. "My hero. It was heavier than I thought carrying this thing all the way from the kitchen."

"Where we going?"

Jenna tilted her head toward a door leading into an area Layne had never been before. "Conference room. They're holding lunch for some potential donors."

Layne raised an eyebrow. "Big deal?"

"I am not the person to ask about that. But, I can tell you this: they're serving steak and foie gras."

Layne opened the door and ushered her in. "After you."

Once they were both on the other side of the door, Jenna smoothed her hair against her scalp, and she held out both hands to take the pot back. Layne shook his head and held onto it.

She stood there, tapping an annoyed foot, insisting he return it to her. "It's just over there, Muscles. I can manage the rest of the way by myself."

Layne handed over the pot. "Suit yourself. Sorry I didn't call you back. I was playing Legos, then we read an extra story at bedtime, then I was wiped. I know that's not a rock 'n' roll kind of answer."

Jenna smiled. "It's okay. A lot of my evenings aren't that exciting, either. I was stuck in a TV binge and didn't get up off the couch for like six hours straight."

She turned to leave but then caught herself. For a moment, she faced the wall, breathing. When she looked up at Layne, her expression wore a grim tint. "I heard about what you did yesterday. Stopping the drug deal in the parking lot."

"Oh, that was no big thing. Everyone's making it into something like a scene from an action movie, but it's nothing. I didn't even know what was going on before I stumbled on those guys. It all just kinda happened so fast."

Jenna shook her head. "I don't think so, Layne. I don't think anything you do *just kinda happens*. You don't strike me as that sort of person."

He started to protest, but she cut him off. "It doesn't matter. But, the thing is, now you've got his attention. I hope that's what you want, and you understand how that might change things for you. I hope you've thought this through all the way."

Before Layne could respond, Jenna leaned up on her tiptoes to kiss him on the cheek. Then, she turned and disappeared through a nearby swinging door.

23

Layne stood at attention in Artyom's office with his hands clasped behind his back. He didn't know for sure if Artyom was ex-military, but he figured it was a safe assumption. Artyom carried himself in the deliberate way Layne associated with non-American soldiers. Standing at attention would be the proper show of respect.

"Do you know why I called you here today?" Artyom asked.

Layne stole a glance to the top of the file cabinet, where the bug was currently sitting. Only for a second, so the look wouldn't be obvious. But, he did want to confirm that the bowl was still there. Obviously, he couldn't peek into it to ensure the flash drive bug was still inside it, at least, not while Artyom interrogated him.

"No idea, sir, but I assume you're going to tell me."

Artyom's chair creaked as he sat back, his eyes like lasers scanning all of Layne at once. He was wearing an unreadable half-smirking expression, his fingers tented. "In a short time here, you have displayed a range of abilities. Raisa says you're excelling and demonstrating your value in all the lectures and workshops, not only when it comes to apprehending drug dealers and breaking up fights. She says you are smart, capable, and discreet."

Layne bowed his head as a show of thanks for the praise. "Winged House has been good to me. I'm just trying to give back when I can." Layne's eyes flicked again to the file cabinet. He wondered about the bug's remaining battery life. A lot of it would depend on how much Artyom spoke in here, causing the recorder to trigger. A few hours worth of capacity, at most. If he didn't retrieve the thing by tonight to swap out the battery, he could lose out on many potential overheard conversations.

"Tell me a story about when you were a boy," Artyom said. "What did you want most in the world?"

Layne launched into a tale without a moment's hesitation. "My father was a hard man. When I was young, my dad would hit us. Me and my brother Randall. I didn't care about my lumps and bruises, but my mom got it so much worse than the rest of us. I would hear her crying through the walls of our little apartment. One night, her eyes full of tears, my mom sneaked us both out to the parking lot, and we went on a night trip. We didn't ask questions."

"And where did you go?"

"Estes Park. Not far from where we lived, but late at night, the trip seemed to take forever. I was very tired but I couldn't fall back asleep. My mother seemed upset, and I didn't know what to do to help her. I was powerless and that filled me with a kind of dread. The next day, we all played hooky, and she took us into Rocky Mountain National Park. It was my first time to go."

"And what did you see in the park?"

"Beauty. Pure, raw beauty, like I'd never seen before. It reinforced how small I was, how little power I had to change things."

Artyom tilted his head. "I'm not sure I follow. How did this relate to what you wanted most in the world?"

"Being away from my father and out in nature, I realized what I wanted most was to stop the ones I cared about from hurting. I wanted to stop the strong from preying on the weak. I'm not a poet, so I can't say exactly how seeing the snow-capped mountains and the waterfalls and the moose made me realize that, but it did."

"Ahh, it makes sense," Artyom said, nodding. "It's not until you see beauty do you understand ugliness."

"That's a better way than I could have put it."

"And did you protect your mother after that?"

"No, not then. I was too little. But, when I got older…" He drifted off, assuming he had made his point.

Artyom sighed and clicked his teeth together a few times, studying Layne. "You impress me, Mr. Haskell. So far, you have fit in well here, and due to some unforeseen circumstances I won't go into, I'm in need of immediate help for a few special projects."

"What sort of projects?"

"First, I need to know how much deeper you would like to go."

Layne scrunched his brow, pretending he didn't know where the conversation was headed. "I'm ready to be useful."

"I'm offering you a job, Layne. A job you can't ever tell anyone about. Do you understand?"

Layne adopted a look that he hoped communicated both gratitude and awe. What sort of unforeseen circumstances would cause Artyom to invite Layne—someone relatively unknown—to conduct a secret operation for him? This probably meant Omega was almost ready, and they were short of personnel to handle it. Maybe some of their crew had been arrested, or they were spread too thin to accomplish everything.

Or Artyom was setting Layne up to take a fall. That was a more likely explanation for why Artyom would invite him into his circle of trust after only a few days.

"This means a lot to me, Mr. Borovitch. I'm not sure what skills of mine you think you could use around here. I'm not qualified as a counselor or anything like that, so maybe in the kitchen?"

Artyom shook his head. "No, I have something much more specialized in mind for you. There is a person who stands in the way of us doing great things. This person needs convincing. You're not opposed to helping me convince someone to stand aside and make the path for progress, are you? To help the strong stop preying on the weak, as you put it?"

He had to be talking about the senator. Putting pressure on him to release the imprisoned Pavel. "I'm not opposed to that at all."

Artyom's expression turned grave. "You understand there would be severe consequences for discussing these projects with anyone else. For even mentioning that I have asked you to consider it."

"Of course. I know how to keep my mouth shut."

Artyom leaned over and thumbed the button on his intercom. "Send him in." Then, he sat back and took a cleansing breath. "Very well. There are some simple tasks for you to complete, and you will begin tonight. It's time to meet your partner, who can explain everything once you are there."

The door open behind him, and Layne pivoted to look. There, standing in the door, was one of the two men Layne had apprehended for dealing drugs in the parking lot, only one day before.

24

As soon as Niran bolted, Serena knew her chances of talking her way out of the situation had plummeted. Across from her were three Thai gangsters, shirtless with machine guns, standing in the backs of Jeeps. They had fingers on the triggers. The expressions on their faces indicated they would have no trouble pumping a few dozen rounds into her and leaving her for dead.

She spoke enough Thai to know they were demanding to know her purpose out here. It's not as if she would inform them about the secret door in the valley to the American dark site location.

This deep in the jungle, with her escort gone, she was out of options.

In a split-second decision, Serena did the sensible thing. She dropped to the ground and rolled off the side of the road, into the thick of the brush. Fortunately, there was a small slope next to the road, so she rolled downward for about ten feet before coming to a stop in the damp muck of spongy grass and tree roots. The density of the greenery would shield her for a second or two more, but not much beyond that.

The gunshots began immediately. They were close enough to her that she wouldn't last long. Chunks of a tree root twelve inches from her face exploded into the air when bullets peppered it. The intensity of the sound was so jarring, she had to force her eyes to stay open.

Serena pushed herself up and launched her feet away from the shots. She stayed on all fours to keep her body low. Hopefully, below their field of view. The tangled mess of vines and shrubs clutched at her like octopus tentacles, but she pushed ahead, breaking through to a small clearing thirty feet from the road.

She dropped to her stomach and looked back toward the Jeeps. One of the men had already descended from the car to venture into the brush after her. Without a weapon and facing three armed men, she would have to neutralize one and take his weapon.

This one currently in motion had earned the privilege of being her *divide-and-conquer* victim.

She skirted back toward the road, keeping the diminutive Thai man in her sights. He was hunched over, the sling of his AK-47 trailing below the gun as he walked, bouncing off the foliage. An unlit cigarette dangled from his lips. His black eyes darted around.

Using the tree as cover, Serena shielded herself, scooting around it to keep her body out of his view. Holding close on the other side, waiting for him to move past the tree so his back would be to her. She looked toward the Jeeps to see where the other two were, but by now they had exited their vehicles and commenced exploration of the other side of the road. Too far away to pose a threat unless this nearby one started squeezing his rifle's trigger.

The muzzle of the AK poked out on her side of the tree. Then, it pivoted toward her. He hadn't stayed on his previous trajectory. He intended to circle around, directly toward her.

Serena whipped a hand out and snatched the barrel of the gun. She pushed it back, hoping to rip it from his grasp and ensure he didn't accidentally pull the trigger. Jerking her hands, she then tugged forward on the gun to knock him off balance.

When she saw his face, an instant of pity throttled her. He was maybe a decade younger than her. Eighteen or nineteen years old, max. Covered in tattoos from his bellybutton to his neck. Bloodshot eyes, a sneer on his face.

Serena jabbed him in the nose with a closed fist. Now she did manage to wrench the rifle free, and she jammed the stock up into his chin, cracking it against bone and knocking him back into the tree. His head banged against it. Black eyes rolled back and then shut. Grunting, he slipped down to the ground, then into the soft mush of the jungle floor. She thunked him on top of the head to send him into dreamland.

Serena checked the AK-47s magazine and found it full. Swallowing hard, she paused for a minute to catch her breath. The possibility of going deeper into the jungle and leaving those two alone occurred to her. But, she didn't want to have to deal with them after visiting the dark site, in case they decided to hang around. Plus, her passport was in the trunk of Niran's car. No sense in leaving it for them to steal.

So, she proceeded to hunt the other two gang members.

She shifted back through the jungle, staying low and keeping plenty of foliage around her to mask her arrival. All the way back, they stayed on the far side of the road.

Crouched, she skulked next to the road, circling the Jeeps. They were a few feet from each other on the far side, their backs to her. Chatting back and forth, waving their AK-47s around, looking for her in the wrong place.

Once Serena was near the Jeep, she popped up and sprayed a line of fire across their backsides, sending them both to the ground.

She waited a few more seconds, machine gun trained on them. The one on the left had died instantly, and the one on the right took a few desperate gasps before he expelled the air from his lungs one last time.

She'd hoped she wouldn't have to kill anyone today, but they hadn't given her that choice. She needed the items in that car.

"Oh, shit," she said as she realized the trunk was locked. Niran still had the keys. He had not returned, which didn't surprise her.

Grunting, she climbed to the top of one of the Jeeps and scanned around the forest. If Niran was out there, she couldn't see him. A light breeze rustled the tree branches, which made the whole jungle seem alive and made it impossible for her to isolate motion.

The idea to call out to him occurred to her, but maybe that wasn't the smartest. Too much noise already. There'd been nothing out here in the jungle to obscure the messy previous few minutes.

All that gunfire would act as a homing signal to any

other gang bangers in the area and shouting would only announce her exact location. No, if Niran had still been alive after his initial flight, the rattle of automatic weapons fire would've only hastened his exit from the area.

Either way, he was probably dead by now.

She could search around him, maybe locate his body to recover the keys, but she was already burning daylight and needed to relocate as soon as possible. If this dark site was indeed nearby, the soldiers within might have also heard the shots.

But first, she needed her gear from that trunk.

After unhooking the rifle sling, she turned the AK-47 around and examined the stock. It'd been strong enough to almost break the first gangster's chin, so maybe it would work.

Serena bashed the AK-47s stock against the trunk lock mechanism on the car. After a few whacks, it finally came open, swinging upward as bits of plastic and metal ejected from the lock. She grinned. One problem solved. Then, she stowed the rifle and retrieved her gear bag.

Serena ventured down toward the area Niran had mentioned. Two hills met in the middle, a couple of miles away. At least, that's where he claimed this mysterious door would be. Of course, her trust in him had disintegrated since he'd abandoned her to avoid facing those gangsters. But, no reason to think he'd led her to the wrong area in the first place.

Unless his entire purpose in bringing her out here had been to deliver her to those Thai men. An American woman, wrapped up in a little bow for them.

She stopped trekking, grunting as she considered this possibility.

As she breathed, Serena took in her surroundings. The chirps of birds and the sound of the breeze rustling the trees. No. This was the right spot. She could feel it. Something was not normal about this place, and she had to keep searching until she found the exact spot.

For another hour, she hiked across the steamy jungle, the hills on either side growing larger and larger. She focused on reaching the valley in the middle, and finally came upon it in her third hour of slogging through the humidity.

Once she was within a reasonable distance, she climbed up onto a mossy boulder for a better look at her surroundings. A few hundred feet to the north, she noted an area with a cluster of trees. Deeply shrouded among the foliage.

Any untrained eye would think them to be a normal part of the valley. But, these trees were thicker than other wooded areas nearby.

Then, she detected the exact thing to make her sure she'd discovered the spot. A blinking light. The reflection off the lens of a tiny surveillance camera, perched high in one of those trees.

Serena climbed down the boulder, stayed low, and hustled in that direction. Always with ears alert for sentries. Taking a roundabout path, she stayed clear of the camera's line of sight.

When she neared it, she pulled back handfuls of jungle detritus at the base of the tree cluster and found her destination.

A heavy door.

25

Layne sized up his partner in crime, Alexander Reznik, also known as "Rez." The day before in the Winged House parking lot, Rez had been the dark-haired one who had fled as soon as Layne had descended upon the drug deal. What the relationship between Artyom and Rez was, Layne didn't know. Rez wouldn't talk about it.

Somehow, tonight, Layne needed to learn new info about Omega. What, when, how, why... anything would be useful. But, getting info out of Rez could be a challenge. Maybe after a few drinks following a successful op tonight, Rez might be more willing to talk.

They'd crouched in the bushes at the edge of Cranmer park, overlooking a particular house in the Cherry Creek neighborhood of Denver. The lights in the house had been off for several hours. No cars parked out front. By all visible evidence, there was no one home.

Rez grunted as he rose to his feet, but Layne grabbed him, pulling him back. Rez was a big guy, but Layne was bigger.

"What?" Rez asked.

"Game plan? We should talk about it, at least."

Rez sniffed. "Nobody's home, bro. We bust in, do our little part, and then we're out of there."

Their "little part" involved planting several items to help the senator understand that Pavel Rusiecki should no longer be held illegally by the Americans at an unnamed foreign site. Pranking with malice, mostly. Things like removing pictures from frames and leaving them in a shredded pile.

"Look, man," Layne said, "I know you've never worked with me before, so you don't know how I like to do things. I'm not the most rigid guy in the world, but I do like to have a damn plan in place before I break into the house of a United States senator."

Layne wondered if Rez believed even an ounce of his spiel. Moving closer to Raisa and Artyom to learn about Omega had been a tricky proposition so far. Making Rez believe he was committed to this cause could become a big part of it.

"Do you need to be somewhere after this?" Rez asked. "Hot date with your boyfriend?"

Layne pursed his lips and said nothing. He was doing his best to play along but damned if he didn't want to punch Rez in the mouth, if only on principle.

"Fine," Rez said as he swiveled his backpack around and unzipped it. He pulled out pantyhose, a lock-picking kit, a couple of hobby knives, and latex gloves. "I got it all covered. Plus, this isn't even the senator's main residence, so there ain't much in the way of security. No cameras inside. A drive by every hour or so. As long as we keep the lights off, we should be fine." Then, Rez drew a Glock 35 pistol.

"Wait a second," Layne said. "Artyom didn't say anything about going in strapped."

Rez sneered. "It's only for emergencies." He paused, then cocked his head and asked, "Where did you serve time?"

"Limon."

"What was your first celly's name?"

Without pausing, Layne said, "A guy by the name of Marcus Wright. Why do you ask?"

Rez shrugged as he returned all the items to his pack. "I've known a couple people at Limon Correctional over the years."

"You probably know more than me, then. I kept my head down and my mouth shut."

For a moment, Rez said nothing. He continued to stare at Layne, his nose whistling as he pushed breaths in and out.

"Do you have a problem with me?" Layne said. "If you do, let's get this shit out in the open now." He pointed toward the house. "When we go in there, I need to know you've got my back. Right now, man, I'm not so sure I can say that."

After another pregnant pause, Rez smacked Layne on the shoulder and let out a little chuckle. "You worry too much. This is going to be fun." Then, Rez stood and handed Layne a pair of pantyhose and latex gloves. With a mischievous grin on his face, he sniffed and flashed his eyes at their destination, the extravagant house across the street. "Time to get it on."

Layne and Rez moved from room to room in the house, spreading mayhem as they went. They didn't have many specific instructions for what to do. Mainly, to ensure the senator would feel their presence in the house tonight.

There was only one required task: they were to place a picture of Pavel on the senator's desk. Aside from that, Layne and Rez had been given free reign to do whatever they wanted.

Layne didn't want to destroy anything, of course, so he did as little as possible. He mostly tried to make it *look* like he was desecrating the house, but he didn't do much actual damage. Undercover operations always contained an element of danger. Maybe you had to snort a little cocaine. Maybe you had to punch a guy in the face to make your colleagues believe you were on their side. But, Layne did have limits. Petty vandalism wasn't as bad as it could have been, though. At least there was no violence; no home invasion.

Rez, however, relished in the mayhem. He destroyed framed canvas paintings that looked like expensive pieces by slashing them with knives and breaking the frames. He emptied the senator's refrigerator, tossing food everywhere. Maniacal giggles often accompanied his actions.

Layne had a hard time figuring out his partner this evening. Rez had a diabolical streak, for sure, but there was something of a childlike and mischievous innocence to him, as well. One thing Layne knew for sure was that Rez was not to be trusted.

After they'd placed the picture of Pavel in the center of the senator's large mahogany desk, Rez lit up a cigarette.

Aside from that being a DNA no-no, the foul smell infiltrated Layne's lungs. Being a former smoker, he'd never gotten used to the odor of other people's cigarettes.

Layne eyed his partner in crime as he puffed and flicked ash onto the mahogany desk. "What is this Omega thing everyone is talking about?"

"Who's talking about it?"

Layne shrugged and didn't answer the question.

"Why are you asking?"

"Just curious. Seems like only important people know about it, so maybe I'm trying to increase my importance."

Rez chuckled, but he didn't provide any further reply to Layne's question. He tilted his head at the two matching cherub tattoos on each of Layne's forearms. "What are those? Like a yin and yang sort of thing?"

"Something like that."

"You get your ink to cover up scars? Looks like it. I can see lines there, under the tats."

Rez was right about that, but Layne didn't want to go into how or why he had collected his tattoos. Instead, he wanted to probe a little further into Omega, but the sound of a car door shutting outside cut through the silence.

Layne and Rez both tensed as their eyes met. Layne knew this would be a possibility, but he'd hoped to avoid it.

Rez dropped a hand into his backpack and withdrew the Glock. Layne put his hands up. "Wait. Let's not overreact."

He rushed over to the window and peeked outside. In the front of the house was the senator's son, the same preppy boy Layne had escorted out of the school almost a week ago. Plus, a woman who definitely looked like the young man's mother. Both of them yawning as they exited a car and strolled toward the front of the house. No sign of the senator, though.

"Who is it?" Rez asked.

Layne paused to consider his answer. Rez was carrying the gun with his finger on the trigger. No doubt, this man would kill the senator's family to impress Artyom. Or maybe he'd simply do it in the name of chaos.

"Security," Layne said. "A couple of them, walking up to the front of the house."

Rez hesitated, sighing at the pistol in his hand. He didn't seem inclined to return it to the backpack.

Layne balled his fists. "If I go back, man, that's three strikes. We need to bail out of here, right now."

"What is with you? First, you're being a pussy about needing to go over every detail of the plan, and now you're scared about a couple of security guards?"

"Look, you dumbshit," Layne said, barely able to contain his anger, "they're going to be here any second. Do you really want to engage in a gun battle against a US senator's private security detail inside his house? How do you think that's going to work out for us?"

"Fine." Rez scowled, making sure Layne saw his disapproval.

Layne exited into the hall first so he could be sure to point Rez at the back exit, away from the Senator's family as they entered via the front door.

Layne and Rez scooted down the hall and entered a utility room just as voices drifted from back down the other hallway.

Rez turned at the sound of the woman exclaiming,

probably noticing a piece of mayhem they'd left behind. He raised an eyebrow at the sound. Layne didn't allow him enough time to hear more. He ushered Rez out the door, hand on his shirt sleeve, practically pushing him. As soon as they'd stepped outside, Rez ripped his arm away.

"Don't ever touch me again," he said, and then strutted off into the dark. Layne considered going after him to try for more information about Omega, but he stopped himself. At least for tonight, as surly as Rez was now, that would be a losing battle.

26

Serena descended a set of concrete stairs down into the bunker. Heart racing, mouth dry, she told herself to be ready for anything. So far, the infiltration had been quiet. Noise from the outside world seemed completely cut off in here, so it was possible they hadn't heard the gunshots outside.

The walls in the stairwell were also concrete, full dark, with only muted orange running lights near her feet to guide her way. Weapon out and ready to fire at the base of the stairs, she encountered a door with a keypad. A few deep breaths calmed her enough to focus.

She withdrew the small electronic device Layne had sent to her. After holding it against the door for a couple of seconds, the door clicked and drifted an inch in her direction. Cool, subterranean air flowed out of the space between the cracked door and the doorjamb. After the last couple of hours sweating through the sheets of jungle humidity outside, the air conditioning felt like heaven on her exposed flesh.

She entered a hallway or a room, or something, but it was hard to tell because it was as dark as the stairs she had come from. No beeps of an alarm or little green lights from night vision goggles. As far as she could tell, she was alone in this room. The half-size crowbar she'd stuck in her belt loop clanked against something nearby as she moved.

Serena let the door close behind her. Careful not to make too much sound, she took a small flashlight from her back pocket and stuck it between her teeth. When she clicked it on, the beam looked like static with all the dust trapped in its path.

Her eyes adjusted to the limited quantity of light inside. This room had to be storage, shelves stacked high with pairs of boots, assorted clothing items, bulletproof vests, utility belts, and so on. She helped herself to one of the Kevlar vests. Never knew when one of those would come in handy.

So far, she had encountered little resistance. No sentries outside, and only a single surveillance camera. The entrance to this place had been well-hidden, but with some direction from Niran and simple tradecraft, she hadn't exerted a terrible amount of energy to find it. The ease at which she had entered meant one of two things: either this was a honeypot, and they were moments away from snatching her, or this was a small, shoestring operation. This room and the materials in here didn't look new.

For safety's sake, though, she told herself to assume a trap. If the above-ground entrance had actually been a *rear* entrance, then she might still have yet to find the real trouble.

Serena noted two doors at the far end of the room.

She approached the one on the left and pointed her ear against it. It was a heavy door, and she couldn't hear much, but she thought she detected the faint and blurred warble of male voices. At the other door, she could hear nothing. The door appeared to be locked, with no keypad entry.

The left door was unlocked.

So, Serena decided to take a chance.

She killed her flashlight and then pulled back the left door a few inches, and then she heard the voices. Calmly, slowly, with her weapon raised, she opened the door a little more, enough to see inside. But she didn't stumble upon enemy soldiers on the other side. Instead, she found herself on a walkway on the second story of a two-story room. A metal, grated walkway that reached from one end of the room to the other. A door stood at the far end of this catwalk.

Twenty feet below her, on the first story floor of this large and open room, sat a cluster of four soldiers. At a round table, playing cards and chatting. A small desk lamp providing an orange glow for their game.

They were Americans. Marines, she assumed. Serena blinked to make sure she was reading the insignia on their uniforms correctly.

This changed everything. Layne had not told her she would face American soldiers. He'd said it was an "American" dark site, but that hadn't necessarily implied she'd find Americans inside it. Plenty of these places were run by locals who were US allies.

Layne also hadn't told her much of anything else. Maybe he didn't know what she would find in here. Only the name of the contact in Patong Bay, that this man named Artyom Borovitch was eager to see his Belarusian countryman Pavel returned to him, and that he was willing to kill people to make it happen.

Serena would not hurt Americans. Not without a damn good reason. But, now she was even more intrigued to know why her own government might be guarding this man with US soldiers.

Why was he so valuable?

At first, the lights from the room down below had ruined Serena's night vision again. But now, as her eyes adjusted to the level of light, she could see the door across the room read *Detainment Area*.

Below her, the men kept talking. They passed a big bottle of brown liquid back and forth between them. No change in their behavior since she'd entered the room.

Serena holstered her pistol and eased across the metal catwalk as slowly as possible. It was not a simple task to cross the grated walkway without making a sound, given that Serena was wearing heavy duty boots for jungle traversing. But, since she was in darkness and the first floor had basic lighting, she didn't know how much the soldiers could see. Maybe she was entirely invisible up here.

Above all, she did not want to kill American soldiers. She would sneak around them and engage in reconnaissance, but she would not draw a weapon against them. If they captured her, though, no telling what they might do. Obviously, no one was supposed to know about this dark site in the jungle in Thailand. Would they shoot her on sight? If they tried, would she shoot back?

At the door, she located another keypad below. After waiting for a round of laughter below to mask the sound, Serena opened the door lock with Layne's device. On the other side, she found a small room with a bank of black-and-white surveillance monitors at a station against the wall. No one monitoring the station.

This place was a shoestring operation. Maybe the four in the room behind her were the only four here. Fewer mouths to spill the secrets inside it.

That made her even more curious.

There were six monitors at the computer station, each showing a cell. Five of the six cells were open. The last cell, the locked one, did contain a person inside it. Above that monitor was a piece of duct tape, with the initials PR written in Sharpie.

Pavel. Serena located the controls to unlock all the cells, but she wasn't sure if she wanted to do that yet. She wasn't here on a mission to rescue him, only to talk to him and learn about him. Then, *maybe* a rescue, if she could figure out what the hell was going on.

First, before anything, she needed to have a conversation with him. Next to the monitors was a metal plaque with a map of the facility. Serena studied it. Once she'd committed the routes to memory, she darted down the nearby hall, toward the cells.

When she entered the open room with the six cells, the man who could only be Pavel Rusiecki lifted his head. Disheveled, thin, dark bags under his eyes.

Serena placed one hand on her pistol but did not draw it. Tentative feet carried her toward the cell. Clearing her throat, she met his eye. "Pavel Rusiecki?"

"You are not one of them," he said, with a meek and gravelly voice.

She shook her head. "I'm not one of your captors, no."

"Then who are you?"

"I'm not here to discuss me, Pavel."

He spread a flat smile. "I see. Artyom Borovitch finally sent someone to kill me, did he?"

27

The security at the Winged House did not completely impress Layne. The front did, of course. That side and the courtyard entrances to the former hotel were heavily fortified. Stealth cameras, motion sensor lights, silent alarm. The side entrance into the residential quarters also looked impenetrable. Layne stayed well away from those areas on his quest to replace the bug's battery and swap out the memory card.

But the exterior cafeteria entrance had only a locked door. The door had an alarm, but Layne could easily trick the device by crossing a couple of wires. Maybe this entrance was last on the list of old hotel old-tech to receive Artyom's security upgrades. It didn't matter to Layne. A way in was a way in.

Inside the cafeteria, he let the door creep shut behind him, as quietly as possible. It still clicked when it closed. Even though it was past midnight, he couldn't be certain there was no one here. Some security wandered the halls during the day, and Layne hadn't spent enough time here at night to know if their evening shift patterns matched. But, so far, he seemed to have the place to himself.

Since the cafeteria was a vast, open space with tall ceilings, the silence of the room boomed in his head. Layne listened to his heart beating in his chest and focused on keeping his breaths slow and even. From somewhere, an air conditioner kicked on, making the ceiling rattle.

Layne checked his phone. No calls or texts from Serena. She should have been inside the dark site by now or at least found it. They'd agreed on limited contact, so he had to hope she was okay.

Layne had so far been unable to learn what Artyom's plan was for Omega and his claim about the "primary target," if not the senator. The memory card inside that bug could change everything. He was also counting on the Pavel angle to provide actionable information. Otherwise, Layne was wallowing in the mud, spinning his wheels, flinging earth as he tried to free himself of this rut.

After a couple minutes had passed in total silence, Layne decided he was alone. In case that changed, he had a backup plan. First, try to convince whoever found him that he was a legit patient here. A random security guard might not believe it. Second, to suggest he was hoping to catch Jenna here on a night shift, to ask her out on a date. People had seen them talking so it might sound believable enough.

Of course, it was always better not to get caught.

He shifted along the darkness, weaving through the cafeteria tables, toward the kitchen and Artyom's office beyond that. On the other side of his locked door, the little recording device disguised as a flash drive sat waiting. Burning through whatever meager battery life it had left, if any.

Layne hadn't known how long the thing would last, to begin with. Harry Boukadakis had given a rough estimate of twenty-four hours, and more than that had already passed since Layne had hidden it in Artyom's office yesterday. Not looking good.

A quick glance down at his arm reminded him of the presence of a streak of applesauce on his shirt sleeve, a leftover from breakfast. He thought of Cameron, sleeping in her big girl bed at Inessa's house. This morning had signaled the beginning of her custody week. While Layne did appreciate that without a preschooler roommate, he could come and go as needed for the next seven days, he missed Cameron. His heart compressed every day she was away.

Ultimately, though, it had been his decision to divorce Inessa, and his decision not to fight her on joint custody. This was just the way things would be, from now on. A regular, weekly heartbreak.

As he entered the darkened kitchen at the north end of the cafeteria, lit only by a meager number of muted emergency lights, he got his first notion that something was wrong. A hint of sound from behind him. Back in the cafeteria. The buzzing, overhead light in that room flicked on, and so Layne ducked behind a stainless steel cauldron of some sort between the food prep tables. The thing was barely big enough to hide his bulky frame, so he drew his limbs close and hunkered down. He leaned around it and considered potential paths out. There were only two: toward the hallway leading to Artyom's office, or back into the cafeteria. Two bad choices.

The front door of the kitchen opened and in strutted Raisa. The fluorescent lights in the kitchen blinked as she flicked on all the switches. The heavy footfalls of her dense shoes echoed around the room as she strutted across the tile. And then behind her, next came Artyom. They were chattering to each other in a language that sounded like Belarusian, but Layne couldn't tell for sure. Too rapid.

He closed his eyes and hugged the cauldron. Straining, he pointed his ear toward them. With the echo and the speed at which they were talking, Layne couldn't make out what they were saying. He caught random words here and there but not enough to string together a coherent narrative. Maybe it was a dialect?

Either way, it didn't matter. Within a few seconds of entering the kitchen, they disappeared into the back hallway, toward Artyom's office.

Layne checked his watch. Just after midnight. How long would they be back there? All night, perhaps?

He entertained the idea of sneaking after them and putting an ear to the door, to eavesdrop on their conversation. But, it wasn't worth it. Not after everything he'd done so far to curry favor with Artyom. Not worth it.

With a sigh, he padded back across the kitchen and into the cafeteria. And with that, he abandoned any hope of retrieving the bug tonight.

28

Serena stared at Pavel through the bars of his cell in the dark site.

"If you are Artyom's assassin," he said, "get it over with. I have no will to fight any longer."

She bit her lip as the weight of his words settled into her ears. "You and Artyom Borovitch are partners or colleagues. Associates of some kind."

"No, not anymore."

When she lowered the pistol in her hand and slid it into the back of her waistband, his head cocked, and he creased his brow.

"You look confused, Pavel. I'm not here to kill you."

"Then why are you here?"

Before she replied, Serena looked back toward the door. As far as she knew, the soldiers were still on the level below her, but it didn't hurt to be sure.

"They are playing cards," he said. "I assume, by the way you entered, the guards do not know you are here. They play every night and will not be around for hours.

When they come back, they will be full of drink and belligerent."

"How many of them are there?"

"Four."

"Always only four?"

He nodded. "Now, please, if you are not here at Artyom's behest, tell me your reason. Are you here to break me out?"

"What is Omega?"

He drew his chin back in what looked like a genuine expression of surprise. "What?"

"Omega. Do you know this term?"

He shrugged. "Of course, I know the term. But I have no idea what you are talking about."

"Artyom is planning something called Omega. A friend of mine needs to find out what it is. Lives have already been lost."

"I am sorry to hear that, but I have no knowledge of this Omega plan. This cell—or others like it—has been my home for a long time now. I have been waiting for someone like you to put a bullet in me, or for the Americans to tire of holding me and inject me with something while I sleep."

"You don't seem too concerned about it."

He flashed a pitiful smile. "My family is dead. My friends betrayed me. I gave up wallowing in the dread of my situation long ago."

"Why are you so sure Artyom Borovitch wants you dead?"

"Because he tried a few months ago in Cairo."

Serena considered his face. Tired, haggard, and seemingly guileless. "Okay, then, *why* does he want you dead?"

"You want answers, I want to leave this cell. I may have let go of optimism, but I know when to grab a rope when I see one. Help me out of here, and I will tell you what you want to know."

"In America, Artyom has been doing nasty things to get you released. Why would I help him by letting you out of here?"

Pavel now laughed, a sickly cackle. "Whatever he is doing in America, it is not to bring home a Belarusian patriot, that is for sure. It is a smokescreen for something else. As for me, he only wants me out so he can hunt me down and kill me."

Serena didn't know why, but she believed him. Something about his face said he was genuinely afraid for his life.

Time to decide. While Layne's request wasn't explicitly to rescue Pavel, or even *not* rescue him, if he would only talk outside this cell, then maybe she had to let him out. What did she care what he'd done or hadn't done to land him in Thailand? He was no threat, as far as she could see.

But, there had to be a good reason the Americans were keeping him here, right?

If her mission was to find out why Artyom would go to such extreme lengths to free Pavel, and he would only talk outside the cell, then maybe she had to let him out. In his weakened state, it's not as if he could overpower her. Worst case, she could turn him back in to the authorities, if she didn't like the way things were going.

Damn it.

Maybe she would come to regret this, but she didn't

have time to sit here and debate with him all night. Sooner or later, those drunk American soldiers would come in here to check on Pavel. And she didn't want to have to make another terrible decision... to shoot or surrender to them.

"Okay," she said, "can you stand?"

He nodded and grumbled as he rose to his feet. She unlocked his cell door, shifted her gun to the front of her waistband, and then rested a hand on the grip. "Let me be clear," she said as his eyes studied the gun. "I'm not your savior. You will stay within my eyesight at all times from this moment forward. Understand?"

He raised his hands in surrender. "Completely. I will give you no trouble."

She guided him out to the hallway. He was thin and frail, like an old man, even though he seemed to be only in his forties or fifties. His face still wore a grim determination as he trudged forward, and she respected that about him.

Maybe helping him escape this secret prison bunker wasn't a good idea. But something about his story intrigued Serena. There were layers of conspiracy present, and she needed a clear head and distance to sort that out. Why had the Americans taken him, why was he being kept in secret, why would some Belarusian ex-pat go to such great lengths to force his release?

And, not to mention, why did Pavel think his employer Artyom Borovitch was intent on killing him? If Pavel would only tell his story once they were out and free, was that a worthwhile risk?

Serena was intrigued enough to actually do it.

He directed her toward a set of lockers to retrieve his possessions and his passport. With some difficulty, he changed out of his shabby clothes and into a set of slacks and a shirt. His ribs were sticking out, but he displayed a surprising amount of muscle definition for someone with such a gaunt face. Perhaps he wasn't as weakened as she'd thought.

Before the door out into the open room where the American soldiers were playing cards, she paused. "You need to be extremely quiet."

He nodded. "This is not the first time I have been faced with a situation like this, believe me."

With a sigh, Serena opened the door. She still wasn't sure if this was a smart thing to do. But, it was happening. She let Pavel go first, and his shaking hands latched on to the railing for help. His feet shuffled along the grated metal floor, which made more noise than she wanted. It would have to do.

On the floor below, the soldiers were making plenty of their own noise, though. The bottle they had been passing around was now almost empty.

She shuffled along after Pavel, hand on the butt of her pistol. The Americans were completely occupied with their own drunken activities at the poker table. She had to ask herself what she would do if she and her new captive were discovered. Draw her pistol?

She honestly had no idea.

Pavel inched along the walkway, the guards chattered about nonsense below, and everything appeared to be proceeding according to plan.

But then, when Pavel and Serena were about halfway

between the door to the cells and their destination, Serena heard the sound of a chair screeching on the floor.

One of the soldiers stood, drunkenly knocking his chair over to make it thwack on the floor below. It appeared that their game had ended. If any of those eyes drifted up, Serena would have nowhere to hide herself or Pavel.

She poked him in the back, urging him to move faster. He did, but his labored breathing was almost louder than the footsteps.

Two-thirds of the way across.

Down below, the guards divvied up poker chips. Shuffling them around the table. Inserting the playing cards back into some kind of card holder device. All of them now standing, finishing the bottle on one last trip around.

Three-quarters of the way across the walkway. Fifteen feet from the door.

"Hey!"

Serena gasped as she looked down to see a single guard with his gaze locked directly onto her. His eyes were light blue, his hair blond, his face chiseled and handsome.

Serena had killed handsome men before.

But, she would not do so today. Not American soldiers just doing their jobs. No matter what came next, she would not aim a gun at these men.

As the other soldiers took notice, two of them ran toward a locker at one end of the room, which presumably contained weapons. Another one sprinted in the direction of a different wall where Serena could see an alarm. If he reached it, would the facility lock down?

Pavel had said there were only four guards here but were there others nearby at a satellite installation?

No sense in sticking around to find out.

"Go!" She shoved Pavel in the back, thrusting him forward at the door. Gasping, panting, he limped at top speed. Within three seconds, they were through the door. Veins on his neck pulsing, bug-eyed and heavy-lidded, but Pavel did not slow down, to his credit.

Serena urged him through a room and toward the stairs leading up. Once they were on the bottom stair, an earsplitting alarm raged behind them.

They raced to the top of the staircase, and she pressed the bar to open the door, but it would not budge.

They were trapped. The alarm had initiated a lockdown.

She withdrew the small, metal crowbar device from the side pocket of her pants and wedged it into the crack between the door and the doorjamb. She wiggled it back and forth to shove it in a little deeper, and Pavel put his hands on it to help her push. In his weakened state, he wasn't of much assistance. As time ticked on, she knew the guards were only seconds away from bursting into this room.

Back and forth, back and forth, crowbar inching deeper into the crack.

After some grunting and sweating, she and Pavel did manage to open the door. Two steps later, they'd fled out into the jungle. One moment, in the comfort of air conditioning, the next, into the intense heat and humidity of a Thai jungle.

The alarm raged as long as the door stayed open

behind them. The instant it shut, they were in total silence.

"Where are we?" he asked, squinting against the sun.

"Thailand." Then, she grabbed him by the shirt collar and yanked him close. "If we can survive long enough to find the car and get out of here, you are going to tell me exactly why the hell I went through all that trouble to break you out of there."

29

Serena saw the Humvee at a distance, but it came no closer than that. As she and Pavel fled for Niran's car, the drunken soldiers drove toward the water. They must have assumed Serena had arrived by boat, so they'd headed to a nearby dock.

But, even as she and her quasi-prisoner found the car and hopped inside, she didn't let up for a minute. The soldiers would find out quickly they weren't on the water.

"Talk," Serena said as Niran's car sped down a bumpy jungle road in the north of Patong Bay in Thailand. Without Niran's keys, she'd had to hot-wire it. Fortunately, the car was old enough that it gave her no trouble. Hot-wiring a car was like riding a bike. Not as fast as her best time back when she was in training, but fast enough, considering she hadn't had to perform this task in years.

Pavel still hadn't quite recovered and caught his breath, but he did as he was told. "I was in Vienna," he said, wheezing. "There was a conference there."

"A conference for what?"

Omega Trap

"How to improve international prescription drug trade. I have been working to get cheaper medicines into Belarus for many years."

"And they detained you at this conference?"

Pavel shook his head. "They arrested me at the airport."

"What was the charge?"

"The assassination of an American diplomat at the US Embassy in Kampala, Uganda."

Serena eyed him. "And I assume your story is that you did not kill this American at the embassy?"

"My fingerprints were found on the knife that stabbed this man, but there is no CCTV footage of me in or around the embassy that day. How is this possible? The footage has been lost, or damaged, or too blurry to make out. This is what they say about it."

"Why would the Americans do this to you?"

Pavel sighed. "They did not do it. They were duped."

"So Artyom is the architect of all this?"

"Yes."

Serena shook her head. "I don't buy it, Pavel. My friend told me you and Artyom have been working together to change the political system in Belarus. That you have been partners for years. Is that not true?"

"No, that much is true. But, when I was in transitional custody in Cairo, a man came to end me. The Americans stopped this man when he had a knife to my throat. They killed him, but not before I could look into his eyes. He was a man Artyom and I both know. Someone from the old country, brought over for this specific task. Artyom sent him so I would know who had done all of this, but never know why. I would never discover why Artyom had turned on me and sent me to my death."

So much didn't make sense. Why would Artyom Borovitch go to such trouble? Would he kidnap the son of a US senator solely to free and then kill this former colleague?

"Why does he want you dead?"

"I told you, I do not know."

"Take a guess. Humor me."

Pavel sighed and ran a hand through his greasy hair. "We were close once. Not as much the last couple of years. Artyom had grown impatient with the pace of progress back home and the failures of my lobbying efforts."

"Did you argue about it?"

"No, never. He never outwardly expressed doubts about me."

She chewed on this for a couple of minutes. Seemed like a flimsy reason to kill him. Especially given all the effort he'd expended to do so.

They undertook the rest of the drive in silence until Serena arrived at the safe house in the northeast part of the island, not far from Laem Sai Garden Resort. A one-bedroom house set back from the road, shrouded in trees.

When she parked, he eyed her. "This is safe?"

Serena held up a hand to silence him, then she lowered her window. Only the sound of birds and water from a nearby creek or river came back. Still, she waited for several seconds as she observed the house.

It appeared empty, but she'd had too many surprises already on this operation.

She rounded the car and opened his door. "It's as safe as we're going to get around here. We rest for a day so I can work on altering your passport. Plus, we make sure no one is on our tail, and then we're out of here."

And, even though she had been assured there would be no one else for miles around, Serena could feel the eyes on her.

30

Crouched behind a tree not far from the Twin Sisters trailhead, Layne glared at Rez. His partner in crime since their home mayhem escapade last night. Rez had taken refuge behind a tree on the other side of the muddy patch between them. Both hunkered down on this hiking trail in Rocky Mountain National Park, an hour north of Boulder.

Rez shook his head and stood up, shucking pine needles from his shins. "Thought I saw something." He crossed the hiking trail and looked both down and then up the trail before fishing something out of his wallet.

"Rez," Layne said as he popped a nicotine lozenge in his mouth. "What are we doing here? Artyom didn't tell me anything."

With a grunt, Rez produced a wallet-sized portrait of a white man, aged about forty. Cropped brown hair, sharp suit, a plastic smile on his face. American flag in the background.

"What's this?" Layne asked.

"The senator's brother."

"Okay, so why are you showing this to me?"

"Our little breaking and entering experiment last night was not a success."

"What do you mean?"

"Apparently, the senator never saw the picture of Pavel Rusiecki we left for him. They thought it was a random break-in from some rich prick kids in Cherry Creek."

Layne's eyes widened as he stared at the photo. "Is the senator's brother here right now, on this trail in Rocky Mountain?"

Rez nodded.

"And we're supposed to kidnap him?"

Rez sucked through his teeth. "Do you have a problem with that?"

"Of course not," Layne said, without hesitation, because he had to say it. Gaining favor with Artyom via following Rez's orders was Layne's best chance at making progress.

Progress that had led him to the prospect of kidnapping a man.

How could he go along with this? When undercover, there was a line that had to remain uncrossed. He'd almost crossed it last night by letting Rez terrorize the senator's family. The senator's wife and son coming home had probably prevented Rez from burning the place down.

If he let Rez take the senator's brother, then too much flew out of Layne's control. But how should he stop it? Talking Rez out of this op wasn't likely.

"Will he have a security detail?"

Rez shrugged. "Probably not. He's on the senator's

legal team, but I don't think that earns him a bodyguard. Not when out hiking in the woods, I'd guess." Rez again looked back and forward to make sure there was no one coming from either direction on this hiking trail. Then, he drew a pistol with a long noise suppressor and offered it to Layne, grip-first. "If he does have a body man, and it makes you feel better, you can carry this."

Something odd flashed in Rez's eyes as he passed Layne the pistol. A micro-expression signal of deceit.

Layne turned the gun flat in his palm as he accepted it, then he let his hand go slack. He was checking the weight of the pistol, an old and scuffed Beretta 92FS. Probably with the serial number filed off.

Layne knew this pistol well, and he could tell what Rez had given him was lighter than it should have been. No bullets in the magazine.

What was Rez's play? To kidnap the senator's brother and get rid of Layne in one move? To flee and let Layne take the heat if things went bad? Maybe these were Artyom's orders.

"Thank you," Layne said. "I'd rather not use this if I don't have to."

"No sweat, bro. He's three miles or so up this trail. He set out alone from the trailhead, but we don't know if he met anyone else along the way. So, we can't say if he's alone now or not."

Layne stowed the pistol in the back of his pants. "Gotcha. Lead the way."

Layne and Rez trudged along a skinny dirt trail cutting between various sections of enormous trees, headed on a path to an unseen peak a few miles away.

They spoke little. Layne hadn't hiked this trail in ten or fifteen years so he couldn't recall the layout.

He kept Rez in front of him the entire time. Thinking, weighing his options, he knew the pistol in his waistband was nearly useless. Well, perhaps not useless. He could always use it to pistol whip Rez, but that wouldn't be effective enough. Rez was a large man, with biceps that rivaled Layne's. Plus a hunting knife strapped to his belt, not to mention a gun of his own.

After about a mile, Rez paused to sip from his water bottle. He eyed Layne as he did so.

"Last night, in Denver?"

"Yup," Layne said as he bent to re-tie the laces of his hiking boots.

"You said a security detail was outside the house. The people in the arriving car that interrupted our fun."

Layne didn't like where this was headed. "I did say that. What about it?"

"You sure about what you saw out there?"

"Yeah, man, I am."

"You don't think it could've been his wife and kid who were coming home from a movie or something?"

Layne shrugged. "I don't know what you want me to say. I saw what I saw. Anything else you want to ask me about it, or can we get back to what we're doing?"

Rez gave a smarmy grin as he screwed the lid back on his water bottle and clipped the bottle's carabiner to his belt loop. "Nope. That's all my questions for the time being, your honor."

Up the Twin Sisters trail, they pushed higher and higher, finally diverting from the trail and reaching a summit at the eastern edge of the park about an hour later. Rez scrambled up the rock outcropping first. When he did, he held a hand out, waving Layne forward.

"There he is," Rez said, pointing to the north, "right beside that small lake."

Layne stood beside his partner, taking in the scene below, still unsure what to do about this situation. Every plan he'd visualized along the way held too much risk.

The senator's brother was not alone down by the water. He was sunning himself on a rock with a woman, both lying flat with arms spread, their faces upturned toward the sun. "What about her?"

Rez made a contemplative *hmmm* sound for a few seconds. "I think she's gonna have to go. It'll be hard enough to get him back to the car without anyone noticing. Don't want to have to deal with a second body."

"Or, we could just wait until one of them goes to the bathroom."

Rez eyed Layne. "Think you're pretty smart, don't you?"

Layne shrugged. "I'm just trying to cause the least amount of chaos."

Rez turned back to staring at the senator's brother and his female companion. "You know what, Layne? I don't think you're interested in controlling the chaos at all. As a matter of fact, I think you're going to try to sabotage me."

"Okay, that's enough. I'm not here to have a pissing contest with you, Rez. So why don't you either put up or shut up."

Rez turned sour, his face falling into a scowl.

In a flash, he reached back to snatch the pistol from his waistband. Layne reacted. He leaped forward and wrapped his hand around Rez's wrist, trying to keep the gun out of his grasp. But Rez was too strong. He managed to draw the pistol. Layne slapped at the top of the gun and knocked it away. It went flying, landing in grass spongy from recent rain.

Layne drove the palm of his fist into Rez's chin, knocking the big thug back a step. Rez responded with a spinning backhand, cracking Layne in the temple. Layne had tried to pull back, but he'd been a fraction of a second too late.

Layne saw the next attack coming, and so he ducked as Rez launched a punch so swift that Layne heard the air whiff above his head. With Rez's body angled, Layne jumped up and wrapped his hands underneath Rez's armpits, securing him in a headlock.

Positioned behind him, Layne pulled them both to the ground, and then he wrapped his legs around Rez, locking his ankles inside Rez's knees. The same move he'd used to neutralize Noah Smith on the gymnasium floor of the high school. Except, Rez wasn't a scrawny teenager.

Layne tensed his arms and squeezed with everything he had in him. The big guy fought back, attempting to wrestle free. Layne gritted his teeth and bared down, like trying to contain a bucking bronco from underneath.

He kept the pressure on Rez's upper arms, which forced them above his head. With his arms locked high, Rez couldn't reach down to the hunting knife strapped to his belt. He tried to punch and dig his elbows into Layne's sides, but he no longer had the leverage. After a few seconds, he slowed.

And, in another thirty seconds, he stopped fighting completely.

His body went limp in Layne's grip, and he ejected one

last breath. Layne pushed Rez to the side, then he scooted out from underneath the dead body. The two hundred pounds of uncooperative weight pressing on him had now slumped into the muck of the trail.

Panting, Layne looked down at the husk of this man, a person inside Artyom's inner circle. A person Layne needed, now dead.

"Shit."

31

Artyom parked under the bridge as cars roared overhead. The giant concrete and metal structure shimmied and vibrated as the interstate's vehicles tested its load capacity. Concrete thundered. The shaded grass area underneath provided respite from the punishing midday heat.

While some people would hate the prospect of meeting in such a loud and distracting location, Artyom loved it. Growing up in Minsk, he called a place like this home for many years.

The bridge near Rudensk Station had kept him safe from the elements until he'd been old enough to join the military. A concrete bridge with angled ramp-like supports on either side led up into small, alcove areas above the ramps, under the actual bridge. He had sometimes had to defend against invaders in the limited number of alcoves, so that is how Artyom learned to fight for what was his.

The need to live at that bridge had arisen after his

parents died. He didn't think of them often, but being in this place now opened the door to a warm cascade of memories. His parents who had taught him right and wrong and how to fight for worthy causes. His parents who had been so insistent that he learn the language of Belarus and speak it, not Russian, which so many in Minsk had adopted as their only tongue. The same parents who would never let him feel ashamed of Belarus, not even for one second.

Artyom looked at his phone and saw no update from Rez. He should have captured the senator's brother by now. Artyom did not like the radio silence, especially hours after the mission had begun. It made him fear something had gone wrong.

Was he a fool to think Rez could handle Layne? With Noah's failure at the school, everything had changed. Artyom had needed a scapegoat; someone to deflect attention away from his own people. With Layne dead and evidence tying him to the break-in at the senator's house planted on him, it would free up Artyom to focus on other tasks without worrying about the police.

But, the whole world now floated like a rudderless ship. They might not even need Omega. So much was undecided.

As Artyom pondered his choice, a car appeared on the far side of the bridge. A truck, creeping through the brush, then settling a hundred feet from his car. Both of the vehicle's noses pointed at each other, dark and silent.

Artyom left his car and crossed the short distance toward the car parked on the other side. The door opened, but no one immediately emerged from the vehicle. When dealing with these people, they often adopted a similar posturing. Artyom didn't mind.

A moment later, someone did appear next to the truck parked there. This man had dark skin, which Artyom didn't much like. But, this was business. Sometimes you had to work with undesirables.

All for Belarus was the mantra Artyom would repeat in his head whenever he had to undertake a distasteful task like this.

"Arthur?" The guy said.

"Artyom, but that's close enough."

The man nodded, then he dug his hands in his pockets. He tilted his head back at Artyom's car. "Anyone else in that ride with you?"

Artyom shook his head. "Yours?"

"Nope. Do you mind lifting your shirt and turning around?"

Artyom untucked his dress shirt and pulled it up past his belly button. Then, he spun in a slow circle. "Are you looking for weapons or government listening devices?"

"Both."

"I assure you, I have neither. I'm here to do business, not play games."

"You can't give me shit for being too careful."

Artyom completed his circle and tucked his shirt back in. "And you?"

The dark one lifted his t-shirt, exposing a pistol grip jutting out of his underwear. "I'm going to keep my piece right here. If you have a problem with that, you can turn around. I don't need your money."

"No, that's fine with me."

The man walked around to the back of the truck and

opened it up. He beckoned Artyom forward, and then he rounded the car, careful to keep the man's hands in view the whole time. A single crate sat there in the truck's bed.

"Just one?" Artyom said.

The man nodded. "Wait until you see what's in it. You'll be happy, trust me."

The man then did open the crate, and Artyom peered inside. He saw what looked like a collection of AK-47s, M4 carbines, AR-15s, a couple Uzi sub-machine guns, and several hand grenades.

Artyom shook his head. "These guns look old and well-used. And where are my explosives? Where is my C4?"

The guy lifted his hands in mock surrender, adopting a smarmy smile. "Old? These are top-of-the-line, my man. And your guy didn't say anything about explosives. This is all exactly as ordered."

Artyom felt his frown darkening into a sneer. This would not do. He needed much more for Omega. He needed bigger. More deadly.

"So," the guy said, "are we going to do business? Do you want these or am I supposed to grab my dick and go home?"

Artyom whipped his pistol out of his concealed ankle holster and raised it to the man's temple. The man didn't even have time to reach toward the gun in his waistband. With one quick press of the trigger, the bullet blew out the back of his head. His hands were still raised in surrender, that smarmy grin still on his face as the light fled his eyes before he'd even fallen to the ground.

"Yes," Artyom said, "I will take them."

32

Layne stood at attention in Artyom's office, legs spread to shoulder width and arms clasped behind his back. He kept his eyes forward on the wall, trying not to look at the bowl where the little bug was hidden. The battery probably long dead by now since Layne had been unable to retrieve it yesterday at his self-imposed deadline. Maybe he could find a way later tonight.

That might depend on how this current conversation turned out.

Artyom sighed. "Tell me again how it happened."

"We spoke on the phone in the morning. We were going to meet at the trailhead at eleven because Rez said he had errands to run first. When I asked him what errands he had to run, he didn't give me a straight reply, which I took to mean he was going to buy drugs."

On the table at the edge of Artyom's desk sat a money roll. Layne hadn't inspected it, but it looked to him like a couple thousand dollars sitting there. The payout for Layne's employment over the last couple days. Artyom had placed it there deliberately, of course, as a means to distract Layne and keep him off guard. Keep him wanting and in need, as a power play.

"What reply *did* he give?" Artyom asked.

"He said he was going to pick up materials. I didn't ask him what he meant by that. He said it in a way that sounded like it was none of my business, which is what made me think drugs. He was pretty high last night when we went into the senator's house in Cherry Creek."

Artyom tented his fingertips and stared at Layne's chest for a long moment. Staring through it. Eventually, he drew a breath and asked, "How long were you at the trailhead waiting?"

"I waited an hour. Maybe ninety minutes."

"And how many times did you call Rez while you were waiting?"

Layne shrugged. "I don't know how many times, maybe three or four. Look, man–"

Artyom slammed his hand down on his desk, making a cup full of pens and pencils rattle. "Where is my god damn asset? Whether Rez was there or not, you should have brought me back my prize. You have no idea the pressure I am under this week. You have no idea how many balls I have juggling in the air right now, and the consequences if I let any of them drop."

"I'm sorry, Mr. Borovitch. Since he didn't show up, I wasn't sure what the protocol would be. And, I knew it wouldn't be okay to call you or anyone at Winged House during the operation."

"Why would you not call here?"

"Because I would never do anything that would reflect

badly on you or this place. Winged House has been good to me. I'm a loyal person."

Artyom dragged his fingers down his face, leaving temporary white streaks behind. "You have done many things well in your short time here, Layne. Aside from your obvious physical prowess, you've shown you have good judgment. Quick on your feet. Also, I like that you don't blather on about yourself. Some might see this as mysterious and therefore a liability, but I like a man who keeps his business his own. It shows respect for the sovereignty of others."

Layne didn't know what 'the sovereignty of others' was, but he dipped his head with modesty. "I appreciate that. I want to find my place here."

"That's why this whole episode today is so baffling. I find your explanation thin, and, to be honest, strange."

"I'm not sure what to tell you. Maybe we won't have the answers until we can get in touch with Rez."

Rez wasn't going to make an appearance any time soon, though. Currently, his bulky corpse was stashed behind an abandoned warehouse outside of Boulder, at the bottom of a dumpster filled with broken hunks of drywall. At some point, Layne would take Rez to a friendly funeral home in Denver, where he would have the body discreetly cremated. Rez was a day or two away from disappearing into ash forever.

Layne hated killing anyone unless necessary, but he hated the idea of going to prison for murder even more. Of course, he could call Daphne Kurek and ask her to make any complications vanish, but Layne didn't want to do that. He didn't want to involve Daphne at all.

"Until we get in touch with him?" Artyom said, echoing Layne's words.

"That's right. I'm not sure what else to say about it right now."

Artyom flashed his eyes as he leaned forward. "Was I a fool to trust you so easily? Perhaps this says more about my desperation to finish this whole business that I would appoint someone I barely know. Perhaps this means it's time to clean the whole thing from top to bottom. I can't set sail with a leaky ship, as it were."

He was talking about Omega, no doubt. And he probably knew Layne had seen through his attempt to turn him into a scapegoat for the attacks on the senator.

Or, maybe Artyom hadn't figured him out yet. The Belarusian was a hard man to read.

Layne tried to keep his face even and neutral while weighing his next words. "Again, I am very sorry, sir. I don't know where Rez went, or where he's been, and I didn't know what I was supposed to do without his approval. I assumed he was running the operation. At least, that's how he acted."

They were both silent for ten or twenty seconds, Layne standing and Artyom sitting. If Artyom had already decided Layne's fate, they wouldn't still be here, talking. Eventually, Layne decided to push a little. "Maybe if you told me a little more about what this is all–"

Artyom flicked a hand as if swatting away a fly. "I've heard enough. Get out. Out of my office. I do not want to see you for the rest of the day. Maybe not tomorrow, either. I need to think about what should happen next for you."

He snatched the roll of cash from the desk and tossed

it. Layne caught it and then stowed the money in his pocket. Then, his eyes flicked to the little bowl on top of the file cabinet. The bug disguised as a flash drive, nestled among the other junk in that bowl. Not only did Layne need to retrieve it now to learn if it had recorded anything useful, but sooner or later, Artyom would find it on his own.

33

Serena made sure she'd locked all the doors. She rotated from room to room in the safe house while Pavel paced in the living room, smoking stale cigarettes he'd found in a kitchen drawer. He seemed terrified. She kept telling him to stay away from the windows since he had a habit of not paying attention to where his feet led him.

"There is someone out there, is there not?" he asked. His lips attacked the cigarette like he was trying to suck the life from it.

Peering out the kitchen window, Serena couldn't be sure. Outside this house in the northeast of Phuket Island, Serena saw mostly trees. Telephone poles clogged with dozens of wires. Stray dogs, mangy and thin, wandering along the uneven and pothole-stricken road beyond the trees.

"I don't know that for sure," she said. "I'm only being careful."

"Did you see anyone on the road behind us? Did the Humvee come back around?"

"I don't know. But until we can get a handle on this situation, you need to keep your head down and take deep breaths."

"How long will we wait to decide if we are no longer in danger?"

She left her perch by the window and joined Pavel in the living room. "That depends on you."

"What do you mean?"

"I can get us out of the country tomorrow, Pavel, as soon as I've had time to make a few changes to your passport. But I need answers before we leave. I didn't *free* you from the dark site. I released you into my custody."

He didn't seem to like her tone, but Serena didn't care about that. Until she could fill in some of these blanks, she had no intention of trusting him.

"What sort of answers?" he asked.

"Why don't you start from the top?"

He frowned and snuffed out a cigarette in the soil of a potted plant, then he slumped onto the couch opposite her. "You would like to hear my entire life story?"

She shrugged and held her tongue, leaving it open to interpretation.

"Fine," he said as he lit up a new cigarette. "I left Belarus twelve years ago. My wife and son stayed behind. Unlike Artyom, who brought his family to America, I was not able to. We did not have the money. I had always intended to send for my family, as soon as I could make enough."

"You and Artyom moved here together?"

He shook his head. "No, we did not know each other in Belarus. When I met him in Colorado, everything changed, and the future filled with so much hope. He wanted me to advocate for cheaper medications. Traveling to conferences and meeting with pharmaceutical companies was his idea. He promised me I would be able to give my family a good life in America as long as I stayed loyal to him."

"Sounds like a good deal."

Pavel dragged on his cigarette, trailing a mist of gray into the air. "For a long time, it was. But, I know now he used their absence and the promise of sending for them as a tool to control me." Pavel paused, staring at the lazy curl of the cigarette smoke. "He paid for me to travel and I could send money back to my wife. After Vienna, I intended to return to Minsk to collect my family. But then, they were arrested, and…"

His words faded as his eyes filled with tears.

Serena waited a few moments for him to continue. Teeth gritted, she could see the pain written on his pallid face. If this was a cover story, it was one of the best performances Serena had ever seen.

He cleared his throat. "And they died while in custody. Since I was arrested the next day at the airport, I was not even able to collect their bodies. They are in what you call paupers' graves in Minsk. At least, that is what the American authorities told me. How could I know if this is the truth?"

"Do you believe it's true, though?"

"I do."

"And all this… their deaths, your arrest for the supposed murder of an American diplomat in Uganda… you think Artyom has done all this?"

He nodded.

"Why?"

Pavel puffed the cigarette, his hand shaking. "I do not know what I can tell you. I do not know. I am not... I do not know how much I can say that I have not already said."

Serena checked the magazine in her pistol and ensured the safety was on. Something about the anguish of his look had seeped into Serena's bones. She couldn't say why, but she believed him. Whatever reason Artyom had to break Pavel free of captivity, it wasn't so they could rejoin forces. Pavel genuinely seemed afraid of this man. And, he didn't know why his friend and boss had betrayed him.

"If you don't have anything more to say, then I guess we wait."

His eyes trailed along the ceiling for a moment, and then he said, "I will make you a deal."

34

Layne skulked through the cafeteria, his movements slow and measured. There didn't appear to be any security in the building tonight, but he wouldn't allow himself to become complacent.

He had to retrieve the bug. Now. While Artyom was deciding if he would keep Layne inside his trusted circle or not, Layne might not be welcomed back tomorrow. Artyom was too hard to predict. He might never allow Layne inside Winged House again.

Layne had even skipped an opportunity to visit ex-wife Inessa's house so he could tuck his daughter into bed. Inessa rarely offered during her custody week, so Layne tried to take advantage when possible. Tonight, though, he had to work.

He moved from the cafeteria to the kitchen in the back and then paused inside the large room. Late night auxiliary lights bounced off stainless steel surfaces.

But there was no motion. No sound. Last time he tried

Omega Trap

this, Raisa and Artyom had appeared out of nowhere, so he wanted to be sure.

He continued to the back hallway and then into Artyom's office. Layne stayed completely silent as he entered. Better to be sure Artyom had no surveillance of his own in his office.

But, if Layne could glean anything useful from his bug's data, maybe everything else would no longer matter. He could finally uncover Omega's purpose and learn why Artyom was working so hard to have Pavel Rusiecki released from a dark site in Thailand.

And maybe learn who or what Omega's *primary target* was.

Layne picked up the device from the bowl on top of the file cabinet. Still there. It would not power on when he pressed the hidden power button, though. As he'd suspected, it had died, but the question was: how long ago? How much had it recorded?

He wouldn't know the answer to those questions until he could smuggle it home and extract the SD card. Layne snatched the bug and shoved it in his pocket, then paused. His instinct was to flee as quickly as possible, but perhaps leaving now was a waste. Maybe he should take advantage of this opportunity.

Alone in Artyom's office, probably for the last time. Previously, he'd rushed in here, dropped off the bug, and rushed out.

Layne looked around and considered his next move. He hadn't brought gloves with him because he didn't figure it would matter. As far as he knew, his fingerprints had been cleaned from any and all government databases, and if they raided Winged House or if the local cops poked around, they wouldn't find traces of him. His real name and Social Security Number were nowhere inside this building's paper or online records.

So, he started with the file cabinet. None of the drawers were locked, which told him he probably wouldn't find much of interest there. And he didn't. Folder after folder of client records, such as treatment plans, behavioral reports, and other documents related to the running of Winged House.

Next, Layne moved to the desk. He checked his watch. Had to hurry.

The two side drawers of the desk were unlocked and contained a few business books on managing companies and people, along with standard office supplies.

The top drawer was locked. Layne snatched a golden letter opener from a desk organizer, and then he slid it into the space between the desk and the drawer.

"Okay, Parrish," he mouthed to himself. "Nice and easy. Leave no marks."

He wiggled it back and forth, wedging it a little further into the space with each thrust. Once it was a full inch in, he slid it over and went to work on the lock. With a couple of sharp motions, the lock clicked. Layne pulled out the letter opener and checked for marks on the wood. None there that he could see.

Sometimes, Layne worried that being retired from the spy game had blunted his skills. Other times, though, those worries were unfounded.

The top desk drawer didn't yield any great results. Pens, pencils, paperclips, Post-It Note pads. All the usual stuff. There was, however, one thing that stood out: a memo pad with a handwritten message on top. Listed there was today's date, along with a single line of text:

Tonight: call from Zabojca. Will call cell, not office.

Interesting. If Layne remembered correctly, *Zabojca* was a Belarusian word for *assassin*. He checked a translation website on his phone to confirm. So who was this assassin and did he fit into Omega somehow?

Layne put the memo note back and shut the drawer. No sense in spending more time for a deeper dive. With a sigh, he strode out of the office and into the hallway. Better to leave the interior before the security guards could complete another pass of the parking lot and notice his car parked in the field beyond.

He crept through the hall, back toward the kitchen. Keeping his footfalls light, his ears attuned to any foreign sounds.

But, he wasn't prepared for what happened next.

When Layne opened the hallway door, the sight of the security guard caught him totally by surprise. North of six feet, lanky, and standing directly in front of the hallway door. The guard looked equally surprised. In the dark, Layne could barely read the man's face.

The guard's hand shot toward a walkie-talkie clipped to his belt. Layne popped him in the mouth with a quick jab, and then he freed the walkie from the guy's belt and flung it across the room. Bits of plastic exploded in all directions as it cracked on the tile floor.

The guard launched a punch at Layne's head, and Layne tried to tilt his head back, out of the way. He caught a piece of the punch, but only a knuckle or two.

Layne readied himself to punch again, but the guard froze. His eyes popped open wide. A strange sound came from his lips like his throat had closed and he couldn't force it open to catch a breath.

The guard gasped, and a spot of blood appeared on the front of his shirt. Then, the spot spread into a circle.

Labored grunts filled the air. A higher-pitched sound, from a woman.

The guard fell to his knees, which revealed Jenna standing behind him, the cute kitchen worker. A bloody switchblade knife gripped in her palm. Chest heaving, eyes dim but burning with intensity.

And then Layne noticed the needle sticking out of her arm, just above the crook of her elbow. A line of blood dribbling away from it. A length of hose had cinched off her upper arm.

She noticed Layne noticing and withdrew the syringe. Layne thought he could see a small amount of brown liquid in the chamber. Not insulin, for sure.

In all the times he'd seen her, she'd always been in long sleeves.

Everything snapped into place.

As the guard died on the ground between them, gasping his last breaths, Jenna took a step back. The syringe fell from her hands and clattered on the floor.

"Sorry," she said, her words slurred and gravelly.

Layne didn't even know which insane detail to address first. "What are you doing here?"

"I come in at night to... do food prep sometimes. I was over there," she pointed at a table up against a nearby wall. "You didn't even... see me when you came in."

"Because you were in the corner, shooting up? This is how you come to work?"

Glassy-eyed, Jenna stared at him. "There's nobody here. I work better without distractions." Her lids almost closed and her head bobbed as if she were about to fall asleep standing up. "Why haven't you called me?"

Layne pointed at the dead body on the floor between them. "Jenna, why did you do this?"

"Did I do that?" she said, her shoulders slumping as her chin dipped. She lifted a bloody hand in front of her face, her head cocked as if confused how she had arrived here. "I thought he was going to hurt you. I wanted to stop him from hurting you."

She swayed and then shuffled a step to the side to steady herself against the dish pit. A bloody handprint on the stainless steel exterior as she gawked at the corpse between them. "Is he going to be okay?"

35

Artyom's phone vibrated on the nightstand. First, he glanced at his wife to make sure she hadn't awoken, then he snatched the buzzing hunk of plastic and glass and pressed the screen to his chest to snuff out the light. He whipped back the covers and slipped out of bed, then he hurried across the room.

"Hello?" he whispered as soon as he'd shut the door behind him.

"It's Zabojca."

"Of course it is you. No one in my time zone would be brazen enough to call me at this hour." He looked at a wall clock in the living room. "You're three hours late."

"My apologies. We need to talk."

"Hold on, my son is sleeping across the hall." Artyom stashed the phone as he crossed the room, and then he slipped out the front door.

On the porch, he lit a cigarette from the emergency pack hidden behind a loose brick. He breathed deeply of the smoke and let it roll out of his mouth and drift up in front of his face. Then, he shuddered, because he was in boxers and a t-shirt and the outside air gripped him like an ice bath. Colorado springtime offered hot days and cold nights, just like the desert.

"Speak."

"The American woman succeeded inside the secret prison in the jungle."

"She succeeded, but you did not?"

"Her guide lied to me. He sent me in the wrong direction. I was quite surprised by his deceit since I cut out one of his eyes. I've never seen someone lie after such a test."

Artyom dragged on his cigarette. "That's an impressive display of loyalty."

"Maybe he felt bad for fleeing and leaving her to die at the hands of a local Thai gang and their assault rifles."

"How many?"

"Three of them, in Jeeps."

Artyom tilted his head, impressed. "The woman killed three of them? Or did she escape?"

"No, she went after them like a surgical strike."

"I see. No wonder the guide remained loyal to her. I wouldn't want to cross a woman so capable."

"When I find him after this," Zabojca said, seething, "I'm going to make him suffer like nothing he's ever experienced."

"Ignore the guide. Don't let your anger at yourself for failing distract you from the mission."

"I have not failed," Zabojca said, bristling at the question.

Artyom grinned. "Then Pavel is dead?"

"No."

"Why is he not dead?"

"I've only recently caught up to them. I've now found the safe house."

"Have you invaded it yet?"

"No, not yet."

"Why have you not invaded it yet?"

Zabojca hesitated, a wispy bit of air escaping his lips. At least, that's what it sounded like to Artyom. Half a world away, he couldn't be sure it wasn't normal static.

"I understand why he has to die," Zabojca said, "for Belarus."

"Yes?"

"But, are you sure this is the right time?"

Artyom took a long drag on the cigarette and then smashed it on the concrete step next to him. His face darkened. "What are you saying?"

"I don't know. Also, I've explained how the woman is skilled. Waiting until they try to leave would seem the smartest move. I don't want to be rash or hasty."

Now, a smile cracked Artyom's lips. He wasn't happy, of course, but he didn't want Zabojca to hear the suspicion in his voice. He didn't want Zabojca to know of his doubts. That Artyom believed Zabojca wasn't telling him the whole truth.

Why was Zabojca keeping secrets? He didn't know. But now was not the time to explore. First, Pavel. Then, he would verify Zabojca's loyalty.

So, with a smile, Artyom said, "do not worry about being rash or hasty. You kill Pavel, and you kill the capable American who is hiding him, and then we will deal with everything after that."

"What is after? The senator?"

"Perhaps. He doesn't *need* to die, but I want him to die

in Omega, anyway. He deserves to die for everything he's done to stand in our way."

"What about your scapegoat?" Zabojca said.

"That has not gone according to plan. But, I'm not worried. He knows little, and I plan to deal with him soon enough. We will focus on what's in front of us. Understood?"

"Understood."

"I know of your sacrifices," Artyom said. "I know how hard you have worked to make our dream come true. We've all worked hard for this. We've all made sacrifices. Pavel doesn't yet understand the sacrifice he has to make for Belarus, so we must help him get there."

"Not long now."

Artyom stared at the smashed cigarette and drew a lungful of chilly air. "No, not long now."

"Goodbye, Artyom."

The call ended, and Artyom pulled the phone away from his ear. He let the cold night air tickle his flesh for a few more seconds.

So much had gone wrong already.

Rez was probably dead. Layne had most likely killed him, for any number of reasons. And that meant Layne had morphed from scapegoat to liability and needed to be dealt with. But how could Artyom control him now, with Omega impending? He didn't trust anyone else to handle Layne.

So many tasks. But, Artyom would make the chaos work for him. He would use it as fuel to destroy everything acting as a blockade to victory.

He stashed the cigarettes behind the loose brick and returned to his family.

INTERLUDE 3

FORT COLLINS, CO | SIXTEEN YEARS AGO

LAYNE MAKES SURE THE SHOOTER HAS NO OTHER WEAPONS on him before he leaves. The way the guy screamed as he clutched his broken arm makes Layne feel like he isn't much of a threat now.

But there is another threat here in the Lory Student Center. Another shooter. And possibly, people in danger.

Layne looks down at the gun in his hand. The early stages of a hyperventilation attack form. People are dying. Guns being shot on his college campus. Only now does he understand how crazy his decision was to run into this building while everyone else headed away from it.

Layne shoves the pistol into the back of his waistband, the same way they do on television. He then turns down the hallway toward the sound of the shots he heard a few seconds ago. There's a second shooter, maybe even more than one.

Now armed, what is Layne going to do? The gunfire sounded like an automatic weapon. Layne has only a pistol. Can he take on multiple armed people?

Hell, can he even take on one? The shooter on the floor with the broken arm now feels like a fluke. Layne surprised him and seized upon that advantage. A lucky break like that will not happen again.

Through the next set of double doors, Layne enters the glass mezzanine level overlooking the main hall. A walkway runs in a square around the length of the area overlooking the food court below. On this level, admin office doors face the center, with a glass railing marking the perimeter edge of the mezzanine.

He sees a large clock hanging on a nearby wall. It's 4:15. Happy hour has begun, and his friends are drinking without him. He doesn't think he will make it to the bar today, after all.

To his right, Layne can hear whimpering, subdued and sparse. After a quick check to ensure no one in the immediate area is pointing a gun at him, he creeps toward the sound. Could be injured. Could be someone who barricaded himself or herself and now can't get out.

Or, it could be a trap.

Layne draws the pistol and keeps it pointed at the ground, with his finger off the trigger. He doesn't know much about guns, but he knows he does not want to accidentally shoot an innocent person by waving the piece around without purpose.

Layne pushes open a door. On the other side of the door is a small office, with a desk and file cabinets and a couple of chairs. His eyes dart around the room, searching for danger.

Huddled between the desk and the chairs are two young white women—a blonde and a brunette—and a young African-American man. All of them younger than Layne; maybe undergrads.

Except for one woman, Layne knows she's actually older than him. The brunette. They met at a party a couple of semesters ago and had a conversation in the kitchen of someone's house. They chatted about hiking and rock climbing. The music was so loud, they had to lean in close to speak to each other. Layne doesn't recall her name, but her hair smelled like vanilla that night. Probably her shampoo. Liking the smell of her shampoo made him feel guilty; he wasn't supposed to be capable of feeling attracted to someone so soon after his girlfriend's death.

This girl looks at him, and there's a half-glint of recognition on her face. But, that recognition pales in comparison to the terror dominating her overall expression.

The young man places his hands in front of the two women. "Please," he says. "Please don't hurt us."

Layne looks down at the pistol and then back at these three. He ponders for a second whether this could be a trap and decides it's not. He stows the pistol and holds his hand out. "It's time to get out of here. I can help you, but we have to go now."

The young lady Layne does not recognize, the blonde with round eyeglasses, shakes her head. "One of them is in the stairwell." Her voice trembles, her words cut with hiccups of panic. "We can't get back down to the first floor to leave."

Layne thinks about this for a moment, then the idea appears. "I know a way you can escape." He jiggles his hand, beckoning them to leave their hiding spot. "Please, come with me. I know how to get you out of here."

Omega Trap

All three of the students stare at each other for a few seconds, frozen. Then, the brunette girl stands and smooths her hands down her shirt and jeans. Her chest hitches and she has to take a shuddering breath to speak. "Okay," she says. "Where do we go?"

Layne turns and draws the pistol again, pointing it at the ceiling. "Follow me. Keep your eyes forward and don't stop. If there are shots, fall to the floor and put your hands over your heads." The words coming out of Layne's mouth feel foreign. He's not even thinking about it, just barking orders, saying whatever comes out.

He tilts his head back to meet their eyes. "Got it?"

All three of them nod.

Layne waves his pistol forward and opens the door. As he guides them out, shots from somewhere not too close ring out. Maybe the first floor. Or, maybe in the stairwell. Too hard to tell.

Three quick blasts of a gun follow, then the sound of a woman screaming and then crashing. Glass breaking.

Layne sets a course to a window near the front of the building at the edge of this mezzanine. As he approaches it, he can see there's no way to open the window. Sealed shut. This is a problem.

"Give me some room," he says, and then raises the pistol. The students gasp and take a few steps back.

Layne knows doing this will bring the shooter or shooters running. But he doesn't think he has a choice. Layne pulls the trigger a couple times, feeling the weapon roar in his hand like a barking pit bull. The glass shatters, and he whips his arm in front of his eyes to shield himself. The crackle of glass as it disintegrates slashes against his eardrums.

He leans forward, through the hole in the glass and sees what he expected to see below. An awning directly outside the window, leading down over the front entrance to the student center. Making the drop at the end only eight feet or so.

He faces the students and says, "Let's go. One by one, down the awning, to the ground. And then don't look back. You hit the grass and keep running."

The blonde woman goes first, and then the brunette pauses. "You look familiar," she says, squinting at him.

Layne shakes his head. "Sorry, I don't think we've met. Time to go." He gives her a little push to hurry her out the window.

Finally, the young man. Before he takes a leap down the awning, he grips Layne by the wrist. "You're coming right after us, aren't you?"

Layne nods. "I'll be right on your tail."

The young undergrad jumps down the awning and then plummets to the ground outside, landing in a patch of soft grass. As ordered, he and the two women break into an awkward sprint away from the building.

Layne holsters his pistol and turns away from the window. He can't go now. Not when there's still an active shooter inside.

He takes three steps along the glass railing around the atrium until a door ahead of him smacks open.

Out marches the second shooter, with an automatic weapon clutched in his hands. A kid no older than Layne. Maybe even an undergrad. Blond hair and blue eyes. All-American, but with black anti-glare streaks underneath his eyes, like a football player.

The kid blares a delirious smile as he lowers his rifle, the barrel pointed directly at Layne.

36

Once Layne had returned to his apartment in Boulder, he could withdraw the data card from the bug to transfer the audio recordings to his laptop. While the data moved from one place to the other, he poured himself a peanut butter and banana smoothie from the jug in the fridge. He contemplated taking one of the Fat Tire beers from the six-pack but opted against it. He rarely drank when in the middle of an operation. As a younger man, sure, but on the wrong side of forty, he would feel even one beer tomorrow morning.

Layne sipped his smoothie as he watched the file transfer progress bar creep from left to right on his laptop screen. His arms and back ached from transporting the body of the guard Jenna had killed only a couple hours before. Twice this week he'd had a corpse to manage.

The bug's battery had lasted for about twenty-four hours and recorded ninety-four minutes of audio. He plugged in his headphones and settled in for a long surveillance review session.

Approximately forty-five minutes of that recorded audio consisted of Artyom in his office, singing to himself. Mostly Belarusian songs, from the sound of it. Layne's Belarusian was quite rusty, but he could pick out some words here and there, especially since most of it sounded similar enough to Russian. Artyom's voice was terrible. Layne didn't know the songs, but he could tell this vocalist was not quite hitting the right notes.

Another big chunk of audio related to Artyom talking to his son on the phone about soccer strategy. The kid's team was apparently quite good. Artyom came across as emphatic and hard on his son, to the point Layne felt bad for the younger Borovitch. Much of the conversation consisted of Artyom criticizing his kid's decision-making abilities on the field.

But there was one phone call in particular Layne needed to hear. One phone call that changed everything.

"Yes, go ahead," Artyom said. "Yes, this line is secure, Zabojca. It is being bounced through so many stations it might as well be tin cans and string from here across the world." A long pause ensued, in which the other person spoke. The microphone on Layne's bug couldn't pick up that end of the conversation. "Yes, well, as I see it, you are in Thailand, so this is your responsibility."

Layne leaned closer to his laptop's speakers, gripping the edge of his desk. Thailand? This was bad. This meant Artyom probably not only knew about the dark site and its location, but he had someone local tracking it.

By sending Serena, had Layne led Artyom right to the dark site? Artyom must have generally known that it was in Thailand, but not the exact location. They probably had a person or persons nearby, waiting for a lead to open the door for them.

Layne paused the recording and rubbed the bridge of his nose. Tension behind his eyes signaled the onset of a headache. Guilt swelled. If Serena died as a result of this, he didn't know how he would recover.

He took out his phone. Off the top of his head, he wasn't sure what time it was now in Phuket, but he had to try. He dialed through to the service to reach Serena and then waited through several beeps and clicks as the call connected. Her voicemail picked up, which suggested Serena was already at the safe house with Pavel. At least, he had to hope that was true.

"It's me. There's a cat on the trail." Layne ended the call. Maybe it was enough, or maybe it was too late.

Layne clicked to continue listening to the audio file.

"No," Artyom said, "I do believe it is your responsibility. And I don't want to hear anything else from you until the job is done. Damn it, Goran, I'm tired of fighting with you about this. Yes, I used your name. This line is secure, as I said."

Goran.

Layne's eyes shot wide open, and he sat up straight. Had Artyom said the name *Goran*?

But Goran was dead.

Goran was Zabojca. The assassin. The high school shooter's father had faked his own death.

Was he actually alive?

It had to be true. It made sense. Goran Smith, the father of the boy who had shot up the school a little over a week ago, searching for the senator's son. The same man who had allegedly died of a heart attack within a few hours in his home. Layne had seen them wheeling a stretcher out, but he had never seen the actual body.

Goran had most likely known about the school shooting all along. He'd probably orchestrated the attack, along with Artyom.

Goran had always been vague about his heritage. He could have been from Belarus, given the flavor of his accent. Never as thick as Artyom's, but that would depend on how long he'd lived in America.

Layne balled his fist and cursed himself for not seeing the connection sooner.

Pieces of the puzzle were falling into place and also creating new questions. The questions were coming in faster than the answers, though. Artyom and probably Goran had sent Goran's son Noah to kill the senator's son to put pressure on the senator. Goran and Artyom were working together, somehow, for Belarus. But why? To what end?

What was Omega?

And why had Goran faked his own death? What could he do dead that he couldn't do alive? That question troubled Layne most of all.

Maybe Goran had done this to avoid speaking with the police after Noah's death. A mountain of attention would have fallen on him as the father of a school shooter.

A knock came at Layne's door. He checked his watch. It was almost midnight, and he couldn't think of anyone who would appear at his apartment with no advance warning at this time of night. Even the mother of his child knew to call first before showing up.

Layne crossed the room and pulled back the picture of Mount Whitney on a hinge, revealing the wall safe behind it. He pressed his thumb against the biometric scanner, and it unlocked. Layne removed his Colt Peacemaker and shoved it in the back of his waistband.

Then, Layne looked through the door peephole to spy the area in front of his door. Jenna stood there, the junkie cook. She was like a ghost, her thin arms crossed, tears streaming down her face.

Layne put the pistol back and then shut the safe, quickly closing the framed picture after it. He took a quick look around the apartment to ensure he hadn't left anything sensitive in plain sight.

He opened the door, and Jenna fell into his arms. Babbling.

"I don't know what's happening to me," she said. "I keep thinking of the security guard in the kitchen tonight, and it feels like a dream. It's like I can see it, but I don't remember doing it. Like it's happening to someone else, and I'm watching it on TV, but I can't turn it off, and I don't know what to do about any of it."

Layne held her out at arm's length and ducked down until Jenna met his eyes. "Look at me. Jenna, look at me. You have to breathe. Breathe. Working yourself into a panic is not going to help anything."

"I killed a guy. We killed a guy. He's dead, and there's nothing in the world I can do to take that back. I saw you sneaking around, and I knew if he caught you, you would get in trouble. I pulled the knife out of my pocket, and then I don't know what happened after that. Why did I kill him? Layne, why did I do it?"

Her chest heaved up and down. Layne realized he was

holding her a little too tightly, so he relented. He wasn't even sure what to say right now, because his brain was still swirling with the revelation about Goran Smith.

"I don't think I can make it," she said. "Maybe we need to talk to the police. I think I need to turn myself in."

"Jenna, do not talk to the police. This is not the time to involve local cops. That will come later. If you do anything right now, the whole situation gets complicated and mishandled, and this investigation slips away from me."

She creased her brow and narrowed her bloodshot eyes up at him. "What investigation? Are you a cop?"

"Please, Jenna, don't do anything rash. I can make this go away. You have to trust me and stay calm now. I need time to make things right."

As her lip trembled and tears made rivers down her cheeks, Layne stared into her eyes, and he doubted if she could keep it together. She didn't have the fortitude and focus.

He didn't have it, either. At least, not right now. While she stood there, only one concern dominated his thoughts: that the cunning and physically imposing man Goran Smith was alive, in Thailand, hunting Serena.

37

Serena stood over Pavel as he slept on the couch, snoring. She'd offered him the bed, and he had declined. Inside that dark site, living in a ten by ten cell, how long since he'd slept on a non-concrete surface?

Maybe busting him out of the secret prison had been a terrible idea. It had felt like the right thing to do at the time. Fortunate that no one had been hurt. A part of her—growing stronger by the hour—believed he had *not* killed the diplomat in Uganda. That this frail and quiet man was not capable of committing the crime.

If Artyom Borovitch was willing to orchestrate a school shooting, he could just as easily also frame Pavel for an international murder.

Or maybe Serena was being duped. She couldn't rid herself of the chronic suspicion living in the back of her mind. Until she knew for sure, she would not let Pavel Rusiecki out of her sight. Maybe the deal they'd made last night had been a mistake. She needed to think that one through.

Serena bent down in front of the couch and put a hand on Pavel's shoulder. She gently shook him awake.

He blinked a few times. "Is it time to go?"

"Yes, to the airport."

"Do we have a flight?"

Serena shook her head. "I don't have Internet access. We'll go to the airport and buy our tickets there."

"Will we be safe at the airport?"

"Probably safer than we are here."

"If you think the presence of law enforcement and airport security makes us safe, then you are mistaken."

She bit her lower lip. "Fair point, but I need you on your feet, now, please. We don't have any time to spare."

Pavel threw back the cover and sat up, rubbing the sleep out of his eyes. He slid on his boots and stood to stretch. Serena wondered about fingerprints in the house, but she had to assume Layne knew of discreet people who could clean the place. Maybe if she could contact him, she could get an answer to that question.

But she was not supposed to contact him.

She would have to tell him about his local contact Niran soon, anyway. He was presumably dead in the jungle. If they were being followed, she had to assume their tail knew about Niran. Since he hadn't been waiting by the car when they left the dark site, he'd been caught somewhere. No doubt about it. And, Niran had probably told their pursuer everything before he'd died. Serena's name, maybe even Layne's name.

She needed to warn Layne. But, her phone still had no service.

"I am glad you did not kill me in my sleep," he said as

he collected his things and placed them in a rolling suitcase they'd found at the safe house. "Thank you for that."

"I have no intention of killing you. It's never been my intention."

"After all the betrayal I have experienced lately, you will understand how I might not trust you."

She nodded. "I do understand. I'm sorry about what's happened to you."

"Thank you for saying so."

Serena snapped her fingers. "We need to hurry, though. I think we might not be alone here."

As soon as the words left her mouth, a window in the kitchen broke. A hole appeared in the couch, six inches Pavel's right. Then, a second later, another. Puffs of synthetic feathers flew into the air from the bullet holes.

Serena grabbed Pavel and yanked him down to the floor, knocking over the coffee table in the process. More bullets broke through the glass on the kitchen window, peppering the couch and the wall above it. Firing in through the window, the shooter would have limited visibility. But, a high-powered rifle probably made up for it.

"I think he's to the west," Serena said. "Out the back." She pointed to the area of the living room she theorized was inside his line of sight. "Whatever you do, don't go over there. When I give you the signal, you stand and run for the door. We need to do this fast before he changes position. Do you have your passport on you already?"

Pavel nodded, his jaw tense.

Then, she realized the car keys were in a bowl by the front door, within the shooter's line of sight.

Serena drew the pistol from her back pocket, counted to three, and then popped up. "Now!" She unloaded the magazine toward the kitchen window. Behind her, Pavel scrambled along the carpet and then broke into a jog past the end of the couch.

She dropped into a crouch as she slammed in a fresh magazine. Staying low, she scurried after Pavel as random shots from the sniper's rifle punched holes in the walls and ceiling.

Serena found Pavel waiting for her by the side door, hands over his head. She grabbed the doorknob. "It's a straight line to the front of the house, and then you turn right and go to the car." She maneuvered her hand through the air to demonstrate his path.

Pavel frowned, eyes wide. "You are not coming with me?"

"I have to get the car keys," Serena said. "When you open this door, it'll distract him, and he'll probably leave his position to move around to the side. I need those few seconds of distraction to pick up the keys. Understand?"

"Yes."

"I'll be there right after you. Stay low and don't stop moving."

He nodded, so she opened the door and shoved him outside. He wasted no time. Pavel sprinted in the direction he was supposed to, as ordered. He moved with great haste for someone so frail and worn.

Serena jerked around and raced through the house, ducking behind the far side of the couch to minimize her exposure. She didn't know for sure that the sniper had stayed in the same place, but he might have. Or, he might have shifted into a different position to follow the door opening. If he were smart, he would have already picked his *bravo* position, one that gave him a line of sight to the car.

Serena snatched the keys from the bowl on the table and whipped the front door open, keys in one hand. She blinked, trying to adjust to the difference in light from inside to outside. The humidity smacked her in the face and made her breaths feel weighted.

No immediate threat outside.

She rushed onto the front porch, pistol up, headed for the car. Pavel was there, on the passenger side, crouched with one hand on the door pull.

A moment of panic hit her. What if the assassin had booby-trapped the car? They could try to flee on foot, but that put them at a distinct disadvantage.

No, she had to trust the car wasn't a danger. If he'd strapped a bomb underneath it, she would have heard him out there installing it.

Serena thumbed the unlock button on the keychain, and nothing happened right away. No *tick tick boom*.

Pavel scrambled inside the car, pulled it shut, and ducked down. Bullets peppered the ground around Serena's feet. So, the shooter had readjusted his position.

Keys in one hand, pistol in the other. She had to hope she could reach the car and hit the road before he managed to blow out the tires or put a few bullets through the engine.

Serena crossed the twenty feet to the car in six long strides. From inside the car, Pavel was yelling at her, but she couldn't make out the words. One big blur of chaos. And as she reached out to open the car door, his eyes widened, and he pointed over her shoulder. While opening the door, she turned around to see the large figure of the man who had been shooting at them.

A nondescript black baseball cap pulled low shrouded his face. Full combat gear, a rifle in his hands. His tall and muscular frame advanced on them while looking down the long nose of his weapon. She couldn't make out most of his features, but the smile on his face stood out.

Serena slammed the door closed behind her and jammed the key into the ignition. A quick flick started the car. She reached over and forced Pavel's head down with her free hand. Bullets clinked off the exterior. One blew out the back window, the screech and clatter of glass landing everywhere.

"Did you see him?" Pavel said.

"I didn't get a good look."

"Neither did I. But it is clear that Artyom has sent a zabojca for us."

"Zabojca?"

"It means *assassin* or *killer* in English. Artyom's assassin. I should have known he would chase me across the earth."

Serena, holding Pavel's head down and herself hunched over, hit the gas with the car in reverse. A blip of thought occurred: the assassin had probably put a GPS tracker on the car. She had to assume he did. It's what she would have done when tracking a target.

That was a problem to deal with in a few minutes, though. First, survival.

The car raced in reverse along the driveway. She knew there were trees and other obstructions behind her, but she couldn't worry about that now. If she raised her head, this assassin would kill her. Or any of these bullets might puncture the car and hit either one of them. So, she didn't look back, and she didn't let up.

The car reversed over plants and mud and bumps, rattling around, the fractured glass on the back seat dancing like rain on a metal roof. Once Serena had backed up what she estimated to be a thousand feet, she whipped up and spun the steering wheel.

She slammed on the brakes, stopping only inches from a tree. Going fully on muscle memory, she slammed it into drive and then gunned the engine. Then, they joined the road headed for the airport.

She assumed he would be there at the airport, waiting, or arriving soon after. And, she had to hope that this assassin wasn't brazen enough to kill them in a public place.

38

THE GLASS WALLS OF THE PHUKET INTERNATIONAL AIRPORT gleamed from the lights within. Airplanes fled the ground and soared, leaving behind an ocean of green trees on the surface.

Serena parked the car at the edge of the lot and settled in with her hands on the steering wheel. A few seconds of quiet to rid her mind of the repetitive thoughts. She had elected not to ditch the car and find another. Whether the assassin on their tail had put a tracker on this one or not, she'd kept the airport locked in as the destination.

Once inside the building, they would reduce their risk. At least, she was choosing to look at it that way. That all depended on whether this assassin would open fire on them inside the terminal, and whether the Thai security forces here would help or hurt in that situation. A lot left up to chance.

"Where is the destination?" Pavel asked from the passenger seat.

"I'm not sure. I was thinking somewhere west. Paris or

Madrid for a couple of days, until we can figure out what to do with you."

He pivoted toward her, intensity in his eyes. "No. Take me to America. We made a deal at the safe house last night, or have you forgotten?"

"After everything Artyom Borovitch has done to find you and kill you, and you want to deliver yourself to him? Do you know how ludicrous that sounds?"

Pavel winced. "I can expose him. I can stop him, but only from America. If we disappear, then I am powerless. If there is a snake in your house, how can you kill it by fleeing down the street?"

"I don't know," she said, chewing on the inside of her cheek. "I'm still not sure if I should even trust you. This is a favor to a friend because he thinks you could be valuable."

"So, I am a bargaining chip?"

"No, not like that. Maybe *valuable* wasn't the right word. I'm not going to let anything bad happen to you, Pavel. We just want to know why this Artyom guy wants you so bad. Apparently, dead or alive."

Pavel darkened as he sat back and drew a finger across the fabric on the ceiling. "Artyom and I were close once, not that long ago. Like brothers. We were set on doing whatever we could to make things better for Belarus. We even decided together to stay in America because we believed we could not do anything from home."

"I get it," Serena said, raising a hand. "You can save the speech this time. I just want to know what you're going to do when we land. *If* I agree to take you to America."

"I will stop him."

She shook her head. "I need a little more than that,

Omega Trap

Pavel. Tell me why, given everything this man is capable of, that delivering you to him is the right idea."

"I am not asking you to deliver me to him. Only to get me to America. There, I can do something about his crimes."

"Do what?"

"I can give you no more detail right now. It is too dangerous. When we are back in America, I will tell you everything."

"You're not worried about being arrested when we land?"

His eyes, unfocused, pointed toward the airport. "No. I do not think anyone will recognize me. I think my arrest and incarceration were secret enough that no one will be alerted."

Serena sighed because she had a feeling she was being played. But, she had to admit she was curious. Beyond curious, actually. Burning to get answers.

If this Pavel character wanted to rush headfirst into the lion's den, it wasn't exactly her place to tell him he couldn't do it. Her job was to contact him and find out why Artyom wanted him. Pavel either didn't know, or he wasn't willing to share.

Maybe he would, in America. Or, maybe men in black suits would haul him away in handcuffs as soon as they landed. Or worse.

She looked around the parking lot, eying the other cars. They still faced a high probability they would both be killed here. She hadn't seen the Zabojca person tailing them, but that didn't mean he wasn't back there, waiting and watching their car's location as a little blinking dot on a tablet or laptop.

She unlocked her phone and tried to call Layne, but it wouldn't go through. Cell service in this country was terrible. One advantage of going back to America would be access to Layne. Pooling their knowledge and resources.

What would Layne think about her choices so far?

Breaking Pavel out of the dark site had been her decision, and now she had to live with it. Pavel's life was in her hands. What good *would* it do to take him somewhere in Europe to hide?

Maybe he was right with his snake analogy.

Time to make a choice.

She sighed. "Okay, Pavel. We'll go to America. But you will stay within arm's length of me at all times and do exactly what I tell you to do. You're still my responsibility, until I decide otherwise, got me?"

"I do get you. Thank you for trusting in me." He paused, his lower lip quivering. "My passport will work?"

"It'll work. They won't know a thing."

He inhaled a shuddering breath and blew it out. Eventually, he nodded.

They left the car, emerging in the sweltering humidity like walking into a swimming pool. Her hip ached. At some point when the bullets had been flying, and she'd been sprinting around the safe house, she'd bumped into something hard. Better a bruise than nursing a bullet wound, though.

Serena adjusted the pistol in her waistband. She'd have to find a place to dispose of it soon, before entering the airport.

Inside the building, they would be both anonymous

and exposed. Unarmed and at the mercy of the local law enforcement to prevent any attacks.

Her head swiveled around, looking for Zabojca. If he was out there, he'd hidden well.

But he probably wouldn't hide for long.

39

Layne tucked in his button-down shirt as he left his car in the parking lot of the Fairmont mausoleum. Usually, he preferred t-shirts and polo shirts, because button-downs didn't fit his top-heavy frame. His lat muscles pulled the shirt too taut across his middle.

But, he was going for a specific look this morning. He considered sliding a pencil behind his ear but thought that might be too much. Simplicity worked out the best. Attitude and confidence sold a cover more than the costume.

He entered the main building of the mausoleum as the sun rose behind him. Properly caffeinated, he blinked away the last remnants of sleep. Last night had been a long night.

Layne crossed the marble floor of the interior and walked right up to a cutout window encased in safety glass. He examined a small hole, wide enough to fit his hands through. It would have to suffice. Why a mausoleum needed such security, Layne couldn't say.

A middle-aged man with a noticeable underbite came to the other side of the glass. He adopted a warm smile. "Can I help you, sir?"

"Yes," Layne said, "my name is Roger Friedland, from Outdoor Magazine. We are doing a story on the recently deceased free climber Terry Owens. If I understand correctly, he's been interred here? I'm not even sure if *interred* is the right word. Can you help me out?"

The man behind the glass cocked his head and creased his brow, appearing deep in thought. "Well, I'm not sure if we have a Terry Owens here. The name doesn't sound familiar, but, then again, my memory isn't what it used to be. Owens, you say?"

Layne nodded. "That's right, man." He hefted the Canon DSLR camera hanging on a strap under his armpit. "Just wanted to get a couple quick shots of his crypt's nameplate for the magazine piece, if that's okay. In and out in two minutes. I have waivers from his family. I can drop the PDFs on a file server for you, or, if we have the same kind of phone, I could share the file over Bluetooth or WiFi. Or, FTP, if you're into that sort of thing. Your call."

The man behind the glass appeared flustered, which had been exactly the goal. He put his hands on his hips and turned all around, lifting various binders strewn about the desks in his little room. "Well, I don't know. I might have to go check the computer, if I can get the damn thing to work, that is."

"That's fine, I can wait."

The flustered man with the underbite left the little area and disappeared into a side room. Layne reached through the slits in the glass and grabbed the biggest binder in view, the one sitting on the desk in front. He turned it around, opened it, and found what he'd been hoping to see. An alphabetical list of all the crypts in the various buildings of the mausoleum.

Layne thumbed open the S section, found the Smiths, and worked his way down to G for Goran. Goran Smith was a resident of 2B3H1R. The second building, third hall, first room. Layne slid the binder back into place and then scooted away from the desk. No point in keeping up the magazine photographer ruse any longer.

Outside, Layne found building 2 next door to the main administrative building. And, as he walked toward it, he again felt that distinct sensation he'd experienced dozens of times in his career as a spy and an assassin for a government agency with no name. The feeling of eyes upon him. The feeling of someone skulking in the shadows, tailing him.

Layne pretended not to notice, for now. If the eyes belonged to a sniper, he would have been shot dead already.

His phone rang, and he slipped it out of his pocket. "Hello?"

"Mr. Parrish?"

Layne recognized the voice on the other end of the line, one of Cameron's caregivers at the daycare. A pulse of anxiety hit him as it always did when they called. "Yes?"

"This is Sheila? From Children's Academy?" She raised her voice at the end of each pause as if it were a question.

"Is everything okay with Cam?"

"Oh, of course, Cameron is fine. We tried to call her mother first, but couldn't reach her."

"Inessa is at a photo shoot in Colorado Springs."

"A *what*, now?"

"She's working today. What can I do for you?"

"Cameron was playing with some of her friends after breakfast, and she bit another child. I don't know if you're on pickup today or her mother, but there's an incident report. Just thought you should know before you see it."

He sighed. They called over every little thing. "Okay, no problem. Her mother will pick her up later today, but thanks for letting me know." He ended the call after saying goodbye and slid the phone back into his pocket.

Whenever something like this happened—which was often—he wondered if his lifestyle had influenced her. Cameron hadn't seen any violence committed by her father in her short life. At least, as far as Layne knew. It's not as if the tendency to violence was genetic.

Someday, Cameron would learn about him. She wouldn't know about his time working for Daphne's team, but she might learn other things. Maybe she would hear of the shooting on campus at Colorado State sixteen years ago. How Layne had run into the building that day and faced multiple shooters, head on.

But, today was not the day for Cameron's education. So, he had to brush off this little incident. Kids figuring out how to play would bite each other from time to time until they learned better. Adults sometimes bit each other, too, and they definitely knew better.

He entered the building and looked around for the numbered halls. Not a single other person here today. He walked toward hall number three and was passing under the threshold when his phone rang. He didn't recognize the number on the caller ID, but he answered it anyway. Probably the daycare again. "Hello?"

"Hey, it's me," said the shaky voice of young Jenna. Panic in her haggard breaths. Less than twelve hours ago she had stabbed someone to death in front of Layne.

She tried to speak, but only a bubble of hiccuping tears came out. It didn't sound as if she were doing any better with the situation than she had been when she'd made a sudden and uninvited appearance at Layne's apartment in Boulder, late last night.

"Hey," Layne said. "We shouldn't be talking on the phone."

"I know, I know. I just… I'm having a hard time. Can't focus. I don't know what to do next. Can I see you?"

Layne entered the hall and then found room number 1 on his left. With the phone up to his ear, he eased inside. Wall crypts lined the room, with little nameplates in front of each one.

He sighed into the phone. "Jenna, we can't talk about this now. I'm going to help you, but I can't right at this moment. I need you to sit tight and find a way to stay calm."

"That's the thing. I don't know how to do that."

His heartstrings stretched tight at the sound of the agony in her voice. The first time he killed someone, he felt the same sort of inner turmoil. And his first kill had been in Seattle, on an assignment. He'd shot a terrorist, a person who'd deserved it. Still, Layne had seen that man's face for months after in his nightmares.

He could empathize with what Jenna was going through right now. Thinking about the security guard she'd killed. Wondering if he had a family, and torturing herself with the possibility. Picturing them in a state of dread, not knowing his fate.

Layne studied the different crypts, up and down the rows. His breath hitched when he found the one he'd been looking for.

Smith, Goran.

"Take a few breaths," he said into the phone. "Focus on something simple to keep your mind clear, like exercise. See if the motel has a gym."

Layne opened the crypt, sliding it out toward him. A body underneath a sheet. He lifted the sheet, staring at the face of a dead man who looked like Goran Smith but was certainly not him.

40

Serena and Pavel swept through the customs lines and then security lines. She felt naked with no weapons. This was, of course, how she had come into the country, but she didn't then know for sure that someone would try to kill her.

Past security, she guided Pavel toward their gate. Rolling bags squeaking along the floor, overhead loudspeaker barking in multiple languages. Certain someone was looking for them.

Her heart thumped. She had to assume, given the secrecy of Pavel's imprisonment, that the authorities wouldn't arrest them both in public. But, she couldn't be sure.

Once they were at gate B6, it wouldn't matter any longer.

To his credit, the weakened and quiet Pavel kept up and caused no trouble. He didn't ask any questions and did as he was told to do. When she bought him food at the airport, he gulped it down.

"What do you like to do in America?" he said between bites.

"Not much. I have a cat at my apartment, so we usually spend lots of quality time together."

"Do you like football?"

She nodded. "Cowboys fan."

"I love American football," he said, with a twinkle in his eye. "The pageantry of it all. Each team with such hopes and dreams every year, but only one can win it all. I love the suspense of waiting to find out." Then, his face darkened. "Unfortunately, I was not able to watch any football this past season. I can't even say who won the Superbowl."

She didn't know how long Pavel had spent as a prisoner in the dark site north of Patong Bay, but he had clearly missed out on a lot of things in that time, not just football. Could he even have grieved for his wife and son while locked away in a dungeon for months?

Serena was about to recap the last Superbowl for Pavel when something in the air changed. The paranoia she'd been feeling coagulated into something solid.

She saw *him*.

The assassin Zabojca wandered around the other side of the large and open terminal, his eyes tracking all around. He had ditched the baseball cap. Although she hadn't seen his face earlier today, she was certain it was the same guy.

Serena grabbed Pavel by the arm. "Your bag. Keep it close. We need to get to our gate, now."

"What is it? Do you see him? Has he seen us?"

Serena couldn't tell if Zabojca had seen them or not, but the assassin started to walk in their direction. A determined look in his eyes as he dipped his head, narrowing the space between them.

Something changed in Pavel's face as he laid eyes on Zabojca. His mouth dropped open. "Goran," he said, musing in an astounded tone. "*Goran* is Artyom's zabojca?"

So, they knew each other, and the assassin was someone named Goran. Useful info for later, maybe, but it didn't matter at the moment.

The man skulking toward them grinned, his eyes locked onto Pavel. "We'll deal with that later," she said, tugging him and his single rolling bag away from the food court.

She had to find a safer place. There was a door to her right, and she snatched Pavel by the shirt collar as she pulled him through it.

They found themselves in a hallway, and Serena tracked it to the end. Practically sprinting, their footfalls echoing in all directions off the shiny floor. Through the next set of doors, they entered an area for luggage processing. Huge conveyor belts moving along the ground, elevating thirty or forty feet into the air. Luggage chugging along on these belts.

"Stay close to me," she said. He motioned for her to lead the way. A few Thai luggage handlers gave them quizzical looks as she and Pavel passed through the various conveyor belt areas, but none of them triggered any alarms or called out.

At the end of the room, Serena peered through a window out onto the runways, where a plane was gassing up. Men with brightly colored vests pulled suitcases from a baggage dolly and loaded them onto the plane.

"That one's ours," she said, pointing at it. "If we can double back and get to our gate, I think we'll be safe. He has to be smart enough to know he can't start firing inside a crowded airport."

But, when she and Pavel looked at each other, she could read the doubt in his eyes.

GORAN SMITH, known on this operation as Zabojca, moved through the airport with his head down and his ears open. In the lot, he'd spotted the car the woman had been driving, but she and Pavel were nowhere to be found.

He wondered what Artyom would think when he discovered Goran had no intention of delivering Pavel to him. That he had betrayed Artyom. He would know why, of course, but would he see it coming? Had Artyom any inkling that Goran would keep Pavel all to himself?

It didn't matter now.

Goran hustled through the airport, and he thought he saw the Latina woman's long brown hair out of the corner of his eye, sitting at the food court. He turned in that direction and met Pavel's line of sight. The shock on Pavel's face cut into Goran, but only for a moment. He and Pavel had never been close friends. They had known each other, both as associates of Artyom, sure. But they weren't anything more than work associates. Pavel traveled too often for he and Goran to develop a friendship. Whenever they were together, Pavel seemed more interested in spending time with his son, Noah, anyway.

Goran gritted his teeth, thinking about his dead child.

He had to put that out of his mind for the time being. The pain was too big. Too distracting.

Too much to do before he could deal with that.

They fled the food court and then disappeared through a door. He followed. When he reached the door and passed through it into a hallway, he found himself alone. The hallway fed into a luggage processing room, and they were nowhere to be seen inside it. Goran reversed course, thinking they might have returned to the front of the airport to lose him.

If they were able to board the plane, no telling where they would go. The smart move would be a trip to Australia or New Zealand or Iceland. But, maybe Pavel would be bold enough to attempt a return to America to take on Artyom. Seemed like just the sort of foolhardy thing Pavel might insist upon.

They weren't at the front of the airport. So, Goran worked his way back through to the main area, where he caught the backs of two familiar heads approaching a gate. A small and weak Belarusian man and the taller, brown-skinned American woman.

He compared their gate number against the departure board, and a smile lit his face. They were going to America. Unbelievable.

Collecting Pavel would be simple and easy in the US. Omega could change from its current purpose to become a trap laid specifically for this brash traveler.

Plus, Artyom would greatly value this information. But, would Goran tell him? He'd have to consider the angles, to see if there was some way to twist the info to his own purpose.

But, Goran believed it would be better to collect Pavel

here and now. Any number of bad things could happen if he disappeared from sight.

Since Goran didn't have a boarding pass, he couldn't proceed. But he did have one last play. If he could make it outside before they shut the doors, maybe he could find a way onto that plane. Or, maybe such a bold move would backfire.

But, letting Pavel flee was not an option.

So, Goran sprinted through the airport, even though the police and airport security gave him funny looks. He'd sneaked a pistol past security by taping it to the inside of his pant leg. Probably best if he did not let them find it in a manual search.

Out the front door, he ducked right and made his way back around to the runways. A nearby jet taking off forced him to come to a halt as the power of the blasting air and the noise made him wince. But as soon as it passed, he sprinted forward again, trying to calculate based on the number of planes and jetways the location of that particular gate.

During all this hustling, he considered his plan. What would he do? Shoot up the plane? That might not be the most effective way to retrieve Pavel.

After rounding the next plane, he saw the one he'd been trying to reach. Just as the airplane door swung shut, and the jetway rolled back, Goran Smith came to a stop in the runway.

As a police car with flashing lights and blaring sirens drove onto the runway, headed straight for Goran, he looked up to a window seat on the plane and saw the Latina woman staring right at him.

41

Layne stepped away from the crypt in the mausoleum, with the phone up to his ear. On the other end of the line, Jenna cried, sniffling softly. Trying to talk to her and process this information about the crypt had muddied his brain.

"Hang on a second, Jenna," he said, and she mumbled something in reply.

Goran Smith was not inside the crypt. Confirmation of the things Layne had overheard on the surveillance recording. That meant he was still alive and had been involved in everything from the start. Allowing his son to die at the school, pressuring the senator to release Pavel Rusiecki... all of it.

They'd never been close friends, but Layne should have seen something. He should have known his acquaintance was capable of such venom and malice. Yet another reason why Layne had been correct to retire from the spy game full time. Ten years ago, he would have detected hints of Goran's double life immediately and put the FBI or NSA onto him without thinking twice about it.

Where was this assassin now?

Assuming everything Layne had heard on Artyom's office recording was true, then Goran was in Thailand, or somewhere else in search of Pavel. Maybe Goran had found Serena. Shit, maybe she had unwittingly led him straight to their target at the dark site. If that were true, then it meant Goran was probably on his way back to the US. Or, if he'd already killed both of them, then he was long gone by this point.

Layne left the room and ventured outside the building at the Fairmont Mausoleum and again felt those eyes on him. Just as before. Someone knew he was here and had sent watchers.

"Jenna," he said into the phone, "I need to go. I have to deal with something."

"What do I do?" she said, sniffling.

"Stay at the motel. Keep your head down and don't talk to anyone."

"Okay, I can do that. How long?"

"I need a day or two. Just stay put, and I promise I will come for you and we'll figure it out together. Don't go anywhere, okay? Can you do that?"

"I can do that."

When she ended the call, Layne stared at his phone. For him, killing had become so automatic over the last fifteen or sixteen years, he barely thought about it any longer. As long as he knew the people he killed were not innocent, he didn't lose any sleep over it.

For someone like Jenna, stabbing a person to death

would rock her world. She probably wasn't sleeping, even with the heroin she was using to numb herself.

Layne remembered those times. He remembered the sleepless nights after the incident at the Lory Student Center in college. He remembered seeing the faces of those school shooters, the faces of the dead students in the hallways. Those three terrified students he helped to escape out the window, down the awning. What if he'd turned to the left in the mezzanine, instead of right? Would those three have been killed due to his inaction?

He caught a flash of clothing out of the corner of his eye. Then, it disappeared.

"Got you," he whispered, smirking.

Layne navigated west from the building and circled around it, with a good idea of the current position of the person conducting this sloppy surveillance.

He took a left turn into a botanical garden area cordoned off from the main walk. Two lines of trees that bent to form something like a tunnel signaled the entrance. As soon as he'd entered the tunnel and ventured deep enough inside to conceal his presence, he exited the other side between a tiny break in the trees, like a secret side exit. He paused there for a moment, waiting to see if his tail would take the bait.

Then, he sprinted to the far end of the tunnel and came to a halt just before rounding the edge. He peered out into the botanical garden to see one young woman in dark jeans and a dark jacket. No gun, at least, not one showing. Plus, she was African-American, which suggested she was not a part of the Winged House crew. Layne had never seen a single non-white person within those walls.

He leaped out and grabbed the edge of her jacket. Before she could resist, he raised it up and checked around her waist for a weapon. She had none. Not an assassin.

"What the hell?" she said, whipping around and pulling free of his grasp.

"You were following me. Why?"

The woman sighed and reached into her pocket. Layne tensed, balling his fists and widening his stance.

"Relax, Boy Scout."

Layne raised an eyebrow at the mention of his old operational nickname. There were only a few people in the world who knew it. "Control sent you?"

The woman nodded as she drew a phone from her pocket and tapped on the screen a few times. She held it out to Layne, showing a phone call in progress.

Layne put the phone against his ear as it rang. The young woman eyed him, a self-satisfied look on her face. A moment later, the call picked up.

"Daphne?" he said.

"Do you have any idea how furious I am at you right now?"

He could hazard a guess based on the current level of grit in Daphne's normally smoky tone. But, he said nothing and waited for her to continue.

"I wanted to send my best operative on an assignment, and guess what? I learned she's out of the country, in Thailand. Do you know anything about this?"

He licked his lips. "You know I do. I asked her to go to Thailand and find the dark site as part of my school shooting investigation. There was a contact in Phuket I arranged for her to meet with."

"I can't believe you. After I asked you to leave it alone, you go and manipulate one of my—"

"I didn't manipulate anyone. I asked Serena for a favor, and she said yes."

"Of course she said yes," Daphne said, her volume rising. "She's got a crush on you! She would do anything you asked her."

Layne opened his mouth to protest, but then stopped himself. Did Serena have a crush on him? Is that why she'd agreed to take on this dangerous mission with hardly any complaint?

He supposed he had to admit it. She was thirteen or fourteen years younger than him, though. Like a little sister in his eyes. He'd never actually thought about pursuing a relationship with her, especially since they'd worked together a few times already. Mixing operations and romance was always a bad idea. He'd learned that one the hard way by dating Daphne off and on for a few years when he'd first joined her team.

"Maybe she has a crush on me, but that doesn't change the fact that I *did not* manipulate her. I didn't put any pressure on her, and I warned her this could be dangerous."

"Who are you trying to convince?" Daphne said. "Me, or you?"

Layne gritted his teeth and said nothing. He took a few breaths to stop himself from lashing out.

"She looks like her," Daphne said. "Don't you think?"

He didn't have to ask for clarification. He knew exactly what Daphne was trying to say. Serena looked like his ex-girlfriend, the one who had taken her own life a couple years before the school shooting in Fort Collins.

"I'm trying to right a wrong here," he said, ignoring the lookalike issue. "I need to to know why Artyom Borovitch wants this Pavel person so badly, and what it has to do with something he's planning named Omega. It's all connected to the school shooting in Broomfield, but there's more to it. I overheard Artyom talking about a *primary target*. It's something else, and maybe Pavel can shed some light."

"Well, you're going to get your wish. Pavel and Serena are headed back to America. They're flying somewhere over the Pacific right now, and then I guess you can ask her yourself soon enough."

42

For a whole day, Layne kept a low profile, waiting for Serena to return. But, he was not dormant. Aside from beginning yet another read-through of George R.R. Martin's *A Storm of Swords*, he made progress on cleaning up the messes of the last few days.

Layne collected the bodies of Rez and the security guard, then cremated them to seal off the possibility of the police finding evidence later. Body disposal work always turned Layne's stomach, but sometimes, it was part of the job. A shitty part, but a part nonetheless.

With a bit of research, he was able to learn that the security guard had no family. Not only that, but he'd had a rap sheet longer than a jumbo-sized family's grocery list. That fact should ease Jenna's mind to some degree.

By now, news coverage of the school shooting in Colorado had dimmed to almost nothing. A brutal shooting in Vermont had captured the nation's attention. Also, detail about the senator's son being the target still had not been released to the media. Curious.

Omega Trap

Layne checked in on Artyom whenever possible, via a network of contacts in the Golden area. During their last conversation, Artyom had effectively banished Layne, unsure what to do with him after the suspicious circumstances around Rez's death. As far as Layne knew, Artyom had decided Layne was to be pushed out of the circle of trust. There had been no contact. That was fine with Layne. While investigating without inner circle access was harder, it was not impossible. Just one new complication to consider.

But, Layne still needed details about Omega. Still needed answers. He had no reason to believe he would be killed or turned away as soon as he set foot within Winged House, so he plotted his return.

In the afternoon, his ex-wife Inessa had to suddenly leave town for the day, so he took Cameron back to his apartment for a daddy-daughter extended play date. They finger-painted and played with Legos and napped and ate fruits and veggies and organic cupcakes.

All the while, Layne considered his next move.

Artyom came in late in the mornings, so Layne figured he could take Cameron to daycare early the next day, and then cruise down to Golden and Winged House and poke around one last time before Artyom showed up. There had to be clues about Omega nestled somewhere within that building.

Maybe Artyom had spread the word that Layne wasn't to be trusted, or maybe he hadn't. Whatever happened when Artyom and Layne met again, Layne could not predict. There had been no proof Artyom had set him up, but that explanation made the most sense.

Layne would have to be ready for a possible

confrontation. If he saw Raisa, he would know what was in store for him by the expression on her face.

The next morning, Layne executed his plan. He made sure Cameron was ready for daycare early. He preferred to deliver her right after opening time, so he didn't end up trapped in conversation loops with the other parents. Not that he didn't sometimes enjoy small talk with parents or the flirty daycare teachers, but today might prove to be a long day.

As Cameron ate her oatmeal and Layne watched, a thought occurred. Layne took out his phone and dialed.

"Hello?" said the voice on the other end of the line.

"Harry Boukadakis," Layne said.

"Ahh, Layne. How goes it?"

"You know… crushing defeat or supreme glory, with not much in between."

"I hear that."

"Your sinus infection?"

Harry sniffled. "Much better, thank you. How did things work out with that little gift I sent you in the mail?"

"Everything worked how it was supposed to. I got about twenty-four hours of battery life."

"That's to be expected with old tech. Anyway, what can I do for you now?"

Cameron looked up at Layne and giggled. He gave her a little wave. "Are you busy over the next couple days?"

"Not really, no. Daphne farmed me out to the NSA for the next two weeks, to help them with a data collection project. No big deal, though. I'm working from home, and it's mostly mindless spreadsheet analysis. Formulas and VLOOKUPs I could do in my sleep. Why?"

"I might need you on standby. Something big is coming, man. Something bad is brewing here, and I'm still not sure what's going on. I only have pieces of the puzzle."

"Sure, Layne. Whatever you need. I'll have my phone on me at all times."

They said their goodbyes and ended the call. As Cameron finished her breakfast, Layne slipped on her socks and shoes. Ready to go.

But, as he opened the door to his apartment, with Cameron dawdling along behind him, Jenna was standing there, on the landing outside his door. Her eyes were bloodshot, her hair and clothes disheveled.

"You have to help me," she said, her lips pulled into a frown.

"Daddy?" asked little Cameron, a suspicious look on her face. "Who is the lady?"

"This is a friend of mine. Her name is Jenna."

"Hi, Jenna," Cam said. "My name is Cameron. Are you sad?"

Jenna glanced at the little girl for a split second and then gave her attention back to Layne. "Please."

"I will help you," he said. "I promise. But you need to be patient. Go back to the motel, and I'll contact you soon. There are things I have to take care of first before we can deal with your situation. The best thing you can do for yourself is to stay out of sight until I tell you it's safe. One more day, maybe two."

Jenna crossed her arms and thrust one hip to the side. Layne could tell she didn't believe him. He wanted to think up some soothing words, but he doubted anything he could say would make much of a difference. Between the life-changing event of stabbing a person and the drugs swirling around in her brain, nothing would calm the storm raging inside her right now.

But, she didn't make a fuss as she turned and strutted away from his apartment door.

43

SERENA EXITED THE GATE IN THE DENVER AIRPORT. The lack of humidity felt like vampires sucking the moisture from her skin. Plus a headache pulsed behind her eyes. Mostly, though, she felt tired. From Thailand to Beijing to San Francisco to Denver. It appeared to be daytime outside, and her watch swore it was early in the morning, but her brain wallowed in a state of total confusion. Serena had made these round-the-world trips a few times in her service to Daphne Kurek's team, but she didn't know if she'd ever get used to it.

Pavel was in tow behind her, dragging his luggage, a semicircular pillow hanging from his neck as he shuffled back and forth. His eyes were haggard, maybe even droopier than hers. She had slept a little on the flight from Beijing to San Francisco, but she wasn't sure if Pavel had slept at all. After months in a cell in an American dark site in Thailand, he had probably adjusted to operating on little sleep.

Did they let him outside for walks? Was he in darkness the entire time? Did they question him or leave him alone with his thoughts all day and night? Did he have books to read? What about the internet or newspapers, or was he cut off from the outside world? So many questions, but Serena knew she'd possibly never get answers to any of them.

"Hungry?" she asked as they collected their belongings. He nodded and removed the pillow from around his neck.

She leaned close and whispered into his ear. "I buy you food, and then you talk. We made a deal at the safe house, remember? I get you to America, and you tell me all about what you think you're going to do to stop Artyom Borovitch."

"Yes, I will tell you. But, food first. I am starving."

She was also feeling famished, so she didn't put up an argument. "There," she said, pointing at a deli once they'd joined the flow of traffic back toward the terminal. "Let's get a sandwich."

They waited in line to buy their food and then settled at a small table to eat. Serena's appetite kicked in as soon as they sat down, and she scarfed half of her six-inch sub in two bites.

"At the airport in Thailand," she said between bites, "you recognized the man following us. Goran."

Pavel nodded through a mouthful of a turkey sandwich. "Goran Smith."

"Smith?"

"He changed his name when he moved to America, obviously. I never knew why, but I suspect he was wanted for crimes in Belarus or Russia or Ukraine. I do not know for sure. He did not like to talk about himself."

"Who is he?"

Pavel shrugged. "What you might call a *fixer*. He works for Artyom. Mostly things related to Artyom's phony halfway house project in Golden. He acts like it is for the good of society, but it is a criminal recruiting operation. To make soldiers loyal to Artyom."

"You knew this before, though, didn't you? When you were working for him?"

Pavel paused. "I did, and I looked the other way most of the time. While I am not proud of my behavior, I did what I did for my family and for Belarus. I believed the end would justify the means."

"And you worked alongside Goran?"

"No, we did not know each other well. Only in passing as two people who both worked for Artyom. I always knew Goran was not a good man. And I feel bad for his son Noah, most of all. He is such a good child. I spend time with him whenever I can."

"Noah is dead, Pavel."

"What?"

As soon as she'd said it, she wished she'd exercised more care with her words. Serena explained about the school shooting and Noah's assassination as the police walked him out of the building, and Pavel's face fell. Tears streamed down his face, faster with each new detail.

He stared at his food, hiccuping breaths and sniffling. "First my family, and now Noah? It is too much. It is too much."

As he set down his sandwich and wiped tears from his cheeks, this was one of those situations Serena knew she was supposed to comfort him. Put a hand on his shoulder? Give him a hug? She was terrible at knowing the right move.

But, she didn't have to choose. He wrapped up his food and cleared his throat. "I am ready to go now. I want to leave this place."

They threw away the remainder of their meals, then collected their bags. Serena guided him to the *people mover*, a moving walkway running along the center of the large hallway guiding them back toward the terminal.

With food in her stomach, the exhaustion of extended travel now weighed on her like chains. She separated from him to lean against the other side of the people mover to catch a bit of rest. But, she caught something out of the corner of her eye. A hint of tradecraft, an unmistakable tell: a woman, averting her eyes, but snatching a glimpse at Serena and Pavel as she did so. Cataloging them.

They were under surveillance.

"Wait a second," Serena said.

"What is it?"

She caught herself before she said more. No reason to set Pavel on edge right now. Plus, she needed more information. The woman who had spied them was no longer there. She had disappeared back into the crowd, likely after detecting she'd been spotted. That meant the woman was well-trained. Not one of Artyom's people. US government, most likely.

Maybe even one of Daphne's? Serena hadn't talked to her boss in a while, and she likely wouldn't be at all happy about Serena gallivanting off for an unsanctioned operation to a dark site in a faraway country. Especially since this op had ended in what some might call "counter-

American" activities, such as helping an enemy combatant escape.

"What is it?" Pavel said.

"Nothing. I'm paranoid."

Something had changed in Pavel's face, though. That sense of panic he'd shown at the safe house resumed. That same anxious expression he'd exhibited in the minutes before Zabojca attacked.

Had he caught the surveillance too?

Pavel's body tensed.

He met her eyes, and then he spun.

Pavel dropped his rolling bag on the floor and sprinted away from her. Serena jumped over his bag, trying to pull her suitcase up to her chest so she could clutch it under her armpit.

"Hey!" she shouted after him.

As Pavel fled up an escalator to the second level of the terminal, Serena tried to duck left and right between the people in the passenger sea. Every one of them staring at their phones as they dragged rolling bags and small children. Serena had to fight the tide. She bumped and knocked people around, endured comments about her rudeness. One large man headed in the opposite direction slammed into her, costing her precious seconds.

And, by the time she reached the top of the escalator, Pavel was gone. Nowhere to be found.

44

Layne stood in the parking lot of Winged House, thinking about strategy. Another crack at Artyom's office sat high on his priority list, but that might not be possible.

Technically, Artyom had not banned him from the organization's employ or even from the grounds. He had not given Layne any decision thus far since the mysterious disappearance of Rez. But, since a few days had now passed and Artyom hadn't called him suggested the boss was not inclined to keep Layne on as a helper.

Or, maybe Artyom had been too busy planning for Omega to decide Layne's fate. Either way, whatever was going on with Omega, Artyom did not seem fit to include Layne in those plans. Layne's goal of pushing himself into Artyom's inner circle had not panned out the way he'd hoped.

Bottom line, Layne didn't think Artyom would banish him from the premises or send goons to toss him out of the building. Layne wasn't worried about goons. Until a couple days ago, he had regularly attended sessions and workshops with all the other ex-cons. As far as he knew, his clandestine missions for Artyom were not public knowledge.

His biggest concern was Raisa. This early in the morning, he wouldn't expect to see Artyom here. But Raisa, she seemed to haunt these hallways at all hours of the day or night. At first ice cold to him, she had softened over Layne's first week as he'd demonstrated himself to be not only a good outpatient participant but a loyal member of Artyom's team. No telling what Artyom had told her after the aborted hiking mission with Rez, though.

Maybe she would smile at him and carry on with her tasks, or maybe she would order security to descend upon him like a pack of wild dogs.

The clock was ticking. Time to put both theories to the test.

Layne marched toward the building and pulled back the front door. Nothing happened. Harmless lobby music drifted from a Bluetooth speaker sitting at the reception area. When he strutted up to the desk, he saw an unfamiliar woman behind the counter, her head down. Past her was an open door, with a mirror in the room beyond. Layne could see the image of Raisa Sokolov reflected in that mirror.

She paced in a back room, one hand on a hip and the other holding a phone up to her ear. He couldn't hear what Raisa was saying at this distance. But, when he focused, he could see her lips moving. Layne had never been skilled at lip reading, and he'd had to use Harry's software program to eavesdrop on Artyom's conversation in his first few days on this operation. But, observing that program in action, he had picked up a thing or two.

When he focused, he could observe the cadence of how her lips moved. After a few seconds of study, these words formed as Raisa spoke slowly to someone on the phone.

No, he's getting ready for Omega. Today. Tonight.

Layne gritted his teeth. Omega was tonight? But where? Layne needed to think this through. Maybe there was something in Artyom's office he'd missed before. Or, maybe something new there could shed light.

He checked his watch. Breakfast had ended, but there would probably be kitchen workers still washing dishes in the kitchen, making a stealthy infiltration of Artyom's office a challenge.

Before Layne could walk away, he watched the reflection of Raisa end the call, and then she emerged into the lobby.

Raisa saw Layne immediately. She straightened up and slipped her phone into a pocket. "Hello," she said, clearing her throat. "We have not seen you in some time, Mr. Haskell."

"Hello, Ms. Sokolov. I've been out of town for a couple of days. I left a note. Maybe you didn't get it."

"I see. Does Artyom know you have returned? He may like to speak with you."

Did that mean Artyom was here early today?

Layne shook his head. His internal warning signals flashed, and an impulse to flee overtook him.

"I don't think he knows. No need to tell him right now, though. I'm going up to the second floor to see someone real quick. Shouldn't take me more than a couple minutes."

Raisa scowled, but she didn't stop him. He pivoted and walked away toward the dorms. Needed to get the hell out of here.

As he was about to head up the stairs toward the dorms to find a side exit out of the building, his eyes trailed back toward the front door, and he saw something to make his heart stop.

Jenna entered, tears streaming down her face. She seemed in even worse shape than when Layne had seen her at his apartment an hour ago.

Why the hell had she come here? This was the last place in the world she should be.

He halted his path to the stairs and headed back toward the front desk area. A burning desire to intercept her crowded out all other thoughts.

She shouldn't be here. Nothing good would come of this.

Jenna glanced at him for a second, then she averted her eyes and marched toward the cafeteria. He picked up the pace. She had her sights set on the kitchen and probably the hallway back to Artyom's office. It had to be her destination.

What possible reason could she have to talk to Artyom, only a couple days after she had killed one of his men in the kitchen?

A terrible idea formed in the back of his brain. If he was right, then this whole situation was about to reach a new level of ugliness.

"Jenna," Layne hissed. "Where are you going?"

She ignored him and pressed forward into the cafeteria. Layne could read the expression on her face, and he could see her next move written there, as plain as could be. She didn't trust him to fix the situation for her. She was going straight to Artyom to throw herself on his mercy.

"This is a bad idea," he said as he entered the kitchen after her. A small crew of kitchen workers milled about, cleaning up after breakfast. "It's not going to work out the way you think. Jenna, please."

She ignored him and jogged toward the back. He called after her again. No answer.

Halfway through the kitchen, Artyom emerged from the back door, via the hallway to his office. At first, looking down at his phone, Artyom then glanced up at Jenna. His eyebrows raised, then raised further when he saw Layne standing a few feet behind her.

"What's going on here?" Artyom said, lowering his phone.

"Please," Jenna said, cowering with her clasped hands out in front of her. She looked ready to drop to her knees. "It was me, two nights ago. Or three nights ago, I don't even remember. The security guard. I don't know what his name was."

Artyom clapped his hands and the half-dozen men and women working in the kitchen dropped what they were doing and fled the room.

"Jenna, damn it," Layne said, "turn around and go home."

For a second, Artyom appeared confused, and then his face changed. He grinned and pointed at Jenna. "You? That was you?"

Before Jenna could answer, the door leading out from

the back hallway opened, and a tall figure stepped through the door.

Goran Smith.

The father of the young man sent into a high school to kill or kidnap the son of the senator. The same man who had faked his death by a heart attack and then disappeared, most likely to chase after Pavel and Serena in Thailand. Layne's acquaintance at the boxing gym for several years now.

Even though Layne had known Goran was still alive, the sight of him in the flesh rippled goosebumps up and down Layne's tattooed arms.

Goran smirked. Artyom muttered something unintelligible to Goran in Belarusian, and the man whipped out a Ruger with a long noise suppressor.

Layne gasped. He bore down, ready to sprint at Goran.

But, it didn't matter. Layne's former friend put two quick bullets in Jenna's head before Layne or Jenna could do anything to stop it.

PART III

SPRING THE TRAP

45

As Jenna crashed to the floor in the kitchen and bits of her brain matter scattered through the air, Layne met Goran Smith's eyes. He and Layne had known each other for years, not quite as friends, but they would occasionally box together at Glazer's Gym in downtown Denver. Goran had a wicked right hook that had bloodied Layne's lip on more than one occasion. Layne had been over to Goran's house and met his teenage son. Charming kid. For a couple of years, they had even exchanged birthday gifts, until they decided they weren't close enough to do that anymore.

"Hello, Layne," Goran said, sporting a demonic sneer.

As he swiveled the pistol in Layne's direction, a million thoughts ran through Layne's head. Foremost was why Goran would go to all this trouble? Why would he fake his own death, flee the country, and then return? It didn't make sense.

As Goran leveled the pistol at Layne, he kicked his legs to the left and pushed himself into a ball to roll along the floor. With the noise suppressor attached to the barrel, when Goran pulled the trigger, the bullet sounded like a car door slam as it screeched across the room and pinged off a stainless steel food prep table on the other side of the kitchen. The ricochet had been louder than the original shot.

"Damn it, Goran, not here," Artyom barked. But, he made no motion to actually prevent Goran from continuing his assault.

As Layne scurried along the tile, he looked over toward Jenna. Two bullet holes in her head. His insides clenched. This was his fault and Jenna would've never stabbed that security guard to death if Layne hadn't been there already, trying to break into Artyom's office. Sure, maybe she would have eventually overdosed on heroin, like many of them do, but were it not for Layne, she would be alive, right now.

Grief and regret would come later. For now, Layne had to survive the immediate threat.

As Goran readjusted his arm to lower the pistol and fire again at Layne on the floor, he twisted out of the way. He rolled toward a stack of plastic bins, a tower stretching from the floor halfway to the ceiling.

Layne put the bins between himself and Goran, the only item nearby to use as cover. Terrible cover, actually, but it was all he had. A few bullets passed through the bins, knocking several of the uppermost ones to the ground. Spongy circles of dough flew into the air and thunked on the tile floor. Looked like they are having pizza for lunch today.

Layne had to take stock. He reached to the back of his waistband where his pistol should have been, but he did not find it there. Gone. When he'd either fallen to the floor or rolled across the room, it had become dislodged and skittered away somewhere. Layne glanced around and didn't see it. If he left cover to hunt around for the gun, Goran would fill him full of holes. So, Layne had no weapon for the foreseeable future.

He had to create a diversion and then make a tactical retreat. It was the only option.

Layne threw a shoulder into the bin stack, pushing them toward Goran and Artyom. The stack toppled, and the two Belarusians had to jump back to avoid a collision.

In the chaos, Layne scrambled to his feet as Goran blasted another couple shots, one of them coming close enough to Layne's head that he felt his hair move. It forced his eyes shut. Dangerous ricochet pings zipped in every direction.

He sprinted away from them, crashing through the door into the cafeteria. There were a few ex-cons and kitchen staff in the room, looking confused, mouths agape. No security yet, though.

As Layne reached the lobby, there stood Raisa, with a walkie-talkie up to her mouth. "All security to the cafeteria immediately," she said, then her eyes met Layne's, and she did a quick double-take. "Correction: all security to the *lobby*, immediately. I repeat: every available security officer to the lobby, now."

Layne didn't wait around to find out how many guards were on their way or what kind of guns they would be sporting. He barreled out the front door of the Winged House, fished his keys out of his pocket, and made it to his car in two seconds flat.

Jenna dead. Goran back in town, trying to kill Layne. Omega happening at some point today.

Adrenaline drove him. His brain had emptied of all thoughts until he finally slammed the keys in the ignition and peeled out of the parking lot.

Layne didn't understand what had happened in there, but he knew one thing for sure: all his plans had crumbled to dust in the last five minutes.

46

Layne eyed himself in the bathroom mirror. In particular, a section of skin above his right eye. The bullet that had been close enough to make Layne feel his hair move had actually grazed him. He hadn't realized it at the time. The cut was only a fraction of an inch deep, more like a scratch. But Layne treated it with antibiotic ointment and a bandage nonetheless.

He kept seeing Jenna, the look on her face as she pleaded with Artyom for her life. The desperation in her eyes. If she only would have waited another day or two, Layne could have fixed everything for her. The body had already been eliminated, and evidence could have been doctored to remove Jenna as a possible suspect. Sure, Layne couldn't have erased her guilt at killing the man, but he could have made it possible for her to avoid jail time.

Or, maybe nothing he could have done would have eased her guilty conscience. Maybe she would have imploded no matter what. Not the first time Layne had seen someone self-destruct in front of him, and not the first time he'd felt responsible for making it happen.

But he had to move on. There were still lives in danger. Still pieces of the puzzle that needed a home before he could act. Too much didn't make sense.

Layne tried to step through the events of the last ten days, starting with the school shooting and ending with Goran Smith returning, bringing everything full-circle. Layne couldn't put the items together in a way that checked all the boxes.

He left the bathroom and picked up a pen and a pad of paper in the living room. Tired fingers popped a nicotine lozenge into his mouth, then he sat on his couch and hunched over the coffee table.

He started by drawing boxes of the major events and major players, at least the ones he knew. Then, he wrote on the pad: *Omega. Today. Failsafe. Primary target.*

The words and shapes swam on the page. A feeling of hopelessness tried to rise from his stomach and bubble into his throat. He didn't know enough, he was running out of time, and he had no clever ideas how to expand his knowledge. All of this felt inches away from slipping out of his reach.

But, he wouldn't let that happen. He sat back and focused on the pad of paper. With his arms together, he stared down at the opposing good and evil cherub tattoos on his forearms, one on each side.

After a few seconds, an idea struck. Going back to the first conversation he'd recorded with Harry's lip-reading software, Artyom had referred to Omega as a *failsafe,* and then he'd said something about moving on to the *primary target.*

Layne had assumed that meant the senator would not be the focus of Omega. That he wasn't the end goal. Pavel had probably always been the end goal, but Layne had assumed the senator and Pavel were somehow linked.

What if Layne had been thinking about the transcription from the wrong angle these last few days?

Maybe Layne had misunderstood the part of the text related to the "primary target?" What if that passage wasn't even related to Omega? The software hadn't been able to decipher the entire conversation, so maybe Layne had stitched the two things together, looking for a connection that wasn't there?

He had shifted his focus away from the Senator, but that could have been a mistake. Maybe the senator was still involved in the final execution somehow.

Layne took out his phone and looked up Senator Carroway's website. Scrolling along the senator's schedule, Layne noted that the man was due to attend a gala event at the new Tuscany Hotel in the little mountain casino resort town of Black Hawk, an hour west of Denver.

The gala would take place tonight.

This was it. So much became clearer in that instant. Omega had something to do with the Senator appearing at this charity event in Black Hawk. A failsafe to put the final squeeze on him.

But it still didn't add up. If the intention of putting pressure on the senator was to force Pavel's release from confinement, then why carry through with this Omega event? Pavel was out. Serena had gotten him out of Thailand. Daphne had confirmed it. Since Goran was back, he must have apprised Artyom of that fact.

Or, maybe he hadn't. Which suggested that if Artyom didn't know Pavel was out, Goran was lying to him.

Goran and Artyom warring over something?

Was this whole thing not about Pavel at all? What other purpose could Artyom have here, aside from the release of his colleague?

What was the goal *beyond* Pavel?

All these things dashed through Layne's mind like lightning bolts in the clouds.

Either way, Layne realized it didn't matter. What mattered was that tonight, men with guns planned to descend on this charity event at a casino in the nearby mountains, and Layne had to stop it from happening.

47

Layne entered the diner and dipped his head at her, seated near the back. She didn't stand or make any effort to greet him. Her eyes flicked around, checking the attentiveness of the residents of nearby tables.

He approached her and held out a hand, which she gripped. "Good to see you, Serena."

Daphne's declaration about Serena's alleged crush on him throttled his brain like a headache. He didn't know if he could see it from her angle, but maybe he had been too flirty with her. Maybe he had misused his position as someone she admired. Serena had, after all, replaced him on Daphne's team once Layne had retired after the horrific London operation, six years before.

She smiled, and for a second, he thought she would pull him in for a hug. But, she didn't. "You too, Layne."

"Thank you. Thank you for all of your assistance and your sacrifices to help me with this."

"Of course. You asked, and I was glad I could do something."

He hesitated over his next words as he sat, and then finally, spat it out. "If I made you feel like you had to go to Thailand, or I pressured you in any way…"

"Pressured?" she asked, raising an eyebrow. "When did you turn into HR?"

The tension boiling inside him snapped like a twig, which made a grin appear on his lips. "Forget about it. Anyway, did I get you into trouble?"

"I don't know yet. I haven't been taking Daphne's calls."

"Do you think that's wise?"

She shrugged. "We're not done here, so that's something I'll have to deal with later. If I had a buck for every time Control has yelled at me in an operational debrief, I would have bought that speedboat by now."

"If that's how you want to play it, then I guess it is what it is. Control can be difficult to work with."

"You're right about that," Serena said.

"Did you know I gave her that nickname?"

"I didn't. It's from that John le Carré spy book, right?"

Layne tilted his head, impressed. "I didn't know you were a reader."

"I'm not. I Googled it. It had to come from somewhere, right? Besides, she gives all the rest of us nicknames, it's only fitting she has one, too. She's taken to calling me *Pepper*."

He nodded. "I can see that for you. Either way, I appreciate the effort you went through to find Pavel."

"I know breaking him out of the dark site wasn't within the mission parameters, but it seemed like the right idea at the moment. There was so much chaos, I didn't have a lot of time to think things through."

Layne showed his palms as a gesture of sympathy. "No, I get it. Sometimes, you have to make a judgment call in the field, and it either works out, or it doesn't."

"Seems like it was the wrong call this time. I haven't been able to find him since he ditched me at the airport."

"More spry than he appeared, huh?"

She gave a grim nod as a reply.

Layne slid a piece of paper across the table with the address. "This is where he will be, though, at this hotel and casino in Black Hawk. If you're right about him, and he's got his heart set on revenge against Artyom, that is."

Serena picked up the paper, glanced at it, then slid it into her pocket. "I talked to Harry this morning. Here's an interesting detail: the senator is going to give a speech at this thing today, and he plans to reveal that his son was the target of the shooting at the school."

"Ahh, I wondered why they'd been keeping it quiet."

"The big reveal for maximum political gain," she said. "I assume you weren't able to get through to his staff to warn him?"

"No, I did. I called the senator's people and told him there will be an attempt on his life at the gala tonight. They weren't interested in hearing about my theories and said they were prepared for any possible security breach. Seems the senator has made a few enemies with some of his recent political moves, so they were expecting protesters, anyway. I think they assumed I was one of them, trying to stir up trouble."

"Locals?"

"I called the cops. They said they would send patrol cars, but I don't know if they believed me."

"Do you think there's someone from Winged House

inside the senator's staff? Why would they and the hotel be so dismissive?"

"Laziness. Cockiness. Tired of dealing with false threats, and probably under a lot of pressure to make sure this charity event comes off without a hitch. Less than two weeks after someone targets the senator's son in a school shooting in his state? These are weird times. Also, with what you just told me about his big reveal, it makes sense he doesn't want to spoil his chance to get some political points out of the day." Layne leaned forward. "But, maybe this will work out for us. With only you and me, we make Artyom and Goran think this will be easy. Maybe they keep it low-key, as long as they don't feel threatened."

Serena swished her lips back and forth. "Possibly. What about a pre-emptive strike on Winged House? I know a couple locals who would be willing to help."

"No, that's not going to work, either. I dropped by a couple hours ago. It's cleared out. Residents, even. Like a ghost town."

"Do you think they will go in with a small team, or does the fact that Winged House is empty mean all of them are going to show up for the assault? Are we thinking ten hostiles, or fifty?"

Layne shrugged. "I don't know. If I knew what their goal was, maybe I could do a legit threat assessment. But it's all so vague at this point."

"Weird. I can ask Daphne about lending us some resources."

He shook his head. "That's not a good idea, either. She wanted to wash her hands of this whole thing from the start, so I doubt she'd be willing to pitch in now. Our best bet is to neutralize Artyom and Goran before anything happens. Cut off the head of the snake. A two-person team is much better suited to that, anyway. We don't want them to see us coming."

She flicked a fingernail against the side of her water glass. "So, we're on our own, as usual."

"Yep. It doesn't look good, does it?"

"Not really, no."

For a moment, they stared at each other. Layne didn't like to poison an operation before it had a chance to succeed or fail on its own, but he didn't know what else to say to rally the troops. The odds were not in their favor.

"Where's your daughter?" Serena asked.

"At her mom's through the weekend."

"Can I meet her while I'm in town?"

"Really? You like kids?"

"Well, I don't have any of my own, but I've been around little ones all my life. Big, Catholic family. So, can I meet her?

Layne considered this. "Sure, if we both survive the evening."

Serena grinned. "It's good to work with you again, Boy Scout.

48

Serena watched the Tuscany hotel from the window of the coffee shop across the street. While the little mountain town's resorts and casinos were plentiful, the Tuscany dwarfed all others. One of downtown Black Hawk's newest hotels, it stood fifteen stories tall, with massive conference rooms and an open gambling area, with ballrooms on the first and second floors.

Local papers had dubbed it the new hotspot and the focal point for political and celebrity fundraisers in the state. Serena didn't know anything about the interior of the hotel, however, only what she'd seen online. She was not the caliber of person to be invited to high society dinners. Fine with her.

A floor plan Serena had found online indicated dozens and dozens of crisscrossing hallways and tunnels and pathways. Securing everything would be impossible.

She wasn't even sure if she could pull off a feat of subterfuge tonight since she was still feeling the dregs of jet lag. In Thailand, she'd been there barely long enough to develop an initial adjustment to the time difference. Now, getting used to it the other way around.

Serena rolled her head around her shoulders, feeling the pain of extended travel in her stiff neck. Her eyes still worked, though. She watched the street leading up to the Tuscany, waiting for any sign of her target. She wished she had handcuffs or zip ties but everything had happened on such short notice. Layne was still in Denver, collecting supplies for their operation tonight.

Layne had worked hard to project confidence at their earlier meeting, but she'd seen the doubt in his baby blue eyes. This had become personal for him, which was probably why he wanted them to go in alone, without calling in favors to add a dozen other experienced operatives to a strike team.

There had been a part of her that wanted to argue with him about bringing backup, but there was honestly a part of her that wanted to see what would happen during a duo operation. A need to find out why Goran and Artyom had gone to so much trouble to spring Pavel from imprisonment at the dark site. Why they'd worked so hard to make it look like they were freeing a political prisoner when in reality, they wanted to kill Pavel. At least, according to Pavel, that's what they wanted.

If fifty G-men poured in through the doors of that casino, she might not get answers to any of those questions.

Maybe Pavel was right, or maybe he'd lied about the whole thing.

Since he had fled at the airport, Serena wasn't sure what to think of his story anymore. She did know that Goran Smith, the assassin known as Zabojca, was associated with Artyom, and he was definitely trying to kill Pavel. The truth about the rest of Pavel's story, though, remained to be seen.

Then, she realized how crazy it was to want to see this scenario play out. People could be hurt. And yet, the adrenaline gave her a rumbling thrill in her stomach.

She took out her phone and dialed the police in Denver, not local. She assumed local would be two guys in a strip mall in nearby Central City. After waiting on hold for a couple minutes, she reported there would be an attempt on the senator's life. The cop on the other end of the line seemed suspicious, but earnest.

If they did decide to take her seriously, it wouldn't hurt to have a few more black-and-whites in the area to keep the civilians out of danger.

Then, Serena saw something. She cut the call short.

A lone male figure strolled up the hilly street toward the Tuscany hotel. Serena couldn't see his face from this angle, but a strong suspicion told her it was Pavel. She waded through the line of coffee shop patrons and exited the front door.

Pulling the hood of her sweatshirt up, she crossed the street. She quickened her pace to cut the distance between them.

He wasn't very observant. Or maybe he was tired.

She shoved the gun into his back and pressed her body against his to shield it from the nearby pedestrians. There weren't many, but no sense in taking chances.

"Hello, Pavel. I'd like you to turn one-eighty degrees and walk with me. I'm going to stay behind you the whole time. If you run, I'll put a bullet in the back of your thigh before you can get three paces away from me. Understand?"

Pavel said nothing, but he did take his hands out of his pockets and turn his palms up to show her that he wasn't armed. She appreciated that. For a double-crossing flight risk, Pavel was quite polite.

And, he did as he was told. She escorted him to the coffee shop she'd used as her stakeout spot, and around to the back of the building. She had already propped open the rear door.

Serena pushed him inside the coffee shop back room and then diverted into a large closet. She sat him down in the chair and trained the gun on him as she took a few breaths to center herself.

"Have you been working for Artyom this whole time?" he asked.

Serena shook her head. "I don't work for anyone. Just doing a favor for a friend, and now that we're in this, looks like we have to see it all the way through to the end." She leaned back against a shelf stacked tall with boxes. "It's time for you to tell me the truth: did you kill that American diplomat in Uganda?"

He held his tongue for a moment, then glanced down at her gun. Her finger wasn't on the trigger, but it was hovering in the air near it.

"No, no I did not. There was no murder of a diplomat at all. There was a CIA agent who had gone into Kampala one night to drink and find a whore. He ventured into a bad neighborhood and met his end when the whore's brother did not like how he ran out on her without paying."

"What does that have to do with you?"

Pavel winced. "I was there, in Kampala. But the death of the CIA officer had nothing to do with me. I was an easy target. The US ambassador to Uganda had a wife there, and she had many contacts in the pharmaceutical industry across Africa. I had been talking to her, building a rapport. You Americans call it *networking*. The ambassador thought we were having an affair."

"Were you?"

He shook his head. "I have never been unfaithful to my wife. When the CIA agent went missing, it was easy to point the finger at me. The ambassador wanted me gone, plus the death of the CIA agent was embarrassing, so they made it look as if I had killed this man. Two birds with one stone."

Serena chewed on her lower lip. "So Artyom didn't frame you at all."

"No, and I am sorry I lied about that. But it is true he has been trying to kill me since I was arrested. What I told you about the attempt on my life in Cairo was real, as were many other details of my story."

"But he did try to kill you? You're sure about that?"

"I think my arrest must have changed his plans at the time. He could not get to me, so the secret prison provided me a refuge. He had to focus on my release. Spending all this time in the cage in Thailand has probably kept me alive because I can only assume Artyom would have killed me long ago, if he could have."

"Why, Pavel? And why did you lie to me?"

"I do not know why he wants me dead. I truly do not know. But I thought I had to tell you it was him who framed me—and not the Americans—so you would bring me back here and I could confront him."

She did lower the gun a little since his body language seemed much more relaxed and he didn't appear to pose a threat. "I just want to know what it is you think you're going to do inside that hotel when you find him."

"I am going to stop him."

Serena took a step toward Pavel and bent down on one knee, shaking her head. "That's not good enough. I need specifics. Why did he work so hard to get you out of that dark site? What does he want from you?"

"He wants to kill me."

Serena kept shaking her head. "That's not the answer I am looking for. Tell me *why*. He's got to have a good reason."

"I do not know."

"Make a guess."

Pavel opened his mouth to say more, then he did something unexpected. With a violent chop, he slammed his teeth together. Serena heard a crunch. She drew in a breath and had just enough time to understand what was happening, but not enough time to defend herself.

He forced out a whoosh of breath. A mist of powdery gas expelled from the broken capsule inside his mouth. This poisonous cloud hit Serena in the face, and although she tried not to inhale, some of it went into her eyes and nose and mouth, anyway.

As she gagged and gasped, she staggered back. Her eyes shut, lungs and nose burning. She lost her footing as Pavel ran past her and out the closet door. She tried to grasp at him, but her reactions were so slowed, he was out of the room by the time she could reach a hand out. Her eyes would not open.

She fell to her knees, heaving breaths. And then, in a

few seconds, the burn lessened. A few seconds later, it dissipated even more.

She was getting better. It was not fatal, this poisonous gas. Pavel had only wanted to flee from her custody.

Serena spent another fifteen or twenty seconds recovering before she was able to open her eyes and rise to her feet. When she staggered out of the closet room and left via the back door, she ran around to the front. Pavel was gone.

INTERLUDE 4

FORT COLLINS, CO | SIXTEEN YEARS AGO

LAYNE MEETS THE SHOOTER'S EYES. THE YOUNG MAN'S finger wraps around the trigger of his assault rifle.

In a fraction of a second, Layne does several things. First, his peripheral vision analyzes the surrounding area. He and the shooter are standing ten feet apart, on the marble floor of the mezzanine level. The doorway to the stairs is on Layne's left. The glass railing lies to Layne's right. This railing is only a few feet away. It's four feet tall, thick glass with a metal bar running across the top.

Second, Layne realizes the quickest way to make an escape is to leap for the railing. Yes, he'll fall fifteen or twenty feet down to the ground floor below, but any other direction is death. With the rifle trained on him, there's nowhere on this mezzanine Layne can flee to stay safe from the shooter's rifle.

Third, Laye knows even if he can raise his pistol in time, the shooter is quicker. He's ready to go. One jerk of his finger and Layne will be dead. This young man has killed already today. He won't hesitate to add one more body to the list.

Fourth, Layne makes a decision. He turns and leaps over the railing, down toward the atrium level below. But, in his haste, he doesn't jump high enough. His knee catches on the glass barrier of the railing, breaking it.

As he falls down to the first-floor area, a stream of glass, crinkling and glittering, follows him. He rotates as he falls. Half a second before he crashes, he raises his hands to cover his face.

He and the river of glass smack into the floor at the same time, his arms receiving dozens of cuts from his wrists to his shoulders. Stray bits pelt him like hail as his body flattens on the cold surface of the food court.

Next, a barrage of bullets rains down from above. The shooter leans over the railing, his rifle spitting a seemingly limitless number of shots at Layne. He's got one finger on the trigger and the other on the stock, swinging it around in a circle.

One of those bullets will find a home, any second now.

Layne doesn't wait. He rolls, crunching over the glass, feeling slick blood cascade over his arms. As he twists, the pistol slips from his bloody grasp, skittering onto the floor. Once he's rolled a few feet away, he looks up and sees the ceiling. He's underneath the walkway of the mezzanine above. Now, he's shielded from the shooter, temporarily.

Layne looks around for his pistol. It's out among the glass, where the shooter is still firing. A trail of blood from the cuts on Layne's arms marks the path he took to roll to safety.

He has to make another decision. Stay safe underneath the lip of the mezzanine, or go after the gun.

Logic tells him to catch his breath, then jump to his feet and turn ninety degrees so he can sprint for the door to the courtyard. It's only thirty feet away.

But if he chooses the gun, he can then make a stand against the shooter. What if more people are hiding in rooms like the trio he helped escape via the awning outside the window?

He chooses the gun. It's sitting among a collection of glass, a couple feet away from a table and chairs out in the open. A study space.

He scrambles toward it, hustling with everything left in his energy reserves. His mouth is dry, and his stomach swirls with queasiness. Abdominals aching. He might have broken a few ribs during the landing.

Layne clears the last three or four feet in a single jump, and he leans down to snatch the pistol before his feet even touch the ground. Bullets plink off the floor around him like hunks of meteorites raining from the sky.

He grabs the gun.

Layne plants his foot to pivot. The logic center in his brain still demands he runs right through the door to meet up outside with the students he saved. He should flee and let the police handle this.

But a nagging thought remains: what if he leaves now, and the body count increases? There are no police outside yet as far as Layne can see. The only one who can stop this shooter from potentially taking more lives in the next few minutes is Layne, and he knows it.

So, instead of dashing to the door, Layne heads for the

stairs. He takes them three at a time until he's back on the second floor. He hurtles toward the walkway to confront the shooter.

When he emerges into the open area, the shooter is still there, leaning over the broken glass railing, looking for Layne. Maybe with all the gunfire, his eardrums are rattling, and he can't hear Layne approaching.

Layne has to take any advantage he can get. He raises the pistol. His finger jerks the trigger once, twice. Both shots fly high, over the shooter's head. Layne is too hyped up to concentrate and aim.

He plants his feet and lowers the pistol, trying to compensate. The shooter turns, the muzzle of his rifle trailing his body by only a few inches. A surprised look colors his face as he wheels around.

Layne is out of time. The next shot has to hit his target, or he's a dead man.

He closes one eye and looks down the sight. He squeezes the trigger one time, making the bullet rocket from the end of his gun.

The blast forces Layne's eyes shut, but only for a second. When he opens them, a puff of blood ejects from the shooter's right arm.

The shooter staggers back a step, but he does not fall. He does not take his finger off the trigger. In fact, he grips the assault rifle harder and prepares to shoot.

Layne knows he's about to eat a bullet. Maybe a dozen, if the shooter has changed out the magazine since Layne crashed to the floor.

Layne does the only thing he can think of, and he falls to one knee as he wraps his other hand around the pistol grip for support. He squeezes the trigger once, twice, three times, and doesn't stop until the magazine is empty.

A few of the bullets hit the shooter. One into his thigh, one into his stomach, but the one that finally sends him to the floor is a bullet that punches through his chest, sending a thin jet of blood like a stream of projectile vomit onto the floor in front of him.

Layne presses the trigger a few times after the magazine empties, the rush of panic pushing him forward.

Don't stop. Keep firing. He could still be alive. You and others are still in danger. Don't let him do this to other people.

After he realizes his pistol isn't firing anymore, and the shooter is on the floor and no longer attempting to rise to his feet, Layne stops. He lowers his arms and lets the pistol clatter onto the mezzanine.

When he tries to stand, he finds his legs don't work, and they give out. He tumbles to the ground, flat on his butt. The shooter makes eye contact with him, his mouth opening and closing. The evil in his eyes now replaced with childlike desperation and terror. Still alive, but bleeding out onto the clean marble floor.

Layne holds the boy's gaze as sirens wail outside, growing louder.

49

The first floor of the Tuscany hotel consisted of a lobby, a casino to the west, and conference spaces and a ballroom to the east. Both ends spread out like the wings of a great bird. The floor plan of the place was a baffling design like Chutes and Ladders, hallways and passages and crisscrossing floors. Keeping their targets within a manageable space would not be easy.

Layne entered to find a grand lobby marked by marble floors and ceiling. He met Serena—both in disguises—at an area populated with seating that fanned out from a central indoor fountain. Serena had donned a short brown wig with tinted eyeglasses. Layne had opted for shaggy auburn hair, with a furry mustache wrapping around his upper lip.

When Serena saw him, she grinned and rolled her eyes. He slid into a lounge chair next to hers, close to the fountain. The sound of the water provided white noise to mask their conversation.

"What?" he asked.

Omega Trap

"Your mustache is ridiculous. You look like a porn star."

Layne shrugged. "Too late now." He flicked his chin at the east wing. "They're setting up for the event but it still isn't for another hour."

"You think that's when they'll clamp down?"

His eyes shifted from the casino entrance to the conference area entrance. "Hard to say. The casino might be a safer bet. With all those people packed in tightly, it would be a much better place to cause chaos."

"Agreed. Senator in the building?"

"I don't know yet." Layne looked toward the casino's closed doors, at the beefy security guards standing outside of it. "He might be in there right now. I've heard he likes the slot machines."

"We should hurry," Serena said as she stood up. Layne tried not to gawk at the slinky and form-fitting gown. Since Daphne's comment about Serena having a crush on him and his influence on her, he'd been in a perpetual state of guilt around this young and attractive woman.

But, he had to put that aside for now. Anything personal between them would only serve as a distraction. He already had enough of that, dwelling on how Artyom and Goran had sent young Noah Smith to die inside the school. If he let those thoughts fester in his head, he'd lose his edge. Become sloppy.

"Can you move okay in that dress?" he asked.

"Sure. It's stretchier than it looks."

She started to walk away, but Layne leaned in and whispered in her ear. "If you see Goran Smith or Artyom Borovitch, you can take them out with these." He slipped two small needles laced with poison into her purse. "You might also consider taking out Pavel if you see him. Whatever Artyom and Goran want him for, I don't think it serves anyone to let them have him."

"You think we should kill him?"

He shrugged. "I'm saying we keep our options open. He's valuable enough for Artyom to go to all this trouble. Plus, Pavel has double-crossed you twice already."

For a moment, she balked. "Despite what he's done I'm still not convinced he's our enemy."

"I know. I'm not either, but we may not have that luxury of choice in the moment."

She nodded. "Understood. Let's keep in touch. And try to not get caught."

They each slipped small Bluetooth devices into their ears, and Layne then made a phone call to Serena. She nodded once the phone call had connected.

They broke apart and walked separately toward the casino entrance.

The bouncers at the door to the casino looked askance at the Bluetooth jutting out of Layne's ear, but none of them said anything about it. If he approached a table, any card dealer would probably make him take it out. Just like no cell phones allowed while at the tables.

Serena entered the casino first, and Layne followed a few seconds later. The bouncer told him to have a good evening as he held the door open.

Layne entered the enormous open room, a mist of cigarette smoke wafting over him as he immersed himself in the social chaos inside. The blinking lights and the beeping of the slot machines, the plinking of poker chips on felt. Not a clock in sight. The scant light from the tall ceilings casting a sickly yellow glow on the hundreds of gamblers milling about, hoping to win big in games rigged against them.

"I will focus on Artyom and Goran," Layne muttered into his Bluetooth to Serena. "You stay on Pavel. You'll recognize him faster, anyway."

"Roger that."

There were distinct areas within the circular casino room. Lining the outer walls were banks of restaurants and food court eateries, as well as a couple of tobacco shops, cashiers, and bathrooms. A ring of slot machines marked the edge of the gambling area. Inside that were the tables for cards, roulette, and other games. Dead center, the banks of televisions and chairs set up for people to engage in sports betting. Concentric circles of open space served as rows between these segments.

Layne decided to focus on working his way from out to in. From a distance, he felt good about his disguise. Up close, it probably would not hold up. He had to find Artyom and Goran first and neutralize them.

He sauntered in a wide arc around the vast room, focusing on keeping track of where he encountered any security. Artyom might not wait until the gala later to unleash whatever it was he was planning. Layne might need allies. Hopefully, these security guards, plus the senator's security, plus any undercover police in the room were prepared for a sudden burst of madness.

Layne readied a couple of his own poison-tipped sticks. If he could deal with Artyom and Goran directly, there was no reason to alert anyone, including the senator's staff. And even though a curiosity burned inside Layne to understand why Artyom worked so hard to spring Pavel only to pursue his assassination, Layne had to resist the urge. He had to accept that he might never know.

Layne caught a few looks from men in suits as he strolled past a fast food Chinese buffet, Mexican and Italian eateries, and fancy sit-down places. Some of these suited men were security for the senator and other high-profile guests, mixed in with regular casino security. If there *were* undercover cops here, Layne hadn't detected any.

After one complete circuit around the outer edge, Layne moved into the slot machine area. And then, out of the corner of his eye to the right, Layne found Artyom.

Omega's architect had the senator dead in his sights as the man was at a craps table, surrounded by his entourage. But, Artyom wasn't yet approaching. Holding there, waiting for something.

At that moment, all of Layne's suspicions were confirmed. He understood why they had proceeded with this Omega plan, even though there seemed to be no point in pressuring the senator since Pavel was no longer in custody in Thailand.

It wasn't about the senator at all. His presence here was a tool.

The gala event was a way of drawing out Pavel. Why that would work, Layne had no idea, but it was all about hunting down Artyom's former friend and colleague. They had set a trap for him. Maybe that hadn't been Omega's original intention, but it seemed clear that's how Artyom meant to use it now.

Alternate target, primary target, failsafe. None of the clues Layne had chased mattered. Pavel was the primary target, and always had been. No one else.

For Artyom, the goal was to get his hands on Pavel through any means necessary.

"Change of plan," Layne said into the Bluetooth. "Focus all energy on Pavel. Whatever happens, we need to find him and extract him from this hotel. This is all a trap to draw him out, and we need to keep him away from Artyom and Goran at all costs."

If Serena replied, Layne didn't hear it. He couldn't hear anything over the sound of two quick gunshots near the front of the casino, and the subsequent screams of several people in the area. A mass of gamblers shifted at once, like a wave crashing.

Layne spun to see a dozen SWAT team members marching into the room, weapons drawn. Apparently, they had taken the warnings seriously. They were armed with M4a1 rifles and ceramic plated vests.

And, before Layne could ponder why they had chosen this exact moment to invade, he saw the bodies. Two men Layne recognized from Winged House were dead on the ground near the doors to the lobby, both of them with weapons clutched in their lifeless hands.

Twenty or thirty people in the crowd unveiled weapons. Cops, ex-cons, private security. Good guys and bad guys blurred in an instant, as soon as the bullets started flying.

Half a dozen civilians died in the first few seconds. Since everyone was packed so tightly in this room, every bullet fired seemed to find a home. The gamblers who hadn't frozen in a panic tried to flee. In the chaos, no one seemed to know where the exits were. People ran in all directions, some in circles.

The senator's entourage forced him to the floor and

crowded around him like a football team's defense dogpiling on a running back.

Cops and Winged House terrorists faced off, guns spitting fire.

Omega had begun.

As soon as the shooting started, Layne palmed the poison-tipped dart, and he ran straight at Artyom. Too many people scrambling around for Layne to risk shooting his gun. He could deal with Goran and Pavel later. Layne wanted to cut off the head of the snake now. Whatever happened next, Artyom would not survive the next five seconds.

Layne was only ten paces away when Artyom looked in his direction, and his eyes jumped wide open. Artyom reached a hand into his suit coat inner pocket and withdrew something. He raised a device like Taser, pointing it at Layne.

Serena barked in Layne's ear as he ran.

Five steps away. Three steps away.

The man's finger closed around the Taser trigger.

Layne diverted a step to his left to avoid the incoming Taser blast. But he'd calculated wrong. Artyom compensated, and the Taser dart pierced Layne's shoulder. A wave of intense electrical pain radiated from his arm down into the rest of his body in a fraction of a second. Layne felt himself stiffening.

And, as he fell to the ground while people ran in a panic all around him, the last thing he heard in his Bluetooth was the sound of Serena screaming.

50

Layne's eyes flicked open, but for several seconds, he could see only darkness. This unknown room was much quieter than the place he'd been before, cooler, with a damp feeling in the air. Basement, probably.

After a few blinks, his eyes improved and he could see this present room was a wine cellar. He'd had to take a guess since the edges of his vision were still blurry. Aside from the Taser blast, he felt as if they'd given him something to dull his senses.

More light filtered in. Racks of bottles lined the walls and shelving areas of this room. Definitely a wine cellar.

Was he still at the casino? How much time had passed?

Something shifted to his right, and Layne turned to see Serena also now stirring. On the floor next to him, her fancy evening gown torn up the side, exposing most of her thigh. Her wig gone. She blinked a few times, squinting against the light.

"Hey," he said.

She shook her head and opened wide for a yawn. "Taser?"

Layne nodded. Now he looked down at her hands and saw someone had restrained them with zip ties. Same with his. But, as far as he could tell, he didn't have any other serious injuries. Neither did she.

His vision now broadened into a wider arc, and he noticed a chubby man in a suit standing fifteen feet away from them. A white guy with a bushy beard and long brown hair corralled in a ponytail. Hands clasped in front, standing at attention, just like the bouncers outside the casino entrance. The man lifted his phone to his mouth and said, "they're awake."

He paused and then nodded. Unbuttoning his suit coat, he walked over to a television sitting on a desk beyond the shelves. Layne could barely see it even though his vision was improving by the second.

The suited man plugged a small device into the television's USB port on the side and then he held his phone out. His thick fingers tapped on it a few times. Then, he held the phone up to his ear "I'll connect you in just one moment, sir."

The guy tapped on the phone a few more times and then turned on the television. The screen flickered to life, showing a video of Artyom in a darkened room, head facing down. He was recording and streaming video from his phone. Layne could hear muffled gunshots in the background.

Layne starting to believe they were still at the casino. In addition to the racks of wine, he saw other clues. On a nearby wall, there was a laminated sheet of paper with a dry-erase marker hanging from a piece of string. A series of dates and initials listed down the laminated paper. Probably a record of who had last cleaned the room.

"You're wondering why you're still alive," Artyom said.

"You piece of shit," Serena growled.

The ponytail man shook his head. "He can't hear you. One-way video chat."

On the TV, Artyom grinned. "I can tell you're angry. That is to be expected. I am also angry, for a number of reasons. Also, I'm quite impressed you were able to find out where we would be today. Layne, you should have been dead by now, but I greatly underestimated you. I should have known better."

Since Layne knew speaking would do no good, he kept his expression blank and calm and stared directly into Artyom's TV face.

"And I know," Artyom continued, "you have lots of questions. We don't have time for any of that right now." He lifted a finger, wagging it at them. "What I do know is that once I have taken care of business up here and finished with my new, altered plan for Omega, I am going to deal with the two of you. I will make both of you feel much, much pain for interfering with me. Especially you, Layne. You broke my plans for you in a grand fashion. A quick death is too good for you."

Artyom leaned back and tapped a button on his phone, which severed the connection. The TV screen turned blue. The man with the ponytail, who Layne now understood was their guard until Artyom could finish with Omega upstairs, unplugged his device from the USB port. He eyed them but said nothing.

Then, he marched over to the room's door and stood in front of it. Legs spread shoulder-width apart, hands clasped in front of his waist, a mute statue with his eyes pointed forward.

The guard opened his suit coat and pulled a Glock 26 from an armpit holster. He pointed it at the ground and then tilted his head toward two chairs next to a row of shelves. "Have a seat, please. I will not tell you twice."

Layne and Serena shuffled over to the chairs and sat. Serena, her chest heaving, craned her neck around, probably looking for something to use as a weapon.

Layne studied the room. Unremarkable aside from the shelves filled with bottles of wine. Except for the main door, there did not appear to be another way out of the room. He considered signaling Serena that they should bum rush the guard, but with zip-tied hands and plenty of distance between them and their jailer, he could easily shoot both of them before they'd reached within five feet.

Serena leaned toward Layne and said, "I have an idea. Follow my lead."

"Excuse me," she said to the guard, "can you help me with something? The zip ties are really tight, and I'm losing circulation in my hands."

"I don't think so," the guard said. "I've heard that one before. Just sit tight, and Mr. Borovitch will be down to deal with you soon."

Layne could now hear the faint echo of gunshots above their heads. If the melee above was still concentrated in the casino area, he guessed they were directly underneath it. Hard to be sure, though.

Serena huffed an angry sigh. Layne knew how she felt. There didn't seem to be a good way to escape, and their guard knew it. He stared ahead, probably daydreaming about what he would have for dinner tonight.

He wasn't paying much attention to them, actually.

Staring at the guard's gun, Layne came to a conclusion. This guy would not shoot them, not after the lecture Artyom had given about how painfully they would die. No way would this guard steal that privilege from Artyom. So, he would resist pulling the trigger, even if confronted. But, the head-on approach still held too many risks. There were no guarantees he wouldn't shoot.

Looking around the room, an idea formed. Layne was only a couple feet away from a wine rack. Since they'd only cuffed his hands and not his ankles, that gave him a chance.

He waited another moment until the guard's head tilted down so he could look at something on his phone. Quietly, Layne lifted a leg and placed it on a nearby eight-foot-tall rack piled high with bottles of wine.

"What are you doing?" Serena whispered.

"When this thing topples," Layne said, "spread out. Make him choose."

As Layne pushed, the guard took notice at the sound of the bottles clinking together. The rack tilted toward him. He proceeded with one hesitant step forward, with the Glock still held low.

"Stop it, right now," the guard said, his eyes watching the rack creak and lean in his direction.

Layne pushed with all his might. The shelf cried and gave way as it toppled over. Wine bottles crashed to the floor. The guard lifted his hands to his face to protect it from splintering glass shards.

Layne jumped up, rushing to the left, and Serena took off to the right. The guard lowered his hands and his eyes whipped around, trying to locate his prisoners.

This spill of red wine immediately created a vast puddle reaching across half of the floor. The guard took one step in it and slipped, arms flailing backward as he fell. Layne and Serena closed in on him from either side.

Layne lifted his hands up over the man's head and neck, using the zip ties to strangle him as Serena freed him of his Glock. She wrapped her hands around his legs to keep him from kicking out of Layne's grasp.

Layne didn't kill him, but he did choke the man enough to send him to sleep. A few seconds more would've ended him. After lowering him to the ground, Layne went through his pockets and found a small knife which he used to cut the zip ties, and another Glock just like the one Serena had commandeered.

"Our phones?" she asked.

"I don't see them. We'll have to do without."

"Understood. Let's move. We need to get back up to the ground level."

They approached the door and found it locked from the outside. The unconscious guard didn't have the key.

"Got any other brilliant ideas?" Serena asked.

"Actually," Layne said, and he reached up and peeled off his big handlebar mustache. The guards or whoever had stripped Layne of his other weapons while he'd been unconscious, but they didn't think to take off his fake facial hair. He separated a lining of C-4 plastic explosive from the inside of the mustache.

"Okay, that's a good one," Serena said, nodding.

"And you made fun of me."

With her hands on her hips, Serena said, "I stand corrected."

Layne packed the C4 around the doorknob, then he

took off his left shoe and withdrew a small wire and a detonator from within the sole. He motioned to Serena to stand back and then he set the C4 to blow.

Both of them rushed around and hid behind a shelf of wine on the far side of the room. A second later, the door blew, an explosion sending a puff of smoke into the room. But it worked. The door bent back on its hinges, letting the faraway sounds of gunfire waft in from the rest of the hotel.

Now armed, Layne and Serena left their basement prison to rush into the melee.

51

They decided to split up to cover more ground. The interior of the hotel/casino was like a spider web, so disbanding made sense. The initial fracas in the casino had dispersed, and now there were dozens of smaller altercations between cops and Winged House people all over.

Someone had confiscated their phones while unconscious, so they agreed to meet in the lobby in thirty minutes if their paths didn't cross sooner.

Serena moved up to the hotel floors to scout for Pavel. As far as she could tell, Artyom, Goran, and the bulk of the cops and Winged House people were either down on the first floor or up on the higher floors. As she stayed on the edges and inventoried the people, Pavel did not seem to be among them.

As much as she wanted to confront Artyom and Goran now, the smarter play would be to find and restrain Pavel. Especially since he was their prize, for whatever reason.

And Pavel would hunt them, probably with the intention of killing both.

She knew he was too smart to go at them directly. So, she figured he might skulk around the floors above, looking for a route around. Waiting to pick them off one by one when there were fewer guns on his side.

Serena was guessing at that detail since she still had no idea *why* Pavel was doing any of this. Layne had claimed Artyom and Goran didn't care about the senator at all; that it was all a ruse to draw Pavel out. She didn't know if that information would prove useful or not.

On the third floor, she exited the stairs to find a man with tattoos all over his neck skulking after a trail of blood along the carpet. In one hand, he held what looked like a piece of a window pane, with a sliver of broken glass at one end. Like a wooden and glass ax.

Since she hadn't expected to find anyone here, she wasn't able to turn and stop the door from shutting behind her in time. It slammed shut, and the tattooed man halted in his tracks. When he wheeled on her, she didn't see anything on his clothing to indicate he was police or some type of government official. A cop wouldn't carry such a strange weapon, anyway.

He took a swing at her, and she leaned back, out of range of his hunk of wood. A quick knee to the groin got his attention. She then slugged him with a left hook since the gun was in her right and she didn't want to start shooting. Not until she knew who else was on this floor.

Also, where that streak of blood would lead.

She jabbed him in the nose and then swept his legs out from underneath him. His weapon went flying from his hand, and the glass part shattered against the wall. He stumbled back and cracked the back of his head against an end table sitting next to the elevators. Eyes shut, he slid to the floor.

Serena waited a moment to see if he would rise, but he didn't. She checked him for other weapons and found none. Then, she turned her attention back to the streak of blood on the floor. Pistol out, she followed it down the hall. Drips and drops painted a trail along the carpet, weaving from one side to the other. Up ahead at a four-way hallway crossing, it stopped.

She squinted and tightened her grip on the pistol as she stepped out into the crossing.

Thunk.

She'd seen the base of the heavy thing only a split second before it connected with her forehead. A heavy brass lamp. The object's base smacked against her a second time, and she became instantly woozy. The gun slipped from her hand, thudding onto the carpet below.

Pavel had been hiding around the corner and had smacked her with the lamp. As she staggered and tried to keep her eyes from shutting, she looked him up and down for injuries. He didn't appear to have any. The blood in the hall had been fake, or someone else's.

Tricky Pavel. Probably his doing, to draw flies into his spiderweb.

She fell to her knees, head swimming. Pavel lowered the lamp and studied her. As she fought to stay awake, she realized this would be the third time he'd swindled her in the last two days. Unbelievable. If this had been an officially sanctioned mission, Daphne would probably never let her hear the end of it.

Serena tried to stand and again slipped, falling onto

her back. Pavel hovered over her, grabbed onto her hands, and dragged her down the hall.

"Why?" she said, her words labored and distant.

"Because of what they have done," he said as he dragged her down the hall. "At first, only because of what they did to my family. That would have been enough. When I would lie awake in my little cell in that dark dungeon, I would think of them, and how I would avenge them. But, you were the one to tell me about Noah Smith. That changed everything."

"The... school shooter kid?"

Pavel paused, his mouth vibrating, on the verge of tears. "He was a good boy. A smart and talented child. Look what they did to him, how they made him do that awful thing inside the school. They will pay for the pawns they have used."

He resumed dragging her.

"Why?" Serena asked again, on the verge of passing out.

"I already told you."

"No, why do they... want you so bad? Why did they go to all this trouble?"

Pavel opened the door of a maintenance closet and shoved her inside. He knelt next to her. "I do not know. And it does not matter. After they are dead, I will be gone. Mexico, then South America, and then back to Belarus. Because, unlike them, *I do* care about home. I want to make it better, not just make talk. When I am free of Goran and Artyom, I can make use of my remaining years."

She checked her surroundings. Pavel noted there was an emergency ax on the wall, and he used the small chained hammer to break the glass. He pulled out the ax. When she shied away, he knelt again. "I am not going to kill you, Serena Rojas. You did me a great service by saving me in Thailand. But, I cannot let you stop me from killing Artyom and Goran. I know that is your goal. You want them arrested so they can enter your justice system. I cannot allow them to slip away, which I know they will do."

Bleary, she tried to concentrate. Her thoughts were like bubbles on the surf. "Don't do this."

"I am sorry that I have treated you this way. You do not deserve this, but I am afraid this is how it has to be."

He stepped back and shut the door. Then she heard the sound of the ax blade wedging into the crack between the door and door jamb, sealing her inside the closet.

And then, she succumbed to unconsciousness.

52

Goran Smith raced across the lobby, chasing after the back of someone's head. He couldn't say for sure it was Pavel, but he had a strong suspicion. The person in question disappeared into the casino, and Goran leaped over dead bodies and skidded through puddles of blood to close the distance.

Artyom's minions were dealing with the police in little clusters around the hotel. Keeping them at bay. The Winged House had proved to be an excellent recruiting tool, based on the sheer numbers of ex-convicts Artyom had brought with him today. Even over the last few days, while Goran had been out of town, Artyom had seemingly doubled their numbers.

Many of them had been surprised to see him when he'd appeared at Winged House after his rebirth from the ashes of his "heart attack." Faking his own death had been an arduous process, but one Goran thought necessary. Had he stayed around, he would have spent days under the microscope of law enforcement for what Noah had done in that school. There were too many other important tasks to accomplish and little time to do so.

But, none of that mattered now. Only Pavel mattered. Especially, finding and killing Pavel before Artyom had a chance to do it.

Pavel had been a fool to return. He should have fled far away from here. But, Pavel had always been a fool.

He wouldn't be a fool for much longer.

After dealing with Pavel, Goran would confront Artyom. They would have a serious talk about Goran's only son, who had been sacrificed for the cause. A bullet from a sniper as he walked out of the school.

It was not supposed to be that way. After Noah's mission in the school, the plan had been to smuggle him out of the country and send him to Belarus, a hero.

Not murdered in the street like a dog.

Yes, Goran would talk to Artyom about that. There would be a reckoning. When Goran had been masquerading as Zabojca in Thailand, it had been easy to downplay the awful thing that had happened to Noah. But now, back in America, there were no excuses.

Artyom would pay for taking his son away from him.

Goran pulled back the door to the casino and stared into the face of a cop in full riot gear. Big yellow letters SWAT across his chest.

The cop gasped and fumbled for the sling of his AR-15. Before he could raise it, Goran whipped out his knife and drove the point into the cop's neck, just under the buckle of his helmet.

"Not today," Goran said as he pushed the knife deeper. The cop staggered back, and Goran kept pace with him. A macabre dance. Blood cascaded down the knife, coating his hand. Arms flailing, the cop bled out as he tried to escape from the blade.

When the cop's eyes turned glassy and the body too heavy to support, Goran withdrew the knife and let the body fall to the floor. The casino room had turned eerily quiet. Artyom's ex-con minions had drawn the police officers into the hotel portion of the building, maybe even into the upper floors. Smart. Keep them divided and out of the open areas of the casino and conference center, to put the police at a disadvantage in a standoff. One of the main reasons they had chosen this hotel as the place to kidnap the senator.

Of course, the senator mattered no longer. Now, with Pavel a free man, the senator could live or die, and Goran didn't care one bit.

For some reason, Marta the Mongolian appeared in Goran's thoughts. A memory all the way back from his teenage years in Belarus. He saw her face, frozen in time from that day at the train station, swaddled in her winter clothing. And, he asked himself why he never tried to track her down after that. In today's world, with the power of the internet, it could have been possible. Anything could have been possible if Goran had made different choices.

None of that mattered anymore. Only finding Pavel and recovering the prize. Recovering the key to everything that would come after.

Goran swept his eyes across the room. No Pavel.

But, within a few seconds, someone came running out from a hallway on the far side. Artyom.

"I saw him," Goran shouted across the distance. He

pointed to the back of the room. "I saw him running that way."

Then, Goran hustled across the room to join Artyom. Because, if he couldn't get to Pavel first, then he could at least be with Artyom when they found him together. Much easier to kill Artyom that way.

———

Artyom exited the hallway after searching the casino bathrooms, and he encountered Goran on the casino floor. Bloody knife in his hand, with a cop at his feet, bleeding out. The line of blood extended up Goran's hand and forearm. Chest heaving, he stood over his victim, glaring down at the dead police officer.

Something in Goran's eyes didn't seem right. Malice there that felt beyond what they were trying to accomplish today.

Artyom's growing itch of doubt had morphed into a festering sore. Goran looked up and shouted something about seeing Pavel, and he pointed toward a side exit. All around them the lights and sounds of the casino still buzzed and beeped.

"You saw him?" Artyom asked.

Goran nodded as he liberated the police officer of his assault rifle. "I came in here to chase him, but I had to deal with that police officer first."

"Good, good." Artyom narrowed the distance between them, stepping over several dead bodies. "Fortunate that I was also here, so we could do this together."

"As it should be."

Artyom jerked his rifle in the direction Goran had previously pointed. "Lead the way. All that's left is victory for us, so let's not wait to find it."

After a second's hesitation, Goran strutted off toward a door in the northwest corner of the room, and Artyom followed, two paces behind. Even as Goran marched, Artyom could feel him hesitant and expectant. Eyes in the rear of his head.

"Question for you," Artyom said. Still walking, Goran tilted his head back in Artyom's direction.

"Yes?"

"When you were in Thailand, you found the American woman and tracked her to the dark site, didn't you?"

"Yes, I did."

"And then, you found their safe house hidden in the jungle, didn't you?"

"True."

"And you even tracked them to the airport before they fled the country, yes?"

"Artyom, you know the answer to these questions is yes. What are you really asking?"

"Why did you not kill Pavel and the American woman, when you had so many opportunities?"

Now, Goran did stop crossing the room, and he turned to face Artyom. Artyom observed that Goran's rifle was still pointed at the ground. Artyom took pains to not look at it directly, but he kept it in his peripheral vision.

Goran winced. "It was not as easy as I had hoped it would be. I could have raided the jungle bunker, but found it much easier to let her spring him from captivity."

"Let her do all the work, then you sweep in like a vulture?"

"Yes," Goran said, "like that. But, the route she took to get to the safe house was too complicated. I lost her. By the time I found them again, she was ready for me. Same at the airport."

"So, you were outwitted by a girl?"

"By a woman who is clearly a highly trained operative."

Artyom hesitated for only a split second. When the change happened in Goran's eyes, Artyom saw it instantly.

Like a slash of lightning, he sprang into action.

Artyom had kept his left hand on the barrel of his assault rifle, and his right hand on the stock. He swung up and forward with his right, cracking the stock into Goran's nose.

Then, with his left hand, he jabbed the barrel of the rifle into Goran's mouth. With a crunch like glass breaking, several of Goran's teeth separated and flew in varied directions like grenade shrapnel.

Goran staggered and tried to raise his weapon, but Artyom was on him in a flash. He leaped forward and hit Goran in the face with his own rifle before lifting the sling over his head and tossing it aside.

"I know you plan to betray me," Artyom said, seething, as he punched Goran in the nose three times in rapid succession. His colleague's nose crumbled under the repeated attacks.

As Goran fell to his knees, Artyom cracked him with a right hook, sending him to the ground. "With Pavel free,

Omega has to change. And part of that change is no longer needing your services."

Goran tried to grip the blade sheathed on his belt, but Artyom snatched the hand and bent it back. Goran cried out, and Artyom used the pressure to turn him face down. Prone on the ground, he no longer had any leverage.

Nearby, clutched in the grip of a dead police officer, were a set of handcuffs. Artyom snagged them and cuffed Goran's hands behind his back.

Standing over him, Artyom gritted his teeth. "Pavel is mine alone, betrayer. His prize is not for you. It is for Belarus, and I alone will make sure everything is as it should be. I knew you would turn on me, but I did not want to see it."

Panting, spitting blood, Goran made no effort to rise or fight back. "You killed my son," he said, blood bubbling from his lips, his speech muddled due to lack of teeth. "You didn't have to do that. We could have sneaked him out of the country. It could have worked."

Artyom swung his rifle around and pointed it at the back of Goran's head. He wrapped his finger around the trigger.

Then, an idea struck. Instead of killing Goran, he might provide a use when the police would come to clean this mess. Pinning crimes on Layne had failed, but maybe Goran could serve that purpose.

Artyom turned the rifle around, hoisting the stock into the air.

"Noah had to be sacrificed. I think maybe he understood that better than you do. But, you're still useful, Goran. You will have one more task to provide for Belarus. And that is to take the blame for all this."

Then, he slammed the rifle stock on Goran's head, sending him into dreamland.

When Artyom stood up straight his back ached. His head swirled with exhaustion. But, it didn't matter. He still had to find Pavel.

53

WITHOUT HIS CELL PHONE, LAYNE WAS IN THE DARK. He hustled into the stairwell on the second floor of the hotel and then dashed up the stairs toward 3. A small Glock clutched in his hand.

In the stairwell, he could hear gunshots and commotion above, on the fourth or fifth floor. The cops seemed to push the terrorists higher and higher, which had been a smart move. Trapped by height.

Serena hadn't been on floor 2. If she wasn't on 3, then he wasn't sure what to do. He didn't want to intermingle with the cops and Winged House ex-cons on the upper floors. Also, he couldn't keep looking for her forever. He had to stop Artyom and Goran before they could flee or find Pavel.

So, if he didn't find her here, he would have to give up.

At the top of the stairwell, a dead security guard sat, slumped over on the landing above the top step. Bullet holes from his stomach to his chest. But, the thing that caught Layne's attention was the phone in his hand, and the headphone cord trailing from the phone to an earbud sitting in the man's ear.

Layne took the headphones and phone and then used the man's thumb to unlock it. Then, he changed the phone's settings so it wouldn't automatically go to sleep and therefore re-enable the security lock. No use carrying around a locked phone. He gave the dead man a moment of silent thanks for donating his phone to the cause, and then Layne rushed across the landing to the next floor.

He paused to press his ear against the door. No sound of gunshots came back.

Out onto the third floor, Layne eased forward. A long window opposite a bank of elevators overlooked the back parking lot behind the hotel. Mountains shrouded in clouds.

And, when he saw the parking lot's layout, an idea formed. Layne inserted the earbud into his ear and made a phone call.

"Hello?"

"Harry, it's me."

"Layne? What's this number you're calling me from?"

"It's a long story. Remember how I said I need you on standby? Now's the time, man. I have an idea, and I need it in the next few minutes."

"Sure, whatever you need. I'm at my computer, ready to go."

"I'm at the Tuscany hotel in Black Hawk. It's a new building, so can I assume that all the building controls are networked?"

"Probably, yeah."

"Do you think you can hack into that network?"

Harry paused, breathing. "It's possible."

"I need better than possible, K-Books. It's important."

"I can't make you any promises, but I can work on it. I'll need a few minutes to investigate, at least. Let me call you back when I know a little more."

Layne thanked him and then ended the call. He left the phone unlocked and the earbud in as he pushed on down the hall, foot over foot. Harry's help could make or break the next fifteen minutes.

A trail of blood on the floor caught Layne's attention, and so he skidded to a stop. Heart thumping, adrenaline throttling his ears. He had to be careful.

His feet pushed forward, tracking the blood along the hallway. Up ahead at a hall intersection, it stopped. Layne eased to the edge and took a breath.

He leaped out into the crossing and spun around. Checked all visible corners for hostiles. No one there.

But, he did note a peculiar door, a few feet down the hall. Peculiar because there was an ax forced into the space between the door and door jamb. Someone had gone to great lengths to keep this door forced shut.

Layne shoved the pistol into his waistband and grabbed hold of the ax handle. Bracing a foot against the wall, he yanked. The wood around the door creaked and groaned and then splintered as the ax worked loose. After one big, grunting yank, it came free, and Layne stumbled back a few steps.

He opened the door. Serena was there, crumpled in a heap on the floor. Motionless.

His throat constricted.

"No," he said, then he knelt next to her. Two fingers against her neck, he did feel a pulse. Dim, but there.

A cleansing breath whooshed out of his lips.

"Come on," he said, giving her light slaps against each cheek. After a few of these, her eyes fluttered.

"What?" she mumbled.

"On your feet, Pepper."

Serena blinked a few times, then her eyes snapped awake. She drew in a deep breath. "Pavel... he sucker-punched me. He is trying to find Goran and Artyom."

"It's okay. You're okay. But, we do need to go."

"Are they still here?"

Layne nodded. "The senator and his people made it out already. There are cops and some of Artyom's people in a bunch of little standoffs on the floors above us. We're not going to worry about them for now."

"Pavel?"

"I can't find Pavel," Layne said. "So, our focus needs to stay on containing Artyom and Goran before they can catch him, if they haven't already."

"How do we do that?"

"I saw something in the parking lot a couple minutes ago. I know exactly what Artyom's plan is. But I need your help." Layne stood and gripped his weapon. "So, on your feet."

54

Pavel Rusiecki exited the back door of the casino as soon as he saw Goran enter the far side of the room. He wasn't ready to confront them yet, not in a large space where anything could happen. Pavel's limbs were like noodles. His pulse thumped in the side of his neck. He needed to take them out one at a time, in a place where he could regain the territorial advantage.

He wished now he hadn't used up his one knockout pill on Serena earlier in the day. It might've come in handy. He now had only her pistol. There were plenty of weapons he could have taken from the dead in the casino or in the conference rooms or in the hotel floors above. But something about that did not feel right.

Besides, he only needed two bullets. One for Goran, for sending his son Noah to die. And the second bullet for Artyom, for his probable part in the arrest and deaths of Pavel's wife and child. For his betrayal.

Pavel couldn't know for certain Artyom had been involved, but he'd spent many nights in that dungeon in

Thailand, trying to puzzle through it. Artyom arranging it all was the only explanation that made sense.

On the other side of the door, he found himself in a long, dark hall. A glowing green EXIT sign lit up the far end, thirty or forty meters away.

Pavel tried to walk normally, but the ache in his limbs and his wheezing breaths made it a challenge. He knew he should turn around and face Goran. The man deserved to die a thousand times for what he had done. As did Artyom. The two of them together had poisoned young Noah's mind. They had made him believe shooting up a school full of children would aid some vague cause in Belarus.

None of it made any sense. Not the shooting, or why Artyom had worked so hard to free Pavel from confinement, only to send an assassin to kill him.

Pavel would force the answer from Artyom as he died. The truth would come out.

At the door under the exit sign, Pavel steeled himself. Based on the curvature of the hallway, he assumed this opened into the main lobby. From there, he would circle back and come at Goran from behind. Only with the element of surprise could Pavel be assured in victory.

He pushed open the door. A fist greeted his face as he stepped into the light.

Artyom's smug smirk appeared behind the fist. In that instant, Pavel knew it all. Everything he'd feared had been confirmed.

This man had sent Pavel's family to their deaths.

He tried to raise his hands to defend himself, but another blow rocked him, making him stagger back a step. His thoughts scrambled.

Omega Trap

He swayed on his feet. Eyes forced shut. Pavel raised the pistol and squeezed the trigger, but it jammed. Not that it mattered since he couldn't see to shoot.

Before he could do anything to stop it, he was spinning, driving forward, being pushed. Strong arms tossing him about like a rag doll. His feet went out from under him, and he sailed downward, smacking against the cold surface. His forehead connected with the marble floor. Instantly woozy. Next, an unbearable weight pressed against Pavel's back. He cried out and craned his neck to see Artyom kneeling on him, forcing him into the unforgiving floor.

"Hello, Pavel. Welcome back to America."

Pavel tried to respond, but with all the pressure, he couldn't open his mouth. The pain had paralyzed him.

Artyom opened a knife, and Pavel felt the blade slice into his back. First, a burning sensation of cutting flesh. Then, the warmth of his blood rushing out, coating his skin.

"Pavel," Artyom said as he sliced open a spot on Pavel's lower back. "Thank you for making my task of finding you so dead simple. I thought we would have to chase you across Europe to recover the data."

"What are you doing?" Pavel asked, grunting against the pain.

"Do you not remember the night we went out drinking, and you probably awoke the next day with a sharp pain in your back? Did you never wonder what this small scar was? Maybe you didn't. Did you not ever see it, coming out of the shower some morning? Or, did they have no mirrors for you to check in prison in Thailand?"

When Pavel responded only with a muted whimper,

Artyom continued. "It's no matter. Storing the device *inside* you was Goran's idea from the start. He did not want the keys anywhere online or kept in a safe somewhere. Always so paranoid, that Goran. And, like I said, we were drunk, and you were passed out, and Goran made the decision.

"I was opposed to it, because I wondered what would happen if you decided to leave, or you were caught up in something and taken away from us." Artyom chuckled. "And that is the great irony, isn't it? You were chosen to carry the data because you had the only legitimate passport and we deemed you the safest of the three of us. I had planned to keep you in Europe, so we could extract the card there and not have to worry about it being confiscated by Customs. Yet, two days later you suddenly left the country, and soon after, you were the one to find yourself arrested!"

Pavel felt Artyom's fingers dig inside his flesh. Pavel tried to gulp air and couldn't catch his breath. This couldn't be happening. They'd put a thing inside him?

"It's no matter, now," Artyom said as he plucked something from Pavel's back. Pavel felt it leave, like a giant splinter dislodging from his flesh. "You have served Belarus, whether you wanted to or not. And, after every futile measure we tried to retrieve you from the clutches of the US government, you came back to us willingly. Goran will not be here to share in the glory, however." Artyom paused, breathing. "You will not share in the glory, either, but your part in this equation is complete."

Artyom bent down and held out his bloody hand, clutching something between his fingers. A MicroSD card, encased in wax.

Pavel's eyes flared. He tried to speak, but words escaped him. The blood rushing under him had now cooled. A shiver ran through him as his body temperature dropped and his eyes wanted to shut.

"Yes," Artyom said, "this was inside you. A card with the bank codes and all the encryption keys. This is a quarter of a billion dollars, my old friend. Enough to make a difference in Belarus. Enough to topple the silly puppet government and set the ship back on course."

The pressure lifted from Pavel's back as Artyom stood. Pavel heaved in a breath, and it came out in a wet cough. Weakness kept him pinned to the floor even though Artyom was no longer forcing him down.

He tried to place his palms on the floor to push, but his hands had no strength.

"Belarus thanks you, Pavel. Your sacrifice will not be forgotten." Then, after a pause, the squawk of a walkie-talkie echoed in the large room. "Raisa, I have it. I am on my way."

Artyom's footfalls bounced off the marble. At first loud, and then growing softer, until a door opened and shut, and the lobby became quiet.

Pavel tried one more time to lift himself. He shuddered, frigid and panicked. All the sensation in his arms and legs had fled.

Pavel blinked once, twice, and then shut his eyes.

55

This was the plan: Raisa would be the bait. Artyom and Goran would emerge out the back door to rendezvous with her, then Layne and Serena would close in from opposite sides. Layne in the front and Serena from behind. Harry would remotely lock the doors from the inside, forcing Artyom and Goran to either engage or to flee to the side, where a collection of cop cars had previously blocked off the exit road.

The back lot of the Tuscany hotel in Black Hawk was a triangle, butting up to a steep and craggy hillside on two sides, which left only one side of the triangle for an exit to the highway. A small thing, not much bigger than a basketball court. Layne had spied the scene out the second-floor window of the hotel a few minutes ago. He'd seen Raisa waiting out there next to the dumpster. She had been sitting on the hood of a Toyota FJ Cruiser, walkie-talkie in hand. The getaway car.

Now, Layne was behind the dumpster, Glock trained on Raisa, with the FJ Cruiser's keys in his pocket. She was next to the Toyota, facing the back door of the casino. A few seconds ago, Artyom had used the walkie-talkie to contact her, and she had performed admirably. If she'd given Artyom a signal, Layne hadn't detected it.

"Harry," Layne said into the earbud dangling from his ear, "you ready?"

"I think so," Harry said.

"Think so?"

"I'm hacked into the building network, but I can't guarantee the locks will respond when I send the command. The system keeps trying to kick me out."

"I see. Well, keep on it, I guess."

"It'll work," Harry said but didn't sound confident.

Layne considered saying a few words of encouragement, but held off. Best to let Harry work in peace.

Then, Layne stood in wait. Serena was a few feet from the door, hiding behind a large rubber bin on wheels, which Layne figured had something to do with the hotel's laundry services.

Ideally, Layne would take Artyom and Serena could handle Goran.

Part of Layne wanted to take on Goran directly, though. To bash in his face for what he'd done to Jenna. For what he'd done to Noah. He deserved to have his face smashed over and over again.

But Layne had to be rational. To keep his wits about him. This was not about revenge, rather, it was about stopping criminals from committing further crimes.

There were four complications. One, Serena had to be able to sneak up behind them without being seen. Two, Layne had to let them both advance far enough to guarantee he could cleanly shoot either of them if something went wrong. Three, the door lock hack had to work to keep them from retreating inside. And four, he needed to keep Raisa compliant and under control long enough to spring his trap.

"If you signal them in any way," Layne said to her, "I'll shoot you in your foot. Is that clear?"

Through gritted teeth, Raisa mumbled her consent to the rule.

The back door opened. Layne retreated behind the dumpster and held out the small pocket mirror, angled to see the door. The other hand on the Glock, with Raisa's foot lined up in the sights.

Only Artyom stepped out through the door. Layne waited for Goran to appear reflected in the mirror, but the door shut behind him. What was going on here?

Layne wanted to ask Raisa, but he couldn't risk it. Was Goran going to sneak around the side? Had their cover been blown?

"Harry," Layne whispered, "how is that door lock control working?"

After a pause, Harry made a quizzical *hmmph* sound. "It's not responding. The door lock/unlock status isn't reportable anymore. I'll work on it, but it might take a minute or two."

Layne might not have a minute or two. He breathed through the frustration, holding the gun and the mirror in place.

Artyom strolled forward, a pistol in his hand. Something else clutched in his other hand, which appeared to be bloody. The object looked small. He shoved the thing into his pocket and picked up the pace.

Layne kept his eyes on Raisa. So far, she'd been a statue.

And then, she gave a subtle shake of the head. Barely enough for Layne to notice. He checked Artyom's reaction. The man's step hitched and his head angled.

He'd seen her warning.

Layne jumped out from behind the dumpster. He wrapped a hand around Raisa's neck and lowered the pistol, using her shoulder to steady his aim.

"Easy, Artyom. Put down the gun."

But Artyom did no such thing. He spread his legs and aimed down the sight, but he didn't shoot. He stood firm, breathing, arms locked and one eye shut.

Although Layne was using Raisa as a human shield, he didn't want to see her dead. He was wagering on the hope that Artyom wouldn't have it in his heart to sacrifice her.

Layne checked Serena out of his peripheral. He flashed his eyes at her to keep her back. If Artyom caught wind of anything, he might shoot. Plus, he needed to keep her in reserve for when Goran showed up.

Raisa bellowed something in Belarusian that Layne couldn't quite understand, and Artyom nodded at her.

"Drop it now, Artyom. It's over. There's no way you're getting out of this parking lot alive unless you put down the gun."

Artyom held steady. "Why do you keep appearing like a neighborhood dog whining for scraps at my door? What must I do to rid myself of you?"

A moment of silence passed. Faraway rattles of gunfire came from inside the hotel. The sound of a siren echoing off the mountain walls in the town.

"Rez is dead, isn't he?" Artyom said.

Layne nodded. "I smelled your trap right away. Were you going to pin the school shooting on me?"

"If possible, yes. But I misjudged your abilities, and that was my mistake."

From somewhere, glass broke. Layne's eyes shot up to see a window on the third-floor shatter, and the barrels of two AR-15s appear in the space where the window had been. Two bald-headed white guys leaned out the window, pointing their rifles at Layne.

Artyom craned his neck to look up above at his two henchmen, then he grinned at Layne. "Seems you are now outnumbered, Layne. Why don't you let Raisa go?"

"I am not afraid to die," Raisa said without a hint of anxiety in her voice.

"Even better," Artyom said. He tilted his head toward the men above while keeping his eyes on Layne. "Men! If this person holding Raisa does not let her go within ten seconds, open fire on him."

Layne's chest tensed. From their elevated position, they had too much of an advantage. If he even tried to lift his gun in their direction, they would blast both him and Raisa. If Serena made an appearance, they'd cut her down, too.

Ten seconds. Nine. Eight.

56

First, Goran blinked, then he drew a breath. Every part of his body hurt. His mouth most of all. The sickening realization that he had lost many of his teeth permeated his brain like the slow ooze of lava cascading down the side of a volcano.

His body urged him to return to sleep and let the world dissolve. But, a voice in the back of his brain screamed at him to rise. It told him he still had tasks to complete. The world was still not right.

No rest yet.

There was still time to exact justice for Noah. Still time to recover the prize from Pavel.

Artyom first, then Pavel.

When Goran sat up, his broken nose throbbed. His jaw felt as if it were hanging by a thread. Head bleary, eyes wanting to shut. He had to spend every ounce of energy to keep himself upright, and he stayed like this for an eternity until he felt confident he wouldn't pass out again.

The outside world faded into existence. The blinking lights, the repetitive sounds of the casino.

When he couldn't move his arms, he realized his hands were cuffed behind him. A flash of panic exploded in his chest. There were police everywhere, and they would sweep through this room at any second now.

Go. Have to go. Now.

How could he do anything with these handcuffs?

But then, Goran's eyes landed on a dead body on the floor, five feet away. A police officer, actually. A set of handcuff keys sitting on the carpet next to his bullet-riddled body.

Plus, a shotgun.

57

An idea jumped up inside Layne's head.

"Harry," he said into his earpiece. "Forget the door. Turn on the sprinklers on the third floor. Do it now, please."

"Uhh," Harry said in his ear. "One second. Yeah, I think I can do that."

A moment later, while Layne's internal clock silently ticked, a sound came from the open window. The armed men looked up as a spray descended from above. They both raised their arms to shield themselves from the foam cascading down on them.

Layne lifted his pistol and squeezed off six shots. Four missed, breaking glass on the fourth floor. But, the final two shots hit home. One smacked into the chest of the man on the right, knocking him back. The other bullet punctured a hole in the stomach of the man on the left. He leaned forward and fell out of the open window, crashing down onto the ground, five feet in front of

Serena. He didn't move at all after crumpling onto the pavement.

Layne had two bullets left in the Glock.

During the shooting, Artyom made no attempt to run or hide or retaliate. Steadfast, weapon raised as if waiting for his turn.

Layne met his eyes, unblinking. "That's it, Artyom. Your backup is gone. Put down the gun."

Again, Artyom declined. Instead, he grinned.

His finger wrapped around the trigger.

Layne tried to move Raisa out of the way, but it was too late. Three quick shots pelted her body. Two in the stomach, one in the chest. Maybe Artyom thought he could shoot through her and tag Layne, but the bullets did not pass beyond her body.

Layne pushed her to the ground, hoping she might not immediately die from the injuries. Once clear, he jumped to the side and aimed down the sight of the Glock. Two more bullets passed directly over his head.

Layne pressed the trigger. A bullet ripped into Artyom's chest, knocking him back. No blood. He was probably wearing a vest.

Serena took one shot, and the bullet cut a hole in Artyom's side. That one had drawn blood. He twisted, heaved a breath, and then fell to his knees.

Layne rushed forward, holding up a hand to keep Serena back.

Artyom sat back on his heels. The gun slipped from his fingers. He opened his mouth to speak, but a gush of blood escaped his lips. Then, he slumped over.

His eyes fluttered as blood rushed out of the hole in his side.

As Layne leaned down to check his pulse, the back door opened. Goran Smith stumbled out. In one hand, he was holding a Mossberg 590A1 Tactical Shotgun. A set of handcuffs dangled from his free wrist.

Goran's eyes were bleary and his gait swooping, like a zombie. Blood caked his chin. But he held the shotgun with the care of a man intent on using it. Pointed directly at Layne.

"You stupid asshole," Goran said, stumbling forward, eyes shooting daggers at Layne. When he spoke, he sounded like he had no teeth. "You ruined everything."

Serena swept into action. Carefully placing each foot, she scooted out from her hiding spot and traced his steps. Light on her feet, she positioned herself in his wake.

Seeing this, Layne set the Glock on the ground and lifted his hands into the air. "I'm not armed, Goran. Let's talk about this."

Goran spat a gob of blood as he lurched forward. "Your lack of a gun doesn't mean I won't kill you."

"Your own son, Goran. How could you do that to your own son?"

"You wouldn't understand."

Goran came to a halt fifteen feet away. With a breath, he hoisted the shotgun high enough to level it with his eye. He sneered down at Artyom. "Is he dead?"

Layne shook his head. "I don't know. If he's not, he will be soon."

Serena closed the distance as Goran peered down at his fallen comrade.

With a quick sweep of the leg, she knocked Goran off balance, then she gave him a shove to send him to the ground. He toppled over and crashed. She kicked the shotgun away and stood over him, pistol in his face.

Layne snatched up his pistol and marched across the parking lot. He stopped in front of Goran, on his back, his eyes swimming as he looked up at Serena.

Layne pointed the gun and wrapped his finger around the trigger. His heart thudded in his chest. So many feelings swirled around in his head. All the years he'd casually known Goran, and he had never seen this side of him. Layne had never suspected he was anything more than a dad Layne would box with at the gym on weekday nights from time to time.

The betrayal gripped Layne like a hand, squeezing him. He pictured a teenaged version of his daughter Cameron, marching into a school with an assault rifle in her hand. That image bled into flashes of Goran sending his son to die at that school. Then, Goran lifting a pistol to put a bullet in Jenna's face.

One bullet left in the Glock.

His anger urged him to press the trigger.

"What are you doing?" Serena asked, scowling at Layne's pointed gun.

Layne took a few breaths. Goran made no move to fight back, or flee, or cower. He was too disoriented to do anything but stare.

Layne stowed his pistol and flexed his hands. Then, he leaned down and punched Goran in the face.

INTERLUDE 5

DENVER, CO | SIXTEEN YEARS AGO

Layne wakes from a nap in his hospital bed at Saint Joseph. As his eyes blink open, he tilts his head toward the window to check the amount of daylight left. The last thing he remembers is finishing his lunch. He would hate to sleep through the day, even though he has nothing better to do as he recovers from his injuries.

The sun filters through the nearby buildings, bits of sunlight reflected off glass surfaces. He can't see the mountains from here, and that's a shame. In the fraction of a second when the gunman at the school pointed the assault rifle at him, he considered how much he would miss the mountains if he died. The prospect of never hiking up a trail or lighting a camp stove ever again.

Next thing, he realizes someone is sitting in a chair on the non-window side. He flinches.

"Easy," says a smoky female voice. "I didn't mean to startle you. You were asleep when I came in."

Layne shifts in the bed to get a better look at her and now takes in the visage of a beautiful woman. For a moment, he's stunned. Tall, shapely, curly brown hair, with a flirtatious smile etched on her face. Maybe a year or two older than him. A perfect ten in a pale blue business suit.

"How did you get in here?" Layne says, and his voice comes out creaky. He hasn't spoken much in the last couple of days since he's been here. "I don't have anyone on my visitor list."

The woman sighs and then flicks her chin at the bandages covering both of his forearms. "Tattoos."

"Excuse me?"

"My uncle Jeff worked at the GM plant in Detroit. There was an accident on the line, and he got nasty cuts all over his arms and hands. He covered them up with tattoos, and you couldn't hardly tell the difference after."

Layne looks down at the bandages. He barely remembers diving through the glass railing, crashing into the floor below as the second shooter blasted shots after him. He knows his arms are cut up pretty bad, but he hasn't seen the extent of the damage yet.

"No thank you. I'm not a tattoo kind of guy."

The woman shrugs. "Just keep it in mind. You'd think arm sleeves would make you stand out more, but not as much as scars up and down your flesh. Besides, girls love a guy with tattoos."

He sits up, which brings a wince of pain to his midsection. "Who are you?"

"Both shooters are going to live, in case you were curious about that. Well, they'll live long enough for the state to put them to death in prison, that is."

He glares. "Who are you?"

"Daphne Kurek. I flew to Denver to see you, Layne."

She extends a hand, and he grips it, despite the pain caused by flexing his wrist. It just happens; he doesn't think about what he's doing.

So many questions run through his mind at once, he doesn't know where to start. Before he can pick one, she digs a business card out of her purse and hands it to him. All it says is *Daphne Kurek - Head of Operations,* with a phone number below that. Not a local area code.

She leans forward in her chair. "What made you decide to run into that student center building on campus, Layne? When everyone else was running away from the gunfire, you ran toward it. What was going on in your head right when it happened?"

"How do you even know about that? I was promised my name wouldn't get out."

"That's another question I have for you. Why don't you want the recognition? You could drink for free in Fort Collins for the rest of your life if you wanted to, but you're remaining anonymous. Why is that?"

He frowns. "I don't know. Fame and glory wasn't on my mind at all. I'm not a hero."

"But you are, and you don't seem to realize it. Why did you run into that building? Did you make a decision, or did it simply happen, like when someone throws a ball in your direction, and you reach out and grab it without thinking?"

"I don't know why I did it. There wasn't a conscious decision before I ran up the steps at the Lory. I just knew I had to go in there and help those people."

Daphne grins. "And you have no military or law enforcement training at all?"

"No more questions. It's time for you to answer some of mine."

She checks her watch and nods, so he continues. "How the hell do you know who I am? How did you find me? My friends don't even know I'm here."

"I work for the government. You've probably figured that out already."

"Are you FBI? CIA?"

She shakes her head. "No, I work for a much smaller organization. So small, actually, we don't have a name."

"I don't understand. What are you doing here?"

"You're almost done with your masters in Psychology, correct? Planning on a Ph.D. after?"

The number of facts this woman knows about him blows his mind. It makes his skin crawl. "I haven't decided yet. I might work in the field for a few years first."

"Interesting," she says, sitting back and crossing her long and slender legs. "I'm here to talk to you about an alternative, Layne Parrish."

"What alternative?"

Daphne offers him a wry smile, and it's equal parts alluring and unsettling. She has an intensity in her gaze that Layne doesn't know how to categorize. She's the sort of woman who gets what she wants. Layne can see that much.

"Layne, dear, I came to offer you a job."

58

Layne pulled his fist back from Goran's face and shook it out. He thought he might have broken one of his fingers against Goran's nose, but it seemed okay. He flexed his hand. The anger dissipated, a little at a time.

"You good?" Serena said.

Layne nodded as Goran, heavy-lidded, stirred below him. His face was a mess, all broken and bloodied.

"Yeah. Thank you."

"I know you wanted to shoot him," Serena said. "You made the right choice."

Layne said nothing. He dropped to a knee and gave Goran a little slap to get his attention. "I need to understand why you did this."

Goran sneered, now seeming more awake. "I did it for Belarus. I was going to keep some of the money, of course. The rest was for Belarus. But, I had to stop Artyom. If he got hold of it, we wouldn't have kept any for ourselves. His stupid principles always stand in the way of everything."

"Money?" Layne asked. "What money?"

Layne looked back over at Artyom, at his corpse prone on the ground. Also, he now noticed Raisa, who had sprawled next to the dumpster. She was motionless, blood pooled around her from the multiple shots. Layne studied her face, her eyes open and lifeless, her mouth still.

Keep some of the money.

Layne took the phone out of his pocket, the earbud still dangling from his ear. "We're all good here, Harry," he said into the phone. "Thank you for your help."

"Any time, Boy Scout," Harry said, and then hung up.

Layne remembered something as he coiled the headphones and put them away. Artyom's bloody hand. Shoving something into his pocket as he'd strolled out the back door of the casino. A tiny object he'd had clutched in his grip.

His prize.

An idea clicked into place.

"Do you have zip ties?" Layne asked.

Serena nodded and pulled out a couple from her back pocket. Layne cinched one around Goran's ankles, then another around his wrists.

With his mouth inches away from Goran's ear, Layne whispered, "Noah deserved a better father than you. If there's an afterlife, he and Jenna will be waiting to settle up with you. You better fucking believe that."

Goran closed his eyes and pressed his lips together, opting to say nothing.

Layne scurried back across the parking lot and knelt next to Artyom. He reached into the dead man's pocket and pulled out a tiny data card, encased in wax. Covered in blood.

When he asked himself why it was covered in blood, he understood why they had wanted Pavel so badly, alive or dead.

All the remaining pieces of the puzzle snapped into place at once. All of this—every single thing Artyom and Goran had done—was to retrieve this tiny MicroSD card, no bigger than a pinky nail.

They never needed Pavel. Artyom and Goran had only needed Pavel's body, to cut out this card. They had planted it *in* him to keep some data safe. Something to do with a large sum of money. Encryption keys or bank account numbers or something like that.

"We need to find Pavel," Layne said, and then he lumbered toward the casino. "If he's not already dead, he's gravely injured."

All of Layne's muscles seemed to seize up and ache at once, but he pushed himself forward anyway. Serena hopped up to follow and they raced inside together. Down a dark hallway, and then into the casino. Pavel wasn't among the dead, so they proceeded into the lobby.

He was there, face down on the marble floor in a growing pool of blood. At first, he was still. Layne and Serena came to a stop near the fountain, twenty feet away.

And then, Pavel blinked. There was a large gash along the rear of his shirt, near the right side of his lower back. Blood leaked out, contributing to a red river flowing out from his wizened frame.

Layne and Serena rushed to his side. Layne put pressure over the wound on his back, which made Pavel gasp and then groan. Serena lowered herself to the floor and held his hand.

"Stay with us," she said. "We're going to get you help."

"Sorry," he whispered. "I am so sorry. I was wrong. I was wrong about it all."

With the crash of glass across the room, a fresh round of cops burst through the door on the far side of the lobby. Shouting, weapons raised, spread out in a line.

Layne cleared his throat. "It's okay, Pavel. What's done is done, but no one else will die today. We're going to get you help."

EPILOGUE

Layne and Serena crossed the grass lawn, with the swing set in their sights. There, Inessa Parrish pushed Cameron in the swing, both of them giggling as her little blonde hair whipped forward and backward with each pass.

"Whoa," Serena said, under her breath. Not yet within Inessa's earshot. "Your ex is tall. Is she a model or something?"

"She is, actually," Layne said in a matter-of-fact tone.

Serena didn't seem to have a response for this, and by now, Cameron had seen Layne. The little girl started yelping for her mother to extract her from the swing.

Inessa caught the swing chair and slowed it, then lifted the little girl out. Cameron, a bit dizzy from swinging, ran in a zig-zag pattern toward Layne, flailing her arms and wailing, "*daddy!*" over and over again.

Layne dropped to one knee and wrapped his arms around her. She folded into him, and he relished the sensation of her tiny frame, each time it happened feeling like it had never happened before. Her little body, so frail and warm and hearty.

Inessa, arms folded across her waist, strode toward them, coming to a stop a few feet away. "Who is this?" she asked in her cutting Russian accent.

Layne pulled back and gave Cameron a kiss on the cheek. Cam also noticed Serena for the first time. She cast a distrustful eye up at this new woman.

"This is daddy's friend Serena," Layne said. "Can you say hi?"

Cam played shy until Serena dropped to one knee and pulled a Tootsie Roll out of her pocket. "Hi, Cameron, do you like Tootsie Rolls? I have one here, if your daddy says it's okay."

Cam's little head jiggled up and down, glee on her face. She implored Layne. "Can I have it, Daddy? Please?"

Layne nodded and rose to his feet to find Inessa scowling at him.

"New friend?" his ex-wife said. He could practically read the insinuation hovering in the air between them.

"We work together, Inessa." He wanted to add, *not that it's any of your business*, but he refrained. No good would come of it. If Inessa wanted to be jealous, then that was her choice.

Inessa pursed her lips for a few seconds and then sighed. "I see."

Serena stood and shook Inessa's hand as she introduced herself, and they all endured a moment of awkward silence. All except for Cameron, who was too busy salivating over the Tootsie Roll she struggled to unwrap. Cam broke the silence by asking, "Mommy, can Daddy's new friend come to the aquarium with us?"

"Going to the Denver Aquarium?" Layne asked Inessa.

"Yes. I know it is not your day, but if you and your *work friend* would like to take her, be my guest. Just have her home by bath time."

"Do you want to go with just me and Serena?" Layne asked Cameron.

The little girl eyed her mom for approval, and Inessa hesitated, then nodded her consent. Cameron giggled with delight as she chewed on her Tootsie Roll.

Then, Cameron took hold of Serena's hand with her left, Layne's with her right, and they all walked off toward Layne's car together.

LEARN MORE

To find out when the sequel is coming, join the reader group at www.jimheskett.com/free

A NOTE TO READERS

Want to know when the next book is coming out? Join my reader group to get updates and free stuff!

For more Layne Parrish, check out MUSEUM ATTACK. It's an intense thriller novella, but it's not available for sale. You can only get it at www.jimheskett.com/readergroup

With that out of the way, thank you for reading my book!

Please consider leaving reviews on Goodreads and Amazon. You have no idea how much it will help the success of this book and my ability to write future books. That, sharing it on social media, and telling other people to read it.

Are you interested in joining a community of Jim Heskett fiction fans? Discuss the books with other people,

including the author! Join for free at
www.jimheskett.com/bookophile

I have a website where you can learn more about me and my other projects. Check me out at www.jimheskett.com and sign up for my reader group so you can stay informed on the latest news. You'll even get some freebies for signing up. You like free stuff, right?

For the survivors.

All material copyright 2018 by Jim Heskett. No part of this work may be reproduced without permission.

Published by Royal Arch Books

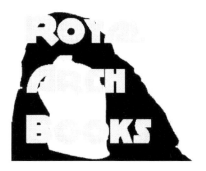

Www.RoyalArchBooks.com
Please consider leaving a review once you have finished this book.
Want to know when the next book is coming out?
Join my mailing list to get updates and free stuff!

BOOKS BY JIM HESKETT

For a full list of all Jim Heskett's books, please visit
www.RoyalArchBooks.com

If you like thrillers, you'll want to take a gander at my Micah Reed series. It's where Layne Parrish got his start, actually. In particular, Micah Reed book #7, Shock Collar, serves as a "prequel" of sorts to the Layne Parrish solo series. See how a dog walk ending in bloodshed sends Micah on a quest for truth, and Layne on a path to reclaim his past and future.

ABOUT THE AUTHOR

Jim Heskett was born in the wilds of Oklahoma and raised by a pack of wolves with a station wagon and a membership card to the local public swimming pool. Just like the man in the John Denver song, he moved to Colorado in the summer of his twenty-seventh year and never looked back. Aside from an extended break traveling the world, he hasn't let the Flatirons out of his sight.

He fell in love with writing at the age of fourteen with a copy of Stephen King's The Shining. Poetry became his first outlet for teen angst, then later some terrible screenplays, and eventually short and long fiction. In between, he worked a few careers that never quite tickled his creative toes, and he never forgot about Stephen King. You can find him currently huddled over a laptop in an undisclosed location in Colorado, dreaming up ways to kill beloved characters.

He believes the huckleberry is the king of berries and refuses to be persuaded in any other direction. If you'd like to ask a question or just to say hi, stop by at www.jimheskett.com/about and fill out the contact form.

- facebook.com/authorjimheskett
- twitter.com/jimheskett
- youtube.com/authorjimheskett

Made in the USA
Middletown, DE
01 October 2018